.to catch a firefly

EMMY SANDERS

Beta Reading by Lauren

Editing by M.A. Hinkle

Proofreading by Ky

Cover Design by Sleepy Fox Studio

ISBN: 9798989542000

Content Warning: This book contains brief mention of miscarriage and cancer, the off-page death of a parent, and a side character who has multiple sclerosis. Please take caution if this subject matter may be triggering for you.

A special thank you to Christie, Heather, Ruth, and Theo, who helped make Ellis's experience as authentic as possible.

For the little girl who always wanted to tell stories but was too afraid to use her voice.

Contents

Part I: Quarter   1

Chapter 1   2

Chapter 2   9

Chapter 3   16

Chapter 4   23

Chapter 5   32

Chapter 6   40

Chapter 7   48

Part II: Waning   56

Chapter 8   57

Chapter 9   64

Chapter 10   71

Chapter 11   79

Chapter 12   88

Chapter 13   97

Chapter 14   106

Chapter 15   115

Chapter 16   123

Chapter 17   130

Chapter 18   137

Part III: Waxing   144

Chapter 19   145

Chapter 20   153

Chapter 21   160

Chapter 22   168

Chapter 23   176

Chapter 24   186

Chapter 25   198

Chapter 26   206

Chapter 27   215

Chapter 28   225

Chapter 29   231

Chapter 30   239

Part IV: Blue Moon   247

Chapter 31   248

Chapter 32   256

Chapter 33   265

Chapter 34   272

Chapter 35   281

Chapter 36   291

Chapter 37   298

Chapter 38   305

Epilogue   312

About the Author   319

Part I: Quarter

Chapter 1

ELLIS

I was ten years old when I met Lucky.

"Ellis, baby?"

I don't answer my mom, too preoccupied with the bugs dancing in front of my face. They flicker yellow and orange in the waning evening light, bodies flashing on and off as if communicating with one another. Maybe they are. Maybe they don't like words, either.

"Ellis."

Her voice is closer now, but I stay still. One of the fireflies is hovering inches above my hand. Flicker on. Flicker off.

I think if I were careful enough, I could cup it in my palm. Would it fly away?

Soft footsteps approach, and then my mom is settling down beside me, legs bent like mine, her feet on the top stair of the deck.

The firefly dances away.

"What're you doing, baby?" she asks, brushing my hair off my forehead.

Another firefly wanders close, and I move my hand below it. *I'm safe*, I try to tell it, but I can't blink like it can.

"Did you say hello to the new neighbors yet?" my mom asks.

I shake my head.

"Their boy is outside," she says. "He's ten, like you. You should go say hello."

The firefly touches my palm, and I hold my breath.

"Ellis?"

"Late," I answer.

She hums. "It is. But it's not a school night." She's quiet for a moment before adding, "You might like him."

The firefly drifts to the left, and I follow it with my open palm. I could trap it between my hands, I think. But then I wouldn't see its light.

"Ellis, honey."

"How do you catch a firefly?" I ask my mom.

She makes a soft sound before standing up and heading back into the house. It's a minute before she returns. When she does, she bumps something gently into the side of my arm. I look over, and she's holding out an empty jam jar, the lid twisted off.

I'm careful to move slowly as I take it from her. The firefly hasn't danced far off. There are hundreds in the sky tonight. Maybe thousands. Countless specks of flickering color dotting the night sky. There isn't much of a breeze, but the crickets are singing loudly. I wonder if the fireflies hear them, too. Maybe that's why they're dancing.

The firefly winks golden at me as I raise the clear jar around its body. It doesn't move away. Doesn't react in any way I can tell. It seems so...easy.

"Here," my mom says, handing me the lid.

I screw it on top of the jar, and then I watch. I watch the firefly flickering inside the glass, wondering what it's saying. Does it know it's been caught?

"Ellis, baby," my mom says, hand ruffling my hair. "Go meet the neighbor boy. His name is Lucky. Maybe you two could be friends."

I set the jar down on the deck and look over at the neighbor's house. It's not far. I counted ninety-eight steps the last time I walked between our yard and theirs. The grasses are tall and wild in the space between—no one has mowed them since my dad left—and the first spring flowers have started to poke through the soil. They're purple in the sun, but now, they're dark.

"Ellis," my mom urges.

With a nod, I stand. The crickets keep me company as I walk the short way to the blue house next to ours. Ninety-seven steps today. I must be getting taller.

The new neighbors moved in this morning. I watched from the window as the trucks came and went, but it reminded me too much of my dad, so I didn't watch for long.

I see him now—Lucky—before he sees me. He's on the old tire swing that hangs from a big maple, not quite swinging, just drifting around and around and around. His hands are holding the rope at the top of the tire, his body through the center, and his head is hanging back, hair dangling toward the ground. It's longer than most boys' around here and shines bright under the moon.

He's nearly upside down when the tire stops and he spots me.

He snaps upright. "Hi."

We look at each other for a moment, both of us seemingly waiting.

"What's your name?" he asks, breaking the silence. He twists in the swing a little, rocking it back and forth as he watches me. "I'm Lucky."

I know.

Lucky hangs his arms over the top of the tire. "Where'd you come from?"

I point behind me, and he nods.

"Don't talk much, huh?" he says.

I shrug.

He tilts his head, hair falling messily around his face. It's blonde, I think. "Well, hello."

I give him a nod and turn to leave, wondering where the fireflies disappear to when it's not dark. Are they still there, blinking uselessly in the sunlight? Can they talk to each other then?

"Hey!" Lucky calls, dropping down out of the swing. He jogs over to me, having to tilt his head up when he gets close. He's shorter than me, but most kids my age are. "Where are you going?"

I point behind me again.

"Do you have to?" he asks, not waiting for an answer before he grabs my hand and tugs. I follow him to the center of the yard. He gives me another tug as he sits down, and I glance back at my house before lowering myself to the ground beside him.

My mom would be proud. I think I'm making a friend.

"It's too quiet here," Lucky says, picking at the grass.

I cock my head, listening to the buzzing crickets, the slow passing of a car on the road, and some sort of bird farther off. Maybe an owl. It's not quiet to me.

"Nebraska sucks," he says. "I didn't want to leave Chicago, but my parents made me."

I don't answer. I wouldn't even know what to say. I haven't known anywhere but Nebraska.

"There's, like, a hundred people here," he adds, sounding glum. "Hey, what grade are you in?"

I hold up my hand.

"I'm in fifth, too!" he says excitedly. "That's awesome. At least I'll know someone."

I nod.

"Do you like school?" he asks.

I shrug.

"My dad got a job at the paper mill," he tells me, heaving a sigh and picking at the grass again. "That's why we moved here."

The paper mill in town is one of the biggest in the state. We learned that in school. Toured it and everything. The people who work there are the pulpers, as our townsfolk would say, as opposed to the huskers. It's either paper or corn here.

I don't think I want to do either, but there's not much choice.

"Do you wanna tell me your name?" Lucky asks. "You don't have to."

I clear my throat. "Ellis."

He grins. "Do you like video games?"

I shrug, and Lucky doesn't push it. He talks a lot, but maybe that's a good thing. I don't talk much.

Lucky continues to ask me questions as the last of the evening light filters away.

"Do you like pancakes or waffles better?"

"Is there anything to do here?"

"Is that silo behind your house haunted?"

"What's with all the corn?"

He doesn't seem to mind that I never say a word. Instead, I listen while I watch the fireflies dance. I've never seen so many before. Our teacher said it's the weather this year.

"Hey, do you think we could eat lunch together at school?" Lucky asks.

I look at him then. His eyes are blue, I think. It's hard to tell in the dark.

I nod, and Lucky beams. I've never had a friend to sit with at lunch before. Is that what we are now? Friends?

"Lucky, time for bed," a deep voice calls. "Oh, is that Ellis?"

"Yeah," Lucky calls back, standing. Mom must have told them my name.

"Hello, Ellis," the man says.

I hold up my hand.

"Time to turn in," he repeats, waving Lucky inside.

Lucky sighs. "I'll see you Monday at school?"

I nod.

"Coming," Lucky calls out. He gets halfway to the house before pivoting. "Hey, Ellis? I'm glad you're here. Maybe this won't suck so bad after all."

My heart beats a little fast at that, but I couldn't say why.

Lucky runs inside, but the man doesn't move. "Need me to walk you home?"

I shake my head, already heading that way. The grass tickles my calves as I walk. It needs to be mowed.

"Goodnight, Ellis," I hear the man say. The door shuts a moment later.

Lucky's dad seems nice enough.

I forget to count steps on the way home, instead watching the moon. It's half-full tonight. I don't know why they call that a quarter.

When I get home, my mom is waiting just outside the door. She must have seen me walking up. "Have fun?"

I shrug, but she looks pleased.

"Don't forget to wash up before bed," she says, walking inside. She leaves the door open for me, and I follow her in.

What kind of name is Lucky?

I go to sleep wondering about my new friend. In the morning, I remember the firefly I left out on the deck. I race outside, picking up the glass, but I don't get a chance to see whether or not it still blinks in the sun.

The firefly is dead.

Chapter 2

ELLIS

I was thirteen when Lucky stared down a tornado.

"Ellis, you in here?"

I grunt, setting down the blue mason jar I'd been examining. It looks nice next to the lavender one I found last week.

Lucky comes through the ground-level access door of the silo, blinking as his eyes adjust to the darkness.

"You weren't on the bus," he accuses.

I had a dentist appointment, so my mom pulled me out of school early. I forgot to tell Lucky.

"What're you doing?" he asks, setting his backpack down against the curved side of the silo. That's when I notice the tear in his shirt.

I point, and Lucky sighs.

"It's nothing," he says.

"Doesn't look like nothing."

Lucky raises an eyebrow. "Four whole words. Maybe I should get injured more often."

I scowl, but Lucky only laughs.

"It's nothing," he repeats.

Lucky starts lining up some of the old, cracked jars we've collected. They're not the pretty ones he knows not to mess with. They're the simple kind people use for canning. Once he has them arranged almost like bowling pins, he reaches for the marbles, but I snag them before he can. At my insistent stare, his shoulders drop.

"Just some guys at school," he says. "They don't like me."

That brings me up short. Why not? I thought everyone liked Lucky.

"You know," he says, waving his hand through the air, as if that explains it.

I don't know.

Lucky expels a big breath. "Because I'm gay, Ellis."

I don't move a muscle, stunned more by the fact that anyone would treat him differently for that than by the news itself. Lucky pushes his hair off his face as I blink at him. The blonde curls wing every which way, wild and long like a lion's mane. His blue eyes drop to the marbles in my hand, and I realize he's waiting on me.

"Assholes," I finally manage.

His eyes widen in surprise, and he huffs a laugh. "Damn. You're full of it today."

I breathe a little easier.

Lucky makes a grabby hand, and I pass over the marbles. He takes a seat a ways back from the jars, and I follow suit, sitting beside him, our knees brushing. He tosses marbles, one after another, rarely missing the jars. I can't stop staring at the rip in his shirt. What happened?

After a minute, Lucky catches my eye. "You didn't know, did you?"

I shake my head.

"Everyone knows, Ellis."

Not me.

He throws another marble. "Does it change anything?"

Why would it change anything?

Lucky must be able to read my face—he always can—because he rolls his eyes a little. "Yeah, yeah," he says. "I'm an idiot."

I bump his shoulder with my own.

"I know," he says lightly, tossing a big red marble. It tinks loudly before settling into the glass. "It's me and you."

Yeah, it is.

When Lucky runs out of marbles, he sighs. "I'm gonna get out of this town one day, El." His words tighten around my chest like a rubber band, but he goes on in a rush. "I have to. You're the only good thing here; you know that. Maybe I'll go back to Chicago or try New York. Or, hell, Thailand even. Anywhere would be better than this."

He's talked about leaving before, ever since he moved here really. Lucky doesn't like our small, rural town, not after growing up in a big city. But this time, he sounds serious.

"You could come with me," he says.

I don't have a chance to reply before a high-pitched siren pierces the air. Lucky and I look at each other in surprise.

"Tornado alarm," he says. "It's not Saturday."

I shake my head, and the two of us bolt.

The wind whips my face as soon as we reach the clearing outside the silo. The sky is darker now, gray and angry, and clouds swirl overhead in a pattern that means danger. The weather station didn't warn about a storm this bad, but that doesn't mean much here.

"Shit," Lucky says, covering his eyes with his arm as some dust kicks up. "Let's go."

Lucky grabs a handful of my shirt as we take off toward our houses. The quickest way is through the cornfields, not around, so that's the way I go. The stalks are head-height this time of year, and the leaves smack us as we run, leaving little stinging bites in their wake. Every once in a while, they blow at a harsh angle before settling.

As soon as we burst from the field, I hear Lucky's mom calling. Lucky yells back as we come around my house, heading for the storm shelter that's buried underground halfway between our two houses. Lucky's dad is helping my mom down the ladder, and her face falls in relief when she sees us running. I can't hear what she says over the wind, but Lucky's mom urges us forward, watching the skyline behind us.

I don't dare look back.

When we reach the shelter, Lucky's dad is the only one above the surface. I don't stop to catch my breath, just dart toward the opening in the ground. I'm about to step down when I realize Lucky isn't hanging on to me anymore.

When I turn back, my heart nearly stops.

Lucky is standing fifty feet away, his back to us. His clothes whip around him in the harsh wind, and his head is tipped up toward the sky. I see it then, the tornado. It looks otherworldly, like it doesn't belong. Black clouds surround the area above where the twister reaches towards the earth, and lightning strikes as I watch, lighting the sky in a brilliant flash of eerie white. A mere second later, thunder booms as the rain reaches us. It comes down in a sheet, soaking me in seconds.

Lucky doesn't move, even as his dad starts to yell. Even as the wind turns vicious. Even as the sky blackens overhead.

Lucky, goddamn it.

He drops his head back, palms up toward the sky, as if he's soaking it in. As if he's reveling in the savage force of nature that's raging ever closer. His hair circles his head, angry like the corn and the clouds and the sky.

He's never looked wilder.

"Luck!" I scream.

He looks back then, and the relief is immense. I don't dare move a step until Lucky is at the ladder. He grins at me, all wide-eyed and excited, and I shake my head, hoofing it down as fast as I can go.

My mom grabs a hold of me as I land, wrapping her arms around my shoulders as we back further into the shelter. It's not large, but there's plenty of space for the five of us to wait out the storm. Along one wall is a bench, and along another is a rack of emergency supplies, including a radio.

Lucky's dad is the last to descend after locking the door tight, and the silence that follows is stark.

"What were you doing?" he asks his son as soon as his feet hit ground. His hands go to Lucky's shoulders as he looks him in the eye. His grip isn't hard. He just looks scared.

"Did you see it?" Lucky replies, not sharing a hint of the same fear as his dad. "It was *beautiful*."

Lucky's dad turns away and scrubs his hands through his hair. He paces a step before turning back. "One of these days, you're going to give me a heart attack. I swear, Lucky, you can't—"

Lucky's mom grabs his arm, squeezing gently. "We're okay now," she says. "Let's focus on that. Get the radio going, Ron?"

Lucky's dad nods, letting loose a breath as he heads for the old ham radio.

My mom presses a kiss against the side of my head. "Okay, baby?"

I nod. My pulse is still hammering, but not because of the tornado. It's not the first one I've experienced, and being smack dab in the middle of Tornado Alley, it won't be the last.

But Lucky...

My mom lets me go as I head toward my friend. His hair is soaked, the curls clinging to his skin. His eyes are bright, almost electric. He gives me a smile when I shove him.

"Oh, come on," he says. "You have to admit that was really cool."

I shake my head.

"Yeah, yeah," he mutters. "I'm an idiot. So you say."

I do.

The radio crackles as Lucky's dad tunes it to hear news on the tornado. Every once in a while, the whistling of wind reaches our ears, and once, there's a thump against the door.

Lucky follows me as I take a seat on the bench. I try to dry my hands on my shorts, but both are wet, so it doesn't help. I shove them in my pockets when I realize they're shaking.

"Sorry," Lucky says, nudging me. He looks a little abashed. "I scared you, didn't I?"

A short, sharp nod.

"I'll try to be more careful."

I nearly roll my eyes. Lucky seeks out trouble. That's how he broke his leg only a month after he moved to town. Despite me telling him the ladder in the silo wasn't stable, he was determined to reach the window at the top. He didn't make it far before a bolt loosened and the ladder jittered, dropping Lucky to the ground in the process.

He went back up once his leg was healed and fixed the bolt. Lucky sighs. "I want to see it, Ellis."

The tornado?

"The world," he answers, despite me not having said a word. "I want to experience life."

There's life happening right here. But I don't think it's enough for Lucky.

"I want an adventure, you know?" he says, eyes bright like the ocean or the clear blue sky. "I want more than corn or paper or five-cent candy at the corner store. I want my life to be...remarkable, El."

It will be. Because it's his. He's not capable of anything else, I know it. I just don't know how to *say* it.

I'll show him; that's what I'll do. I'll show Lucky there's adventure to be had right here. That he can have his remarkable life.

And then maybe, just maybe, he'll stay.

When we leave the tornado shelter a half hour later, debris covers the ground. The sky is startlingly bright, as if it didn't just rain destruction down all around us. Our houses are fine, apart from a single shutter at Lucky's that's hanging loose.

But the corn... There's a long, warped path carved into the field that starts not 300 paces from where Lucky was standing.

I've never been more afraid that, one way or another, I'm going to lose my friend.

Chapter 3

ELLIS

I was fifteen when I got into my first fight.

"Come on, asshole! Is that all you've got?"

I rush toward the sound of Lucky's voice, gut dropping when I find him surrounded by three guys from our class. Brandon has a hold of Lucky's shirt, pressing my friend against a locker as other students stand back, creating a wide arc around the scene. Brandon's hand is clenched at his side, and Lucky is smiling around a split lip.

"Hey," I bark, pushing my way through the crowd.

Brandon has only a moment to look over in shock before my fist is connecting with his jaw. He drops Lucky but recovers fast, driving his shoulder into me in a move that might work out on the football field, but I'm bigger than Brandon—his friends, too—and I barely sway an inch. It's all too easy to press my weight forward and connect my fist with Brandon's nose when he takes a stuttered step back.

"Oh shit," his friend, Riley, hisses.

I look his way next, and the guy's eyes widen. He holds up his hands quickly, backing away and grabbing for Jace, their third, to follow. The two guys take off as Brandon groans on the ground, and when I look up, our classmates are holding up their phones, varying degrees of surprise and awe on their faces.

I grunt, and half of them flinch away.

"Hey," Lucky says in a soothing voice, his hand landing on my arm. My pulse comes down as I turn, but only slightly. Lucky is grinning, blood smeared over his lower lip.

"Why are you smiling?" I grit out.

His grin widens as someone behind me gasps.

"Is your hand okay?" Lucky asks, taking a hold of my tightened fist. He cringes slightly, looking at the damage, but I shake my head. It's fine. Lucky rolls his eyes. "Okay, tough guy."

Brandon groans again from the ground as our classmates whisper behind us.

"Did you see that?"

"I've never seen the dude angry before."

"Did you know he could talk?"

"Hey," Lucky says again, hands on the sides of my face. He looks up at me with those clear blue eyes. I still haven't figured out what to call them. Azure? Cerulean? "You okay?"

I nod, scoffing and touching the side of his lip.

"I'm fine," Lucky says.

Right.

"Don't give me that."

Smartass.

"El, I—"

"What is going on here?" our teacher, Mrs. McMillan, says. She rushes up to us, parting the sea of gawking students, and her hands fly to her mouth when she catches sight of Brandon on the floor.

"He attacked me," Brandon says, hand over his bloody nose.

"He did not," Lucky fires back, stepping around me. "You hit me first, jackass."

Mrs. McMillan's hands wave in the air for a moment before she says, "Principal's office. All three of you. *Now*."

The rest of the students scatter, and Lucky gives my uninjured hand a squeeze as we walk down the hall, that wild grin back on his face.

I can't help but smile, too.

"I just want to understand why you did it," my mom says. From the moment she arrived at the principal's office to now, at home in our living room, she's looked more astonished than upset. "You're not a violent person, baby."

I shake my head.

She sighs, sitting down next to me. My right hand is wrapped, and my mom picks it up between her own, rolling it gently and checking to make sure I haven't bled through the bandages.

"Ellis," she says quietly, setting my hand down. "You know I don't like to push you, but I'm asking for an explanation. Please."

I give her a slow nod.

It's not that I don't *want* to talk, especially to her. But words, for me, have never been easy. They don't always come out right, as if having to wade through a bog from my brain to my mouth, and it's exhausting having to constantly make that journey. People don't often like to wait for me to get it right, and I've learned it's easier to stay quiet.

Besides, the important people understand me anyway.

"He was hurting Lucky," I finally tell her. It takes a minute.

My mom nods, patting my cheek and looking resigned. "Don't make a habit of it, yeah?"

I nod my agreement.

"You can wash the siding this week while you're on suspension," she adds.

I groan but nod again.

My mom ruffles my hair before heading down the hall, and I look out the window toward Lucky's house. Grabbing a jacket, I head outside.

Lucky's bedroom is on the far side of the house, so I make my way around with our bikes in tow. He's lying on his bed when I tap the window, but his head pops up immediately, and he jumps to the floor. His smile is wide when he opens the window.

"What are you doing?" he asks.

I nod down to the bikes.

Lucky shakes his head, but his eyes are bright. "I'm supposed to be grounded."

I raise an eyebrow, and Lucky rushes to his closet. He grabs a sweatshirt and tugs it on before popping the screen out of his window and climbing through. He lowers the glass from outside and replaces the screen, and then we're on our way.

Neither of us says a word as I lead him along the cornfields that run behind our houses. Eventually, we reach a dirt road, and Lucky's bike clangs behind mine as we turn onto it. The sun is riding low in the sky, and I pick up the pace, not wanting to miss it set.

When I turn off onto a private property, Lucky doesn't question me. He follows me past a darkened house to an old windmill I've gone past a million times since I was a child. When I stop my bike, Lucky skids up next to me.

"El," he whispers loudly, sounding excited. "Are we trespassing?"

I touch my finger to my lips, and Lucky laughs.

We set our bikes against the outside of the windmill and walk around to the door. It creaks loudly when I tug it open, but we're far enough away from the house that I doubt anyone would hear anything, even if they're awake. Lucky grabs his phone from his pocket once we're inside and turns on the flashlight. Cobwebs cover every surface imaginable, and I swipe my arm through them so we can walk forward.

The stairs are just as rickety as the rest of the structure, so I go first, stepping slowly to make sure each can hold my weight. Lucky is quiet behind me, our breaths and footsteps the only sounds in the still night air.

At the top of the windmill, there's a small platform. I have to climb through a hole to get onto it, and then I help Lucky up. His eyes are big and round as we crawl under the short, pitched roof to the small window at the top of the structure. The countryside stretches out before us, far and wide. We're not up all that high, but the land is so flat, it feels like we can see for miles.

Lucky settles in front of the window, legs pulled up in front of him. I squeeze close, my hip against his. There's not room to be any further apart and still see out the window, but it doesn't matter. It never matters with Lucky.

"Why'd you do it, Ellis?" he asks. "Why'd you defend me?"

What's he talking about?

You're my friend. Of course I defended you.

He sighs. "Yeah, okay."

I'm not sure why he seems almost sad, but then I catch sight of the color that's starting to light the sky and point it out to Lucky.

"That's pretty," he says, leaning against me, his shoulder pressed to mine. We watch the oranges and purples streak across the sky for a couple minutes before Lucky pulls out his phone. He takes a few pictures, but my mind keeps tumbling over what happened today.

"Brandon?" I ask.

Lucky snorts. "He won't be bothering me again."

I'm glad he understood what I was asking, but I still raise an eyebrow, which Lucky catches.

"Ellis, buddy, I'm not sure if you've looked in the mirror lately, but no one at that school is going to touch me. Not ever again."

My chest warms at that, and I feel a strange sense of pride that I could give that to Lucky. Hopefully, he's right, and the assholes in town will leave him be. Why they care about his sexuality in the first place is beyond me.

Lucky's eyes are aimed out the window when he says, "You don't know what you look like, do you, El?"

I'm not sure what he means. Of course I know what I look like. Brown hair. Brown eyes. My dad's nose, my grandpa's height, and my mom's eyebrows. I'm part of those who made me, but I'm just *me*, too.

I don't have golden curls like Lucky that seem to glow in the low evening sun. Nor his bright, piercing eyes.

I'm just Ellis.

Lucky sighs, leaning his head against my shoulder. "Yeah. Okay." I think I hear him say *my hero*, but it's so soft, I can't be certain.

As the sky turns from a painted masterpiece to blackened night, the stars start to emerge. There's so little light pollution here; they're easy to see.

"Thanks for bringing me here, El," Lucky says.

I nod. *Of course.*

"Days like this make me think..."

He doesn't finish his sentence, so I give him a nudge. His smile is a little off when he looks my way.

"They're just good," he says. "You know?"

I touch his lip, and his smile wobbles, breath leaving him in a rush.

"Yeah," he says softly. "Even with the split lip."

Are they good enough to stay?

He doesn't provide an answer.

When Lucky turns away, he fiddles with his phone. After messing with his camera settings, he props the device in the corner of the old, dusty window, steadying it with a stone that was beside his foot. "Slow exposure," he explains, pressing the record button. "You don't mind sitting here for another hour, do you?"

I huff.

"Good," he says, laying his head back against my shoulder.

I wonder, when he's done getting his picture, if he'll be able to see the world spinning.

I wonder how many more revolutions Lucky will be in mine.

Chapter 4

ELLIS

I was seventeen when things started to change.

"Look at this one," Lucky says, showing me the photos he developed from inside his closet. He turned the small space into a darkroom earlier this year. "Isn't this neat?"

The picture is of Chimney Rock in western Nebraska. We drove out that way with his dad two weekends ago, visiting some of the more notable rock formations along that portion of the Oregon Trail. Lucky took this shot at night, such that it looks like the tall, pillared rock is holding the moon aloft. A streak of star-littered blue runs overhead, and the rest of the sky is black. It's stunning.

"Luck," I manage to say.

He beams.

Lucky wants to go into photojournalism. It's an idea that's stuck ever since he got it into his head a couple years back.

"It's my ticket out of here," he told me. Photojournalism could take him around the world. His remarkable life.

I think I knew he'd never stay.

Still, I cant my head toward the door.

"Yeah," Lucky says, packing his photos away. "I'm ready."

The pair of us get in my truck, and I lead us north. Lucky hums along to the radio as we drive, his window rolled down and his hair whipping around his face. The sight makes me smile, and when Lucky catches me watching, he sticks out his tongue.

As his hand weaves through the air outside the window, he says, "Did I tell you Jace wanted me to give him a blowjob behind the bleachers yesterday?"

I sputter, unintentionally twisting the wheel. Lucky laughs as I right the truck.

"I didn't, obviously," he says, and my heart rate starts to come down. "The guy's a dick whose dick I want nothing to do with."

Jace is one of the guys who used to hassle Lucky. Not anymore, but he's certainly not out, as far as I'm aware. Lucky is alone in that respect.

"I told him if I can't kiss him in the hall, I'm not going down on him behind closed doors," Lucky says.

Jesus. There goes my heart again. At least he said no. The idea of Lucky with someone like that...

"Have you ever thought about it?" he asks.

I'm sure my eyes are wide when I glance his way.

He laughs again. "Not *me*, El. Have you thought about...you know. Getting with someone?"

Oh.

I shake my head because the truth is no, I haven't.

Lucky hums. "I have."

I squirm a little, not sure why thinking about that makes me...unsettled. We've talked about sex before. Or Lucky has talked, and I've listened. Neither of us has had it. Lucky wants to.

"It's okay, you know," he says. "If it's not something you're interested in."

I shrug.

"Maybe I should try an app," he muses.

My fingers grip the wheel tight.

"You don't think I should?"

I shake my head. *Too dangerous.*

With a hum, he lets the subject rest.

When I pull up to Smith Falls State Park forty-five minutes later, Lucky looks around.

"Hiking?" he asks.

Not quite.

I grab the bag I packed from the back of the truck, and we make our way to the north end of the park. After crossing a footbridge, we reach the wooden boardwalk that leads to Smith Falls, the highest waterfall in the state. Lucky's eyes are wide when the rushing sound reaches our ears, and as we round the final corner, the waterfall comes into view.

Lucky hops excitedly, grabbing my arm, and I can't help but chuckle. He has his camera out before we even reach the end of the boardwalk, shutter clicking away. I watch Lucky, chest feeling tight.

A few other people are visiting the falls, so we have to wait before we can stand up front. Once we're at the rail, the water mists us gently. Lucky has to stop to clear it from his lens.

"This is great, El," he finally says, his forehead and hair dotted with moisture. His cheeks are bright and his smile wide. "Thanks for bringing me here."

"Not done," I tell him, giving him a little tug.

Lucky looks curious as he follows me back down the boardwalk. He looks even more curious when I lead us down an unmarked trail. Several minutes later, I catch sight of the landmark I'm looking for.

Lucky lets out a whoop. "Please tell me you brought our swimsuits."

I pull them from my bag.

The next couple minutes are a rush of changing beneath the privacy of beach towels and then clambering into the cool water. Lucky doesn't hesitate to make his way to where a lower portion of the falls slides gently over rock, emptying into a natural pool. There's not another soul in sight down here.

"This is awesome!" Lucky yells, wading deeper into the water and climbing up a slope of rock beneath the falls. He's dunked in seconds, and all I can do is watch as he shakes his head and laughs and lets out a battle cry that surely scared away any birds nearby.

When he turns around, arms out to his sides, I have a moment of deja vu. Behind Lucky is a tornado, not the falls, and for a heartachingly long second, I fear for my friend. I'm scared because he's brave and curious and likes the thrill of danger, even though he's never outright said so. Those qualities I love about my friend, those things that make him so uniquely *him*, are the things that scare me.

There's no tornado today, of course. But Lucky looks free as he stands outstretched beneath the water, and it hits me that I can't compete with that. I can drag Lucky all over Nebraska or even further, show him the wonders in his own backyard. But whatever this feeling is he's chasing, it's bigger than me, bigger than this place, bigger than anything I know. What I have to offer won't ever be enough for my free-spirited friend.

The realization hurts more than it reasonably should.

"Ellis!" Lucky yells. "Get your ass over here."

Shaking off the phantom pain, I follow Lucky into the falls. The water is slightly biting as it pelts me from above, but through the sheet of the downpour, Lucky's smile is like the sun. His face falls a little when he sees my own.

"What is it?" he asks, tugging me to the side. The water rushes down next to us, the force of it causing us to speak louder to be heard over the noise.

"Why go?" I almost shout. It's useless—I know it is—but something about this moment feels urgent. Like if I don't *try*, I'll always regret it.

Lucky watches me for a moment, eyes pinging between my own. "What?"

"Why?" I repeat, frustrated that I can't get the rest of my question out. Lucky waits, his chest rising and falling. "Why do you need to leave?"

"Ellis," he mouths. I can't even hear the word. I can only see it.

"Am I not..."

"What?" Lucky says urgently, taking a step forward. "Are you not *what*? Say it."

I can't.

I know I'm not enough. I'm being selfish and childish, not wanting to let go of my one and only friend. But that's not fair to Lucky.

"Is there a reason for me to stay?" he asks, his breath rushing out fast, like my own. When I don't answer, he shouts, "Ellis!"

"You're..."

"What?" he says, putting us toe to toe in the water. He reaches out slowly, hands settling on my waist. It's a jolt to my system, even though his skin is warm. My heart pounds, and I can't pull in a big enough breath. "I'm what?" he repeats.

My best friend.

Lucky closes his eyes in an extended blink, as if pained. He looks down, looks away from me, and I don't understand. He shakes his head before brushing his hair out of his face, and then he takes a step back. I feel it like a loss.

"It'll always be me and you, El," he says. "But I can't... I can't stay here. I've never even been kissed, you know?"

My breath catches in my throat, and it takes me a moment to make the connection. Even if Lucky did stay, who would he date? Who could he kiss and fall in love with, not to mention have sex with? There are no options for him here, and it never truly occurred to me before. Of course he'd want a boyfriend. A partner to build a life with.

Of course Lucky needs to leave.

I've been foolish to hope otherwise for all these years. Just a foolish boy who didn't want to grow up. Not if it meant saying goodbye.

But I set it all aside because the way Lucky looks right this instant—how his face is downcast, how his arms are around his stomach as if holding a wound closed—is not something I can bear.

Taking a step forward, I tip Lucky's chin. His eyes catch mine and his lips pop open, and when I lean down to press my mouth to his, his fingertips dig into my arm. Not pushing, though, holding. I've never kissed before, either, but Lucky deserves a first with someone who loves him. At least I can give him that.

His mouth is warm, soft even, but his nose is cold as it brushes against my own. It's just a press, really. Innocent. But Lucky sighs, tipping his head back and opening his lips, and...

I don't remember jumping back, but the next second, I'm looking at Lucky's blinking, blue eyes and his slightly parted mouth, wondering why my hands are shaking. Wondering why that show of trust had me wanting to press into Lucky and...I don't know.

"Ellis." Lucky steps forward, hand reaching out and touching my stomach for just a moment before his arm falls lax at his side. "Should I stay?"

Yesterday, I would have said yes. I would have told him I could make it worth it. That *I* was worth it because we're best friends, and best friends stick together, right?

But today? Today, everything is different.

Would Lucky be happy here, really? I don't think so.

I shake my head, and Lucky closes his eyes. He nods several times before opening them and flashing a crooked, cheery smile.

"Right," he says, tone teasing. "Are we going to talk about the fact that you kissed me, El?"

I roll my eyes, but at least my feet are on solid ground again.

"Are you going to give me my first blowjob, too?" he asks, and suddenly, the ground is whooshing out from under me.

Lucky laughs as I slip on the rock and fall chest-deep into the water, even as he rushes to help. But then we're both falling, slipping under the surface where sound cuts out and there's only the all-encompassing feeling of being weightless and surrounded in cold. For a moment, with only Lucky's hand in mine, I feel lost in the cosmos. Drifting, but not alone.

When we break the surface, Lucky is laughing again. We end up on our knees—the water isn't deep here—and I wipe my face.

"El," Lucky gasps, hand on my shoulder. "One day, someone is going to corrupt you, and I can only hope I'm there to see it."

I scowl, but it makes Lucky laugh harder. I turn away so he doesn't see my lips twitch.

When he finally quiets, he gives me a little shove. "Hey."

I turn back around.

"I'm glad it was you," he says. *The kiss.*

I nod, eyes dropping to his lips again. They're bowed on top and the bottom is fuller. I never quite noticed before.

When my gaze rises back to his eyes, Lucky looks serious. We're still near the falls, the sound of the water a constant drum, but I can hear him just fine when he says, "Come with me."

He's said it before, but I've never seriously considered leaving Nebraska. I'm not like Lucky; an adventurer at heart. A wild thing. I like my home and the comfort of this land. I like the ever-present earthy smell of the corn and how I know when I enter town, Maisy's Diner will be there waiting.

I like my life here, but for the first time, I consider Lucky's words.

He can tell. His eyes light immediately. "We're applying to colleges this year," he says, fingers running from my shoulder to my hand underneath the water. He grabs on tight, nails digging in. "Let's send applications to the same places at the very least, okay? There's still plenty of time to decide."

I nod—because what's the harm?—and Lucky grins so wide my breath catches.

"It'll be great, El. You'll see."

And I don't know what to say, so I hold on to Lucky's hand and hope he's right.

Chapter 5

ELLIS

I was eighteen when my mom got her diagnosis.

"Ellis, baby, would you sit down? You're making me dizzy."

I huff. How am I supposed to sit right now?

"Honey," my mom persists.

I go to her, slumping down on the couch. She immediately reaches for me, squeezing my arm. I notice the tremor in her hand, and my anger drains instantly.

"It's going to be okay," she says.

How? It's not okay.

"It's not so bad yet," she goes on, soothing me. "And the doctor says I'll have years before the symptoms worsen enough that I'll need to make adjustments."

But she's already had symptoms for years. She just didn't know the tingling in her hands or pins and needles in her feet were the beginning stages of multiple sclerosis. Shouldn't the doctors have caught it before now? Couldn't they have done something?

"Ellis, look at me."

I do. My mom's steely hazel eyes catch my own.

"I refuse to let this stop me," she says. "It's a bump in the road, nothing more. You hear?"

I nod, and she squeezes my arm again.

"Okay. Now I need to make some phone calls, so I want you to go out and scream a little or do whatever you need to do. And then, when you come back, we'll talk about next steps."

Without a word, I wrap my arms around my mom, and she exhales heavily.

"Oh, honey. We'll be all right."

Her hand rubs circles over my shoulder blades as I will my eyes to stay dry. When I pull back, she pats my cheek.

"Love you," I say.

Her chin wobbles. "Love you more."

When I get outside, my feet carry me toward the silo. It's sat unused on our property for as long as I can remember. My dad told me his grandfather stored corn in it a few generations back, but when bigger companies bought most of the land in town, small farms gave way to mass production. The silo has been empty since, and the land that once belonged to our family—the cornfields behind our house and Lucky's—was sold decades ago.

I never understood why my dad—a husker himself—up and left the way he did. Didn't he have ties to this land? To the memories made here? To *us*?

I guess maybe some people just aren't meant to stay.

When I get to the silo, I feel restless. Unsettled. Inside, the air is balmy and still, and I head to the shelves of colored glass I've collected over the years. Jars, mostly, but the occasional plate or bowl, too. Usually, the colors soothe me. I like examining the different shades and the way the light plays off the surface. Today, it doesn't help.

Spotting the discarded jars on the ground, I pick one up, weighing it in my hand. It's grimy, the clear glass clouded over from years of being exposed to the elements. There's a chip along the top, too. I run my finger over it before chucking the whole thing at the wall. It explodes in a shower of fragmented glass. Picking up another, I send it flying.

"Ellis?"

I ignore Lucky's call, eyes prickling as I grab two more jars and hurl them. The sound as they hit the curved metal of the silo is satisfying. The clang and crash and answering echo.

Lucky's eyes are wide as he comes to a stop inside the door. I pick up another jar, turning and throwing it at the opposite wall. It doesn't hit as hard, but it still breaks, sending glass skittering to the ground.

"Your mom called," Lucky says.

I'm not surprised.

"Said you might need me."

Always.

Lucky steps forward as I send another jar flying through the air. "Hey." *Crash.*

I shake my head roughly, reaching for another only to realize they're gone. I broke them all already.

"What's going on?" Lucky asks, sounding surprisingly calm. Or maybe it's just that I'm *not*.

When I reach for a blue jar off my shelf, Lucky's eyes shoot wide.

"Hey," he says again, almost a warning.

I chuck it at the wall. Lucky grabs my arm, but he's not fast enough to stop me. Sky blue glass litters to the floor, joining the remnants of the clear jars like little supernovas in a sea of jagged ice. I stagger a step when Lucky tugs me around to face him.

"Ellis," he says, shocked.

I pull from his grasp, my hands shaking, and toss another—the lavender jar I found when I was thirteen. And another—a bowl I picked up at an antique shop that's the color of sea glass. Now it joins the discards in the dirt.

I'm reaching for a light brown mason jar when Lucky inserts himself in front of me, shoving me back with all of his weight. It's the surprise of it more than anything that has me taking a step back. He does it again, his hands pressing hard against my chest.

"Stop it," he gets out.

I try to brush him off, but Lucky comes at me again.

"I said *stop.*"

I ready myself for another shove, but it doesn't come. Instead, Lucky wraps his arms around me tight and plants his face against my chest. He murmurs calming words into my shirt, his grip unrelenting, and like the snap of those glass jars against the wall, every ounce of fight in my body shatters to dust.

I cry as Lucky holds me, my back heaving with the force of it, his hair collecting my tears. My friend is the only thing keeping me upright.

Lucky shushes me, his hands clutching my shirt tight. It lifts under the strain, and his palm ends up on my skin. I focus on the feel of it, on the tether it provides. On how, for a few endless moments, I can almost imagine everything will be okay, so long as Lucky is here.

When Lucky turns his face up, putting us nearly nose to nose, I realize his eyes are wet, too. I rub my thumb underneath each, marveling at the color. I've never been able to find anything remotely close.

It's the reminder of the shattered glass on the ground that has my thoughts turning back to my mom. Lucky watches me closely as I take a step back, dislodging his grip. His hand brushes my side before falling away, and I swipe at my face.

"Are you going to talk to me?" he asks.

And I know what he means. It's not about the words; it's about letting him in. I tilt my head toward the door and walk outside, where the air is cooler. It blows across my damp cheeks the moment I step from dirt to grass, and I turn my face up to the sky, inhaling the scents of earth and machine oil and citrus. The last one is Lucky.

Lucky and I sit on the ground, our backs to the metal silo. It's later than I realized, the sun having dipped beneath the top of the fields. An orange glow lights the horizon, and my house stands in the distance, not terribly far off. Beyond that is Lucky's. We're the only two in this stretch. It's always made it feel like it was just us, ever since Lucky arrived when we were ten.

"My mom," I finally say, my voice sounding hoarse.

"Is she okay?" Lucky asks, but I can see it on his face. She's not, and he knows it.

I shake my head, and he sighs, long and low.

"Tell me?" he requests.

I nod, and in slow, stilted intervals, I explain what we learned today. That my mom has primary progressive MS. That she's had weird symptoms for years, but she always chalked them up to other things. The tingling in her hands could be carpal tunnel because of her office job at one of the town's corn processing plants. The muscle spasms were only diet related. The fatigue was normal. Who doesn't get tired from time to time?

Lucky listens patiently, never rushing me, never looking frustrated that it takes so long. When I finish, he reaches into my lap for my hand, curling his fingers around my own.

"I'm sorry," he says, and it's all there is to say. It's enough.

I nod, eyes stinging.

"You broke your collection," he adds quietly.

I shrug. I might regret it later, but... It's only broken glass. It can be repaired. Reformed. Unlike certain things.

I clench my eyes shut, replaying the decision I know I already made. I think I knew it the moment I tossed that first jar.

"I'm staying," I tell Lucky.

His hand twitches against my own. "What?"

I'm not sure he heard me, but when I find Lucky's eyes, I know he did.

Still, I repeat myself. "I'm staying."

He swallows several times, nodding slowly. I can see the gears turning. "Okay," he says. "We'll go to UNO, then. It's only a few hours away and—"

"No," I tell him.

"No?"

"I'm *staying*," I repeat.

His breath comes short as he digests what I'm saying. "You're dropping out?"

"I'll get my GED."

"You know what I mean, Ellis," he says hotly, his hand nearly crushing mine. "You're going to...what? Skip college and become a husker? A pulper? You really want that?"

I shake my head in resignation. It doesn't matter. I never saw myself getting out of Nebraska until recently, anyway. I always figured I'd be a lifer. Now I will be.

Lucky's nostrils flare, and he turns his face away. When he looks back, his eyes are on fire. "No," he says. "No. I won't let you."

It's not for you to decide.

"You don't get to throw your life away—"

"She's my mom!" I nearly yell. "I had to...to *carry* her this morning, Luck. She..."

I shake my head. The pain was so severe in her legs that she fell getting out of bed. I had to help her get dressed and out to the car so we could meet with her doctor about her test results. I can't go. Not now.

Lucky sets his jaw. "Fine. Then I'm staying, too."

"No."

"No?"

I shake my head roughly.

"It's not your choice, El," he says. "It's mine."

And you've always wanted to go.

"I can get my degree anywhere."

But you don't want to do it here.

"It's my choice," he repeats, sounding more stubbornly determined than I've ever heard him.

"Go," I tell him.

"No."

"Go."

"*No.*"

I let my head rest back against the silo and blink up at the sky. It's fully dark now, and a few fireflies are out, winking in front of the rows of corn. They look almost green tonight, haunted. When one flashes right beside my head, I lift my palm, holding it beneath the flicker of light, my hand cupped in invitation.

The firefly moves farther off, and I let my hand drop.

"You should go," I husk out.

Lucky doesn't respond, and we spend the next hour listening to the crickets sing. In the morning, I drive to my mom's employer and apply for a job.

Chapter 6

ELLIS

I was twenty-one when I got drunk with Lucky.

"Come on, Ellis," Lucky urges. "It's a rite of passage. Go ahead."

I pick up the pack of beer, feeling all sorts of wrong. But it's my twenty-first birthday, which means I can buy it legally now.

Lucky follows me to the counter. The cashier checks my ID, mumbling an unenthusiastic *happy birthday*, and then Lucky and I are on the sidewalk, heading toward his dorm at University of Nebraska Omaha. He's holding a pint of Jack Daniel's.

"Are you excited?" he asks, grinning.

I raise an eyebrow.

"Yeah, yeah, you've had beer before," he says, bumping me with his elbow. "But you've never been drunk."

I cut him a sharp glance, and Lucky rolls his eyes.

"Come *on*, El. Let loose this once. You're staying the night anyway, so just...drink a little. Have fun. Maybe find a sweet girl to kiss?"

The last suggestion is given with an eyebrow waggle, but I shake my head. I have no interest in girls, sweet or otherwise. No interest in anyone, really. Except...

I cut Lucky another glance as he tells me about his friends that are coming to my unofficial birthday party tonight. His hair is long, like usual, the wild curls hitting his shoulders and spilling free around his hoodie. His lips are turned in a smile as he talks, and his cheekbones cut a sharp line across his profile. He catches my eye for a second before walking around someone on the sidewalk, and yet again, I wonder at the blue. Lapis?

I've always thought Lucky looks ethereal, like he was cut from glass and smoothed to a polish. But somewhere along the way, what was fascination for color and form became...something else entirely. I don't know when it happened, exactly. When I started dreaming about his lips and how they felt against my own. When I started *wondering* every time Lucky would talk about blowjobs and the men he found here at college. When I started wishing those other men would simply disappear because Lucky is supposed to be mine—*my* friend, *my* person—and don't they know that? Doesn't he?

Except that's not fair. I know that. And what would Lucky say if he knew? What would he think of these feelings I've been hiding?

Would he—could he—feel the same?

I suppose, in the end, it doesn't matter when things started to change. Because Lucky's path has been set from the moment he came into my life. *"I'm gonna get out of this town one day, El."* He never was mine to keep. No matter how much I wish it.

"You okay?" Lucky asks, nudging the side of my arm. We're walking up the steps to his dorm now.

I give him a nod.

"Would you rather it just be me and you?" he asks, coming to a stop. "I didn't mean to invite so many people, but you know how it goes. You tell a couple friends, they tell a couple friends, and then all of a sudden, it's a party."

I don't really know, no. But it's fine.

I shake my head and give Lucky's arm a tug to keep going. He follows me through the door, and this time, it's me leading the way to Lucky's room. It's not the first time I've visited.

The party is already underway when we arrive. Lucky's room and the one next door are opened up to one another, both packed like sardine cans and buzzing with noise. People mingle with cheap beer in hand while a bottle of Jägermeister makes the rounds. Lucky clears a path through it all, dragging me to the back of the room. I lean against his desk as he starts mixing his whiskey with Coke and chatting to one of his friends. I recognize a few of the partygoers, including Lucky's roommate, who gives me an up-nod from across the room. Popping open one of my beers, I take a sip.

Guys and girls and one self-introduced nonbinary person come up to me throughout the evening. They give me drinks because Lucky tells them it's my birthday, and they make small talk. Or, at least, they try. They never stick around long when they realize I'm not talking back. Lucky comes over at one point to apologize to me, but it's not his fault. Still, he's never far off, and his eyes find me often.

It's somewhere around my fourth beer—I lost count of shots—when a guy shows up and attaches himself to Lucky's side. Lucky welcomes it, smiling and laughing along as the guy dips his head to Lucky's ear, saying something charming, it would seem. His palm slides low on Lucky's back, his hold possessive. Familiar.

My hands clench into fists.

Lucky introduces us before long, his cheeks a little flushed from drinking. "El, this is Andrew."

"Ah, the best friend," Andrew says, his arm tucked around Lucky's waist. He smiles at me, but his gaze isn't friendly.

I tip my head in a nod.

"So Lucky tells me you're a corn farmer," the guy says, taking a swig of his beer. His thumb sneaks under Lucky's shirt, and he grins a little wider when he sees me watching. "What's that like?"

I shrug, and he narrows his eyes.

"It's hard work," Lucky fills in for me. "A lot of physical labor."

"Is that why your friend is built like a brick house?" Andrew asks.

Lucky snorts a little. "No, that's just El."

Andrew's eyes run over me, but it's nothing like the way he looks at Lucky. "You play football?" he asks.

I grunt, and Lucky cracks a smile. He knows I couldn't care less about sports. Andrew, though, bristles, looking between the two of us.

"What?" he asks. "Is that a no?"

"Ellis doesn't play football," Lucky answers for me.

"What, he can't speak for himself?" Andrew tosses back.

Lucky stiffens. "Don't be a dick."

Andrew turns away from me, bending low to say something in Lucky's ear. I can't make out the words, but Lucky rolls his eyes. It mollifies me some, but when Andrew's lips travel downward, pressing to Lucky's neck and Lucky's eyes slip closed, I have to step away.

My heart is pounding when I climb up the ladder to Lucky's loft. His and his roommate's beds are up on a platform built over the room, which allows for more standing space but makes for tight sleeping quarters. I stoop low, slipping onto Lucky's mattress and rolling until I'm tucked up beside the wall. I don't think anyone saw me leave.

I stare up at the ceiling as the sounds of the party continue below. There's a mark in the plaster over my head that looks almost like a windmill, and I trace the shape with the tip of my finger. My world spins just a little, and for a moment, I imagine I'm one of those stars Lucky captured with his camera.

He won't be here much longer. He's graduating next year, and then he'll be gone. He stayed for college out of guilt. Obligation. A fact that never ceases to make my gut tighten. But soon, he won't have an excuse. He'll have his degree. He'll be ready to chase his dreams. And me? I'll still be here, tethered loosely to my friend no matter where he goes.

I let out a breath. We've been on borrowed time. But Lucky will go—he was always going to go—and I can't even fault him for it. I want him to be happy. Simply, truly happy.

"El?"

I turn toward the sound of my friend's voice, finding him regarding me with a small frown. It smooths out, though, as Lucky climbs the remaining step into the loft. He settles on his knees beside the bed, and I realize the room is quiet. How long have I been up here?

"I'm sorry," he says.

My brows draw together.

"For all the people," he clarifies. "I know it's not your thing."

I shrug.

Lucky exhales, scooting onto his stomach beside me. He settles his head on his arm, riotous golden hair everywhere, and I turn on my side to see him better. My world shifts again, like I'm a ship at sea, and I realize maybe I am a little drunk, after all.

"They're gone now," Lucky says. "Party moved next door."

I nod. I won't complain about having Lucky to myself. Not ever.

"Andrew?" I ask.

Lucky cringes, almost. "Yeah, uh. He's gone, too."

I shake my head. That's not what I meant, and I think he knows it.

"We're friends. Mostly," he says.

Mostly. They're sleeping together.

My gut cramps.

"You didn't like him," Lucky notes.

No, I didn't. I didn't like the way he was touching Lucky, but I don't tell him that.

"It's not serious, you know?" he says, almost like he's pleading with me to understand. As if he would need my permission in the first place. "It's just fun with him. Just some meaningless fun."

I don't get it, not fully. I've never wanted something meaningless—sex for the sake of sex. What's the point? The only person I've ever wanted to touch is right in front of me, and anything between us could never be meaningless. Not to me.

It's a souring reminder. I know I'm not like most. My wires run a little differently. But even if Lucky could ever look at me the way he looks at guys like Andrew, what good would it possibly do? It would only hurt more, in the end—having a taste, only to lose it. I'd rather never know.

I think, maybe, this is all I'll ever have. Because who else is going to take the time to understand me like Lucky?

When I don't say anything, Lucky lets out a breath. "You're not interested in girls, are you," he says, not quite a question. More like he's confirming something for himself.

Still, I shake my head. *No, I'm not.*

He licks his lips and swallows hard. "And...have you ever wanted other guys?"

My heart kicks, and Lucky watches me, waiting for an answer. After what feels like an eternity, I shake my head slowly.

"No," I manage to say.

Only you. There's only ever been you.

Lucky nods, looking at a point over my shoulder, and for once, I'm grateful he missed the words inside my head.

"How's your mom?" he asks.

I nod a little. She's been stable these past few months, which is about the best we could ask for. "Got the wheelchair ramp in," I tell him.

It's been a slow process, outfitting the house for when my mom will eventually need accessibility. We're getting closer to that stage, but we're not quite there yet.

Lucky gives my arm a squeeze, leaving his hand there afterwards. His palm is warm against my forearm, and his thumb brushes my skin almost absentmindedly. I close my eyes for a moment, letting the sensation—that slow, sweet, drugging *want*—wash through me before I push it away.

"El," Lucky says, and I open my eyes. "It should've just been me and you tonight. I'm sorry."

I shake my head, grabbing Lucky's hand and giving his knuckles a quick kiss. His breath catches.

"If you ever decide to love someone," he says slowly, "they'll be very lucky."

He already is.

Lucky turns onto his back, settling on the narrow mattress, his head on one side of his pillow. The rest of it is for me. "Happy birthday, El."

And maybe it's the alcohol still running through my system that has me acting without thought, but I lean my forehead against Lucky's shoulder and throw my arm over his chest, hand settling at his heart. He doesn't move for the longest moment, but then his head leans against my own, and his hand curls up over my wrist, holding me in place.

For one night, I hold Lucky like I want to. And in the morning, I go.

Chapter 7

ELLIS

I was twenty-two when I said goodbye.

I hear Lucky's car pulling up his parents' drive before I see it, but I'm nearly done replacing the belt on the lawn mower, so I focus on my task. When I finally turn around, Lucky is standing beside his vehicle, looking at me, and I *know*.

Heart heavy, I right the mower as Lucky strides over through the too-tall grass. He walks past the hatch of the tornado shelter before reaching the backyard, and then he stops five feet in front of me.

I bring my eyes to his slowly, doing my best not to flinch when he opens his mouth.

"I got the job," he says.

I nod, using a rag to wipe the oil off my hands before I pocket the cloth and step toward him. I tap the side of his lips, and Lucky frowns harder.

"I'm happy," he claims.

I raise an eyebrow, keeping my own feelings locked down tight. Because I knew, I *knew* this day would come, and Lucky deserves nothing but my support. But he surprises me, storming a step away.

"I *am* happy," he huffs, hair whipping around his face when he turns back my way. "This job is unreal. I'll be flying all over the world. They're starting me in Norway. *Norway*, El. You know how much I've wanted this."

I nod once. Lucky's been set on being a photojournalist since his mid-teens, and starting out at a prominent nature magazine like he'll be doing is a big deal.

He'll see the world. His remarkable life.

I'm not the least bit surprised he got the job. Lucky is immensely talented, and when he sets his mind to something, there's no stopping him.

But he's also sad. I can see that plain as day, despite what he himself claims.

"I'll miss you, too," I tell him.

He croaks, his arms hanging limply at his sides. "*Damn* it, El."

What...

Lucky stalks over, shoving my shoulder. "You...you can't just..." He huffs again, and I have no clue why he's so put out. "I'm going to call. And you're going to talk to me."

It sounds like a threat.

"Yes," I say.

"And sometimes, we'll email."

I nod.

"But we're not done," he says vehemently, stepping into my space. "We'll *never* be done. Me and you, we don't have an ending."

And what do I possibly say to that?

When I open my arms, Lucky falls into them. At some point in the past couple years, he grew into a man, but right now, with him tucked against me, his head under my chin, it feels as if we're boys again. Just two young boys with no responsibilities or duty, in a time where dreams ruled the waking world.

But we're not boys anymore, are we? The world spins, and with it, we move forward.

"I'm going to miss you, El," he finally says, voice cracking alongside my heart.

I wipe my cheek before pulling back. "Tell me," I say.

So he does. The pair of us sit side by side on the overgrown grass as Lucky tells me about his new position stationed out of New York City. He tells me about the second interview he just arrived home from and how he checked out an apartment there before he flew back. He tells me about his first assignment in Norway and how he can't wait to see the fjords. And the more he talks, the more animated he gets, and the wider his smile. It's good, seeing that. It's right.

He'll move later this week, and he promises to visit lots. "You better visit me, too, Ellis," he says, sounding stern.

I cross my heart, and Lucky snorts.

"Promise me something," he says suddenly.

What's that?

"I need you to be happy," he says. "Promise me you'll be happy here."

"I will," I tell him. I like it here. I always have.

He nods, swallowing and looking away. When he looks back, he says, "I have an idea. Feel like trespassing for old time's sake?"

I huff a laugh, and Lucky's smile widens.

Before we go, I stop inside to check on my mom. She's already set up in bed, reading before sleep. Even though she insists she's fine, I get her a small snack and a glass of water, leaving both on her nightstand. Once I meet Lucky back outside, we head toward my truck.

Lucky rolls down the window as I drive, and I can't help but glance at him as we bump down the dirt roads. There's an ache in my chest every time I catch the corner of his smile, but I do my best to ignore it.

I park a ways down from the house with the windmill, in a spot where my vehicle won't be visible from inside any of the nearby homes. The sky is only just now darkening, so Lucky and I are extra careful to sneak our way across the property, and I feel more than a little ridiculous while we do so. It seems worth it, though, when we crawl up onto that platform at the top of the windmill. The sky is lit with pink and orange tonight, and through the small, open window, we watch the colors spread and dissipate like we did so many years ago.

"Do you remember when we were twelve," Lucky says, "and you convinced me to race our bikes down the rows of corn behind Mrs. Brown's house, and we almost didn't make it out in time before the combine harvester came through?"

I stare at him, unimpressed.

"*Yes*," he insists. "*You* convinced *me*."

We seem to have very different recollections of that day. I remember racing after Lucky, who thought it would be fun to tempt fate. Any Nebraskan raised around these parts knows you stay out of the fields when the harvesters are running.

Lucky simply chuckles as he knocks his shoulder into mine. He nearly gave me a heart attack that day, but I admit it's made me extra vigilant when working the land now.

"Remember...the mud slide?" I ask him.

Lucky barks a laugh, his eyes sparkling. "We were sixteen," he says. "And they were doing construction down by the railroad."

I nod. It had been raining really hard for days when we stumbled on the fenced-off construction site. We only meant to take a peek, but then we noticed a huge mound of dug-up dirt. And, well, when Lucky found a piece of perfectly bent sheet metal, we had to ride it down the hill. A few times.

Lucky's whole body shakes as he laughs. "We got so dirty, we had to hose each other off outside your house," he says, wiping his eye. "I had mud up my ass."

He laughs harder when I snort, nodding my agreement.

"Remember..." He has to start over, humming a little to disperse his laughter. "Remember a couple weeks after that when you took me to prom?"

My gaze snags on his, and his expression is so warm that my heart starts to pound in my chest. I hadn't felt...different toward Lucky at that point. He was my friend. *Just* my friend. But he'd seemed so sad, and I didn't want him to miss prom just because he didn't have anyone to go with.

"You wore a blue boutonniere," he says quietly, his eyes dropping to my chest as if remembering. I tried to match the color to his eyes, but it wasn't quite right. "You were really handsome that day. I never told you that."

I swallow roughly, my pulse doing its best to drown out everything else.

"You looked—" I cut myself off, not unable to finish my sentence, but stopping myself from doing so at the last moment.

Lucky smiles a little, giving me another nudge. "Okay?" he asks.

Beautiful.

I nod, and Lucky sighs, looking back out the window. "Things are going to change," he says simply.

They already have. Lucky has been drifting steadily away from me for years now, ever since he left for college. Our paths split back then, and I don't begrudge him living his life, but he's right. Nothing will be the same after this. This is...bigger.

"I'll call," he says, repeating his words from earlier. "And you'll answer."

Every time.

When Lucky lays his head on my shoulder, we fall silent. The sky is navy, stars shining like littered glass, and eventually, when Lucky's head rolls forward and he jerks back to consciousness, we lie down, knees bent toward one another in the small space. Neither of us suggests leaving.

As we resist sleep at the top of that windmill, Lucky reaches out his hand. Without hesitation, I twine my fingers with his. Blue eyes blink at me in the dark, and I don't dare look away. For once, Lucky stays silent with me, neither of us speaking a word.

My mom's voice enters my head then, a whisper of memory from when I was seven. *"Not everyone is going to understand you, Ellis. But it's not your job to make them."*

Lucky has always heard me. From the very first time we met, he's heard me. He knows me, unlike any other.

He squeezes my hand then, as if to say *yes*, and it takes everything in me not to break.

No, this isn't our end. Never that.

But it is goodbye.

I don't remember falling asleep, but it's still dark out when Lucky's hushed voice whispers my name. I blink my eyes open.

"We have to go," he says, face hovering over mine. "It's almost sunrise."

The pair of us sneak down the spiraling staircase inside the short windmill, our steps light. Lucky snickers when I nearly trip as we're running past the house like the trespassers we are. When we get to my truck parked along the side of the dirt road, Lucky looks at me, and we both break into laughter.

There's a grin on Lucky's face as we drive back home. It wanes a little the closer we get, but I try not to focus on that.

When I park in front of my house, Lucky's hand lands on my own. I see it then, his fear. His worry over the unknown.

"It'll be good," I tell him, my voice sounding raspy after the little sleep we managed.

He nods in a jerk, and we exit the truck. Lucky isn't leaving for a few days still, but I know they'll pass quickly. He'll be packing and getting everything set up, and there might not be a chance for another night like we just had. The thought makes me almost unbearably sad, but I shore myself up tight, refusing to crack in front of Lucky. This pain, it's my own, and I'll work through it.

It's not his fault my feelings grew to...this.

We stand opposite one another for a long, stretching moment. "See you later?" Lucky finally asks.

I nod, and then so does he.

"Yeah," he says quietly. "Me and you, right, El?"

"Me and you," I answer.

Lucky smiles, and, as he turns to go, the morning sun crests the top of the cornfields. For a mere blink in time, he's set alight, his hair a halo of burnished gold. He stops in front of his house, looking back at me, and then he's gone.

I was ten years old when I met Lucky. I knew it then, and I know it now. He's a firefly. Luminous and wild. He was never meant to be trapped. Not here and not with me.

And in a few days, I'll finally watch him fly away.

Part II: Waning

Chapter 8

LUCKY

"Holy shit, that was fantastic!" Danil says, lowering a hand to help me up into the boat.

I pull out my mouthpiece, giving my partner-in-crime a grin as I make room for our scuba guide to climb up the ladder after me. I work on catching my breath as I tug off some of my gear, not because I couldn't breathe down below the surface, but because diving in the Great Blue Hole was an immense rush, and my body is still buzzing with the high of it.

"Did you get the hammerhead?" Danil asks, grabbing a towel for his face. He tosses one at me, too, which I snag from the air.

"What do you think?" I retort, pulling my diving camera free. I flip through the shots before angling the screen Danil's way.

He whistles. "Thought it was going to take a bite out of you."

"They're not dangerous," I say of the hammerhead shark.

"Maybe not, but you got right in its face," he points out.

I shrug. "Had to get the shot."

"Uh-huh," he says, as if he isn't just as big of an adrenaline junkie as me. "Well, I'm just glad I didn't lose my new partner."

Danil and I have been working together for five months now. He wasn't my first partner at the magazine. That was Geoff, and I was paired with him for two-and-a-half years before he retired. Geoff was in his mid-sixties, and the man was an inspiration. After huffing and puffing up the Aconcagua mountain in the Andes while Geoff himself barely broke a sweat, I gained a new idol. He was the journalism half of our photojournalism partnership, and now that position is filled by Danil.

While Geoff was a more professional, calm presence in my life, Danil is a whirlwind. He's twenty-eight to my twenty-five, has never met a man, woman, or child he couldn't charm, and is an in-your-face out-and-proud pansexual. We're a good match.

"Well, lucky for you, no shark bites today," I tell Danil.

He snorts indelicately. "Lucky for you, too, Lucky-boy."

I chuck my towel at him, and Danil laughs. He knows I hate that nickname.

As our guide gets the boat ready to bring us back to shore, Danil plops down on the wooden deck beside me. He nods in the other man's direction.

"I'm meeting up with Tomasz later," my coworker says quietly. "Come to my room with us?"

I turn my gaze his way slowly. "When did you possibly have time to flirt with our scuba guide?"

Danil gives me a rakish grin, and I shake my head. The guy is something else, but I can't blame Tomasz for his interest. Danil has that tall, dark, and handsome allure that traps partners like flies. I've been trapped once or twice—or half a dozen times—myself.

"Is that a yes?" Danil asks, knocking his leg into mine.

"We should probably stop sleeping together, Dani."

He looks affronted. "What on Earth for?"

I laugh, and the boat kicks into motion. "You don't think it's a bad idea, mixing business with pleasure?"

"Pleasure is never a bad idea," he practically purrs.

I push his face away, and this time, it's Danil laughing. But then he pouts. "Fine. But I'll have you know you're breaking my heart, Lucky."

"Somehow, I think you'll survive."

He lets out a long-suffering sigh. "Yes, well. What are you going to do instead? Call your Ellis?"

My Ellis.

The thump in my heart that accompanies those words is as familiar to me as the man himself. Ellis, who's tall, dark, and handsome in his own right, but whose strength lies in his steady calm and unwavering dependability. Ellis, whose rumble of a voice is like distant thunder, so rarely there but impossible to ignore. Ellis, my...friend. Above all else, he's my best friend. Still. Always.

"Yeah," I say on a breath. "That's what I'm going to do."

Danil watches me closely before he shrugs, looking off over the bow of the boat. "Well, I hope the phone sex is worth it."

"We're not having phone sex," I say, smacking his arm.

One of his eyebrows arches. "What the hell else are you doing on those hours-long calls?" When I don't answer, his second eyebrow joins the first. "You just talk?"

"We just talk," I confirm.

Well, more like I talk, and Ellis listens.

Danil and I bump along as the boat rolls over waves, but then we're slowing down, approaching the dock we set off from half a day earlier.

"Well," my coworker says, "if you change your mind, you know where to find me. And Tomasz."

"Yeah," I tell him, but when it comes down to catching up with Ellis or having sex with Danil, there's no competition.

When we reach the shore, Danil has a quick word with our guide, and then the two of us head off to grab some food. We stop at the first place we reach: a small shack of a restaurant set right on the beach with its sides opened up to the warm evening air. I get a fish-of-the-day sandwich, and it's so good, I could weep.

The sky is turning pink by the time Danil and I get back to our lodging. He gives me a salute as he heads into his bungalow, and I carry my tired and aching body into my own. I should shower off the ocean, as well as the exertion of the day, upload the photographs I took, and even go through tomorrow's itinerary. But I don't do any of it. I power on my phone, flop onto the hammock on my porch overlooking the Caribbean Sea, and call Ellis.

He answers on the third ring.

"El?"

There's a soft hum, and every muscle in my body relaxes as if I'm still floating in deep, dark blue.

"Hey," I say softly. "How's it going?"

A small grunt.

"Good. And your mom?"

"Yeah," he says. "Good."

I smile into the phone. Ellis can't rely on physical cues when we're talking so far away, so he's had to get used to speaking more. It takes a while, sometimes, but I don't mind. Never have.

"You'll never guess where I am," I say.

A curious hum.

"Belize. It's beautiful here. I think you'd really like it."

He hums again, but it's a question.

"There's so much color everywhere," I explain. "The water, the sky, the plants. Even the shops. Everything is washed in vibrant pinks and blues and oranges. And *God*, the crab. Have you ever had crab?"

I don't think he has, and a small grunt confirms it.

"It's so good," I say. "Sweet, almost. They catch it early in the morning and serve it that day. You have to watch out for shell because there's always shell, but it's worth it. And it's so cheap here, it feels like a steal."

Ellis makes a sound like he's getting ready to say something, so I wait. The breeze blows through the palm trees on the beach, making the large fronds wave gently, and the water crashing on shore is a constant soundtrack, the repetitive whoosh easy to forget about if you're not listening for it. I wonder what sky Ellis is looking at right now. I'm an hour behind him in Belize, so he's probably staring at black night. If he's outside at all.

"Maisy's had a clam...special last month," he says, his words coming out a little stilted with the occasional pause.

"Uh-oh," I say.

Ellis laughs, and *God*, it's such a good sound. "People got sick."

I groan. Maisy's Diner serves great breakfast and lunch food, but I can't imagine any clams they would have access to would be fresh. The poor people of Nebraska.

"Did you have any?" I ask.

There's a grunt, which I take to mean yes. Ellis huffs when I start to laugh.

"Sorry," I croak out.

"Not," he counters.

He knows me well.

I let out a measured breath, using my foot to push the hammock into motion as I rein in my amusement. "I *am* sorry you got sick," I clarify. The *but not sorry for laughing* part goes unsaid. It's what friends do, after all.

Ellis huffs again, but it's a gentler sound. "Belize?" he asks.

"Yeah," I say, a smile on my face. "I went down the Great Blue Hole with Dani."

When there's silence, I stutter out another laugh.

"It's one of the largest underwater sinkholes in the world," I explain. "It was..."

How to even describe it? It felt like I was exploring the great unknown. Like I was an interloper into something vast and foreign and beautiful.

"It was blue," I start with, to which Ellis snorts. I chuckle with him. "No, stay with me. At the top, the water is this stunning Caribbean blue, right? So clear and nearly turquoise. But the sinkhole, it was this big circle of deep, dark blue, like a vacuum of space dropped straight into the sea. And when you get down there, there are these caves. And fish everywhere. Parrotfish, angelfish, reef sharks. It was..." I shake my head a little. "I was just there, in their home, surrounded by endless blue, and it was beautiful."

"Luck," he says quietly.

I close my eyes tight, breathing in the sound of my name and letting it cocoon me.

"Yeah," I say. "You'd like the parrotfish best, I think. Some of them are as bright as a rainbow."

"Tell me," he says. So I do.

We talk for hours, like we usually do when I call. And I realize, not for the first time, that my favorite part about all of these adventures is when I get to go back to whatever temporary home I have at the time and share them with Ellis.

It's nearly midnight when we finally say goodnight, and I cringe a little at how late I kept Ellis up, knowing he rises with the sun. But, like I told him, I have a busy week planned, and I likely won't have a chance to call again for a while.

After dropping out of the hammock, I head inside, ignoring the quiet sounds I can hear coming from Danil's open window. I transfer today's photos to my laptop and send a couple to Ellis that I think he'll enjoy, and then I strip down and wash off the day. When I sink into my surprisingly comfortable, narrow-as-can-be bed, I think about Ellis doing the same.

It's dangerous, letting my mind go there, but I can't drum up the willpower to stop myself tonight. I think of him beside me, those deep, brown eyes of his soft as they gaze my way. I think of his big hands—*God*, those hands—and the massive breadth of his shoulders. I think of his jaw and his steady heartbeat and his arm slung across my chest.

And with the last of my waking thoughts, I think about going home.

Chapter 9

ELLIS

"Oh, this one is lovely," my mom says.

I take a look at the bowl she's pointing at and nod. It is pretty, but it's not what I'm looking for.

We continue along the zigzagging aisles of the antique shop, my gait slow to match my mom's. She's using her walking aid today, and the wheels squeak lightly when she turns. I stop to look at an old set of Stanley Bailey woodworking planes as she examines a teapot with a scrolling blue design along the side.

"How's Lucky?" she asks, splitting the silence.

I catch her eye and nod.

"Where's he at now?"

I clear my throat. "The city."

"Ah," she says. "Back in New York."

I give a nod. He's never there for long between assignments. The magazine sends him out a couple times a month. With Dani, his new partner.

"I saw that article on the sea turtle migration," she says. "Where was that?"

"Indonesia," I answer after a moment, stepping along with my mom as she walks into a new aisle. There's furniture here, and some old, ratty dolls.

"That's right. His pictures were beautiful."

Always are.

I know the ones she's talking about, though. Lucky must have been right down in the sand with the turtles because it looks like they're straining toward him, not the ocean. One of the pictures in particular made headlines. In it, the turtle, newly hatched, had wire hanging from its flipper. Lucky told me after the fact that they removed the trash before the turtle could make it to the water, but it was a stark reminder of how humans are impacting the environment, and more than one talk show featured the article with the photograph Lucky took.

"I talked to Marcus yesterday," my mom says, throwing me for a loop. She glances at me before going on. "Put in my notice."

"Mom," I say a little sadly.

She shakes her head. "It's time, baby. And don't give me that look," she adds. "You'll always be my baby, you know that."

I nod, and my mom sighs.

"My legs are going," she says factually, "and I can barely type anymore." To prove her point, she holds out her hand. The tremor is more pronounced than it used to be, but when she grabs onto her walker again, I can barely see it. "I'm finishing out the month, and then I'll be done."

I'd tell her I'm sorry, but I know she doesn't want to hear it. And at fifty-four, maybe she'd be ready to retire, even without the MS spurring her on.

"Gabby will be taking over for me," she says.

Gabby has worked in the office for over a year now. She moved to town from South Dakota and has a dog named Toodles—facts I know because Gabby likes to chat in a friendly way. I don't mind it when I'm in the office, and she doesn't seem to care that I don't say much back.

"She's cute, don't you think?" my mom says, shocking me to a standstill. She stops, turning to look at me. "No?"

When I continue staring, she huffs a laugh and walks on. My mom never asks me about dating or girls. Or guys, for that matter.

"That's a no, then," she says, almost to herself.

I catch up quickly, and my mom gives my arm a shaky pat.

"I won't pry," she says. "You're an adult, and we had the talk long ago, so I know those bases are covered."

We had quite a few talks, actually, when I was a teenager. My mom lectured me on safe sex (of all kinds). She gave me a box of condoms (that I never used). And she explained consent to me numerous times (including the fact that *I* could say no, too).

But beyond that, she's never tried to meddle in my love life. Until—maybe—now.

"All I want," she goes on, "is for you to be happy, whether that's with someone or without. But you know I'm here if you ever have questions. You're never too old to need your mother."

I give my mom a sharp nod, and she reaches up to brush my hair behind my ear. She can barely manage it these days while we're standing, now that I'm a good foot taller than her and she's a little more shaky on her feet. But it feels familiar, that action, and my heart aches.

"Cora and Ron invited us over for burgers tonight," my mom says, continuing down the aisle. One of the wheels on her walker catches on the corner of a rug, dragging a little before popping free. "I told them we'd be there. I hope you don't mind."

I shake my head. Of course I don't. I like Lucky's parents. They've always been kind to me and my mom. Good neighbors. Good people.

"Maybe I'll make those lemon bars," she says, but my mind is suddenly elsewhere.

On the shelf in front of me, tucked away and nearly hidden behind a few hardcover books, is a pink glass vase. It's big, bigger than most pieces I find in places like this. But the color is perfect. I'm careful as I move the books aside so I can reach it. There's a slight dusty sheen covering the glass, but it's otherwise in impeccable condition. Not that it would make a difference, really. The color is right, and that's all that matters.

"Found one?" my mom asks from further up ahead.

I nod, my eyes on the vase as I turn it in my hands. There's a sticker on the bottom. Twenty dollars. Well worth it.

I check the area we're in for any more hidden treasures, but not finding any, me and my mom make our way slowly back to the front of the store. I pay with cash before we exit, and then I help my mom into the truck. Not for the first time, I think about switching it for something with handicap accessibility. Soon.

It's a forty-minute drive back home, but it passes quickly, my mom talking about some of the people she works with that she'll miss. Not that she won't still see them, she makes sure to tell me, but it'll be different.

I know the feeling.

The air is on as we drive, keeping the cab cool, and my mind keeps straying to the pink vase sitting in the backseat, wrapped carefully in paper. I already have the rest of the colors. This is the last piece I need.

When we get home, it's late afternoon. Mom settles into her wheelchair without a word, and I watch her maneuver into the kitchen with a pinch in my gut. After a day like today, it's no surprise she needs the added support, but it never fails to make my stomach knot, seeing her in that chair. She sets about making lemon bars as I pull out my laptop.

I check for messages first. With Lucky having gotten home the night before, there's likely nothing, but I check all the same. I try not to be disappointed when I see the empty inbox. I know Lucky's too busy to message or call every day.

Even so, I start a new email.

Hey, Luck. When I woke up this morning, the sky was a gentle cyan that made me think of you. Not that it takes much for that to happen. But I woke with you on my mind, all the same. It's been six months since I saw you last. Since I saw your smile with that hint of incisor. Saw those golden corkscrews floating around your face in the breeze. Saw your eyes, so bright and blue, looking at me the way you do. Six months since I hugged you to me and told you, once again, goodbye. It's never good when you go, but I know it's good for you.

I hope you're happy. I know you are. I hope you're living. I have no doubt of that, either. I hope, sometimes, that you think of me like I think of you. But then I hope you don't because I miss you, Luck. And I don't want you to miss me the same.

I think it was at thirteen that I first felt my heart beat for you. And break, just a little. Because I knew, like that tornado, you'd leave destruction in your path, and I'd be your willing victim.

I'd do it again.

I love you, my brilliant firefly.

I close the email when I'm done, and just like all the others, it sits lifeless in my drafts. I don't know what it accomplishes, writing to a ghost, but it makes me feel...maybe not better, but a little lighter each time it's done. Like I've shed some of the weight of all those unsaid words residing inside my head.

When I close my laptop, I face my mom. "Need help?" I ask her.

She looks over at me with a hum. She's in front of the counter that sits lower than the rest, mixing bright yellow ingredients in a bowl. "I've got it under control," she tells me. "Go on. I know you're dying to take care of that vase. Just remember, dinner at the Buchanans' in an hour."

I give my mom a nod before grabbing my keychain and heading out the door. The vase is in the truck where I left it, and after tucking it under my arm, I make my way to the silo. We never used to keep it locked, but I added the precaution a couple years back. Not that we've ever had issues with theft around here.

I unlock the heavy door when I get there and throw it open, blinking a few times to acclimate my eyes. Flicking on the lights inside makes the interior marginally brighter, but even so, it's dimmer than outside.

Glass runs along the curved interior wall of the silo, sitting atop shelves that I designed to fit the space when I started the upgrades in here. Every color imaginable rests along those shelves. Pinks and purples, yellow and blue. Red, black, green, white, gold.

My collection has grown quite a lot in the last few years.

I bring the vase over to my workbench. The tabletop is wood, worn but sturdy. Carefully, I unwrap the new piece, leaving the paper beneath the glass as I look it over again. The pink is exactly what I had in mind, brighter than the options along the wall.

Grabbing a cloth, I clean the dust off its surface. I give it a few passes before using water and then a dry cloth to make sure it's spotless. When I'm done, it gleams under the low light. Cerise, maybe. It really is quite beautiful.

Satisfied, I set the vase on its side and put on my gloves. Without an ounce of hesitation, I pick up the hammer sitting at the edge of the workbench.

And I break the vase into pieces.

Chapter 10

LUCKY

"Fuck," Danil groans, his mouth near my ear as we dance. His hands are on my hips, some other guy's hands are on his hips, and with my eyes closed, all I hear is the pounding beat of the music and Danil's occasional swear in both English and Russian. Until he says, "Let's get out of here, Lucky-boy."

I let my eyes open and give Danil's nipple a good twist.

He grunts before laughing. "Do that again later."

"Stop with that nickname," I tell him over the hammering pulse of the club.

"Come on, Lucky," he croons, seemingly uncaring that the guy behind him is slipping his fingers in the front of Danil's jeans. "Your place, my place, doesn't matter."

God, I could really use the release. It's been weeks.

"Tim can come, too," Danil says, as if trying to sweeten the pot.

"Tom," the guy behind him corrects.

Danil's eyes widen, and I have to work hard not to laugh at his *oops* cringe. Luckily, Tom can't see it.

"Tom, too," Danil says quickly. "What'cha say?"

Danil is smiling before I've even nodded my yes.

The three of us make our way out of the club, Tom looking as if he won the lottery. We grab a cab out on the street and head toward Danil's. While Danil and Tom kiss in the backseat, I roll down my window and inhale deeply. The air smells of exhaust, spiced meat from a street vendor, and something I've never been able to name in all the time I've lived here. It's nothing like Nebraska.

I never thought I'd miss the earthy-sweet scent of corn.

Danil's apartment is in a high-rise much nicer than my own. He comes from money—something that's evident in those fancy watches he rotates through and the fact that his building has not one, but two pools—but he's surprisingly down-to-earth, all things considered. Still, it's always a bit of a shock stepping into his three-bedroom home with world-class views and trying to reconcile that level of wealth with my coworker who has no problem following me into grimy caves or along three-day hiking trails for our assignments at the magazine. Heck, he's usually the first one leaping into semi-danger.

Now, though, Danil is all suave sophistication as he leads Tom into the living room, his eyes on me all the while. Even as Danil undresses Tom, and even as he kisses down his neck, those dark eyes stay locked on mine.

I blow out a slow breath as I approach, and Danil grins, like the cat who caught the canary. I can't blame alcohol on my decision to keep up this game with Danil—I didn't drink anything at the club—and I can't even say I don't want it. It's thrilling every time I let him drag me into his web. It might not mean anything, but who says it has to?

I strip off my shirt as Danil sinks to his knees in front of Tom, and for a blissful reprieve in time, there are no fields of green and maize in my mind or memories of waterfalls. No worry that I'm somehow making a mistake with my life or longing for things I told myself were off-limits. For a little while, I let myself feel nothing but good. I even almost convince myself it's enough. That it doesn't all feel a bit...empty in the end.

When the rush has swept past and the three of us lie sprawled out on Danil's plush living room rug, Tom is the first to speak. "Shit. Holy fucking shit."

Danil chuckles, his arm over Tom's waist but his thumb running a circuit on my hip. "That good?"

Tom blinks up at the ceiling. "Shit."

"Excuse me," I say, extracting myself from the pile. Danil frowns, but I grab my shorts, pulling them on as I make my way to his balcony. The air is crisp when I step outside, and I almost go back in for my shirt, but in the end, I hunker down in a chair and wrap my arms around my knees to ward off the chill.

I'm not surprised when Danil joins me a few minutes later. "Here," he says, dropping a blanket over my shoulders.

"Thanks," I mumble.

Danil sits next to me, shirt and jeans in place. He pulls out a pack of cigarettes, extracting one and tucking it between his lips as he flicks on a lighter.

"You really should stop," I tell him.

He hums, shrugging as the cigarette lights. His inhale sounds like a sigh. "I like it."

"It'll kill you."

"So glad to hear you care about my health," he says, flashing me a smile.

"You're my friend," I reply, tucking the blanket more firmly around my shoulders. "Of course I care."

Danil makes a soft sound, stretching his long legs out in front of him on the chaise. When he speaks, his voice is far away, as if he's talking to only himself. "And high above, the moon sits round, and we, in its light. Waxing, waning, never gone. A gift to see the night."

I look over at Danil as he brings his cigarette back to his lips. Smoke drifts lazily into the air when he blows it from his lungs.

"I forget sometimes," I tell him.

"What's that?" he asks, dark eyes meeting mine.

"That you're a poet."

He scoffs, arm resting on his chair. "I'm a journalist, not a poet."

"But you have a way with words," I counter.

And he does. Danil is a damn good journalist, as compelling in written word as he is in person. It never ceases to amaze me when I read his articles, that the fuckboy I know is capable of such insightful reporting. And—apparently—spontaneous verse.

"Do you like that, Lucky-boy?" he asks me lazily. "Is that what you're telling me? Shall I whisper sweet nothings in your ear?"

I nearly scoff. "Sure, Dani. As if you need sweet words to woo me into your bed."

He watches me for a moment, gaze narrowed, until something seems to click. "No," he says slowly, stubbing out his cigarette. "For fuck's sake, Lucky, don't tell me you're a romantic? I mean, you're nearly as big of a slut as I am—no offense, of course—and that's saying something."

This time, I do scoff, but Danil is not to be deterred. He swings his legs to the ground, leaning my way.

"Why don't you date?" he asks.

"What?"

"In all the time I've known you, you've not once gone on a date," he points out.

"Why don't you?" I combat.

"No, no," he says. "This isn't about me. I can't believe I didn't see it before, but you're waiting for that perfect romance, aren't you? That's why you never let people in. That's why it's nearly impossible to get you to open up."

"What are you talking about?" I ask him. I don't shut people out, do I?

"No one can measure up to the ideals in your head," he goes on, nodding to himself. "You're a hopeless romantic, parading around behind a shield of flippancy."

I flounder for a moment, completely caught off-guard by Danil's assessment. "I'm not... You're wrong."

"Am I?" he presses, dark eyebrow winging up.

"Fuck, Dani," I practically growl. "I'm not..." Frustrated with him or myself or who knows what, I throw my hands into the air. "Okay, *fine*, maybe I was a romantic once, but not anymore. It's different when you're young, you know? The world is this sweet, shiny thing and you think you *know* how everything is going to turn out. But then you grow up and realize real life is messy and unpredictable, and no guy is going to show up at your front door with two blue boutonnieres just to make you happy. Because seriously, who the fuck does that?"

Danil blinks at me as I suck in a breath. My heart is pounding, and I look away from him as the sound of city traffic filters up from below.

"That was incredibly specific," he finally says. "Your Ellis?"

"Not the point," I huff out, trying to clear the memory of six-teen-year-old Ellis in a rented tux from my mind. "Just...stop trying to psychoanalyze me. Plenty of people prefer casual sex to dating." I give him a pointed look.

He ignores me. "You're hung up on him."

"I'm not—" *Fuck.* "I'm not *hung up* on Ellis. He's just my friend."

The whisper in my heart tells me I'm a liar.

"Then explain it to me," Danil says. "Because I'm not sure if you've noticed, but you talk about him every single day. You don't talk about your parents that much or even our job. But every day, I hear about Ellis."

I swallow roughly. "He's my best friend, Dani," I say, trying to get him to understand. "When I moved to Nebraska, he was all I had. I was in this new place with new people, and *God*, I hated it at times. I hated that I didn't have a say in my life being uprooted. In leaving my friends and everything I'd loved behind. But then..." I look out over the balcony railing, remembering that night I met my new neighbor in our sleepy Nebraskan town. "Then there was Ellis, and he made me feel like everything was going to be okay. I was safe, and I had someone who was just mine, and...and he was always there for me. Even still, he's always there for me."

"He's your anchor," Danil says quietly.

"No," I whisper, my eyes lifting to the full moon. "He doesn't fight the tide. He controls it."

My coworker-turned-friend sighs, and I bring my eyes back to him. "A romantic," he insists.

Maybe he's right.

"You left Tom alone," I say, desperately wanting to move us off this topic.

Danil snorts, looking back over his shoulder through the glass before giving me a smirk. "Tom is passed out in a pool of his own cum."

"Jesus, you can be crude."

He winks proudly. "A poet, as you said."

"Mhm," I mutter. "Please, gift me more of your poetry."

Without missing a beat, Danil says, "There once was a god named Dani, with a cock as long as his hami—"

"Oh my God."

"And he made the boys scream as he sucked out their cr—" Danil's words cut off when I slap my hand over his mouth, and he laughs against me.

"Christ," I moan. "This is my life now."

Danil waggles his eyebrows before licking me. He doesn't even seem to care that I wipe my palm on his shirt. "You know," he says, reclining back in his seat, hands behind his head and legs crossed at his ankles, "one day, *far* in the future, if I ever do settle down, I will gift my beloved with my poetry. And they will adore it."

"I don't doubt that," I admit, wrapping the blanket back over my arms. "You're smooth when you want to be."

He flutters his lashes at me. "Thank you, Lucky-boy."

"And also a dick," I put in.

He places his hand over his chest. "Thank you."

We're quiet for a while after that, and try as I might, there are no crickets to be heard. Not here.

Just when I'm about to stand up and head back inside, Danil's voice halts me. "Tell me the truth," he says. "Did you ever have a crush on your...friend?"

My swallow is rough. "Maybe once upon a time," I admit. It's not exactly a lie, even if that crush never quite went away.

"And Ellis?" Danil says. "He didn't feel the same?"

"No," I answer, my heart clenching tight. "No, he did not."

Danil doesn't stop me as I stand, blanket around my shoulders, and I walk through the door, ignoring his lightly spoken, "Shame," as well as the moon at my back.

Chapter 11

ELLIS

"And I wasn't sure about it at first," Gabby tells me, recounting the story of her dog's new hairstyle. Apparently the Lhasa Apso gets groomed every six weeks. "But I think I've warmed up to it. Sometimes you just have to trust the groomer, you know?"

I don't, but I hum, and Gabby nods, looking lost in thought.

"Yeah. And Toodles seems happy. Not that she's ever unhappy, mind," she says with a chuckle. "She's the nicest dog. If you ever meet her, you'll see."

I nod along, bending low to get a look at the hitch system of the tractor I'm working on. It's been clinking lately when it engages the bucket, and the last thing we need is the front-end attachment falling on someone's foot. Or worse.

Gabby goes on as I eye the machinery. "Did I tell you about the new high-protein diet I switched her to? I swear she's got an extra pep in her step lately. It's like she's a pup again."

Ah, there's a loose bolt on the stabilizer arm. I give it a wiggle.

"God, it's hot today," Gabby says. She pulls her hair back, holding it off her shoulders in a loose ponytail. "What are you doing?"

Pushing myself off the concrete warehouse floor, I step over to the tool chest. Marcus doesn't want us doing any major work on the machinery—he calls the guys from the company for that—but I know he won't mind me tightening a bolt. When I grab the wrench, I hold it up to show Gabby, and she nods, dropping her hair and fanning her face instead.

"Are you going to the corn festival next weekend?" she asks.

I shrug as I walk back to the tractor. Our town has held a summer corn festival for longer than I've been alive. I used to like going when I was a kid, sampling the different flavors of popcorn and going through the corn maze. Lucky hated that festival on principle, but he made it more fun, too, once he came to town. Lucky's always had the ability to make just about anything fun.

These days, the festival has lost its luster for me. Maybe that's simply because I've grown up—how excited can an adult get about corn, after all, especially one who works with it day in and day out? Or maybe it's because I know no new memories made there could hold up to the old.

Either way, it's been years since I went.

"I heard they're doing a cornbread cook-off this year," Gabby says as I lower myself to the ground. It's an awkward angle, getting my arm in the spot needed to tighten the bolt. "I was thinking I might enter. I have this recipe from my gran that, uh... Um..."

Gabby trails off as I find the right angle to reach the bolt. I'm on my side, one leg forward for balance and arm stretched high. It only takes a few twists before the bolt is snug in place, and then I look back at Gabby, who's stopped talking.

Her eyes snap to my face, and she gives me a quick smile. "Um, yeah. It's good. A good recipe."

I nod before giving the other bolts a check, but none of the rest are loose. Gabby is quiet as I stand back up and right my shirt.

"Hey," she says, fanning her face again. "I was sorry to hear your mom is leaving."

My sigh comes from deep within, a feeling more than a sound. I give Gabby a nod, and her face pinches in sympathy.

"She's such a nice lady," she says. "Always patient."

That she is.

"It doesn't seem fair..."

Gabby doesn't finish her sentence, but she doesn't need to. No, it's not fair what my mom is going through. But life doesn't operate on fairness, does it?

"Right," Gabby says, her voice soft. "Well, I should probably get back to work."

I give her another nod as I put the wrench away. She takes a step before stopping, her sundress floating around her knees.

"Hey, Ellis?"

I wait.

"I was wondering if you'd want to go with me. To the festival."

It takes me a moment to react, but Gabby waits, a gentle, hopeful smile on her face. "I..." And then it clicks. "Friends? Or...a date?"

Her head tilts to the side just a little, an action that feels somewhat vulnerable, although I couldn't say why. Her smile stays in place. "A date, if you want it to be. And, if you don't, then as friends."

I don't know what to say. Well, that's not entirely true. Instinctually, my reaction is to tell her no to the date, that I'm not interested in her that way. Except—what if I could be? I've wondered, on occasion, what creates attraction. I've only ever felt it for one particular person, but I know, for others, it's not the same.

Attraction can be swift, instantaneous and all-consuming, like wildfire. It can be slowly crafted and tended to over time, an ever-changing canvas, brush strokes built over one another until the picture is clear. It can be lost, I think, for some.

But what makes one person look at another and think *yes, this one. I want this one?* What makes their heart beat faster? What makes their body react?

Is it our atoms, working on a level we'll never understand? Is it fate or kismet or something out there pulling threads together? Or is it simpler than all that? Is it our humanity, our need for connection and closeness with others?

I don't think I'll ever know, but maybe that's exactly why I should say yes. Could I find that something in Gabby that feels like home? Maybe.

Do I want to?

It's not a betrayal.

Feels like it, though.

In the end, I nod slowly, and Gabby's smile widens.

"You'll be my date?" she checks.

I clear my throat. "Yes."

She looks so happy, and I hope I'm not making a mistake. I don't want to hurt her, but one date isn't a promise. People date all the time.

Not that I'm familiar with it myself.

Gabby hops a little on the balls of her feet, reminding me momentarily of Lucky. "Great," she says. "See you tomorrow?"

I give a nod, and with a final, beaming smile, Gabby twirls away. I watch her go for a moment, trying to imagine us together. Trying to imagine her hair between my fingers or her lips on mine. I think about her eyes—what color are they, green?—and what they might look like lost in pleasure. But all I can picture is sparkling blue and corkscrewing blonde, and I quickly wipe the images from my mind.

Alone again, I climb up onto the tractor. It whirs to life, and this time, the hitch attaches to the bucket without a single extra clunk. I smile, making sure the front end is lowered before I turn off the tractor and climb down.

The rest of the afternoon passes quickly. I work with Riley to clean up the farm equipment that's onsite, scrubbing dirt and all manner of gunk off the machinery and down the drain. Like many of our classmates, myself included, Riley stayed in town and became a husker. Brandon, from what I heard, is over at the paper mill. I can't say I ever did forgive him for splitting Lucky's lip. Riley, at least, apologized for being a part of it. We get along well enough now.

Some days, I don't spend any time here in the warehouse or at the adjacent corn processing plant where Gabby and my mom work. During planting and harvesting seasons especially, it's not uncommon to be out in the fields for days or weeks at a time. I think I prefer it that way, just me and the land. With the exception of Lucky, I've always preferred my own company to others'. It's easier when I don't have to worry about my words not coming out right. Or not coming out at all.

That's never been a problem with Lucky.

Riley, at least, doesn't seem to mind my lack of conversation, unlike some of the older farmers who avoid me or think yelling will make me hear them better. I hear them just fine, but I'm used to that reaction from people who don't know me.

Most people in town are kind, and truth be told, it's not so bad here, corn-husking included. The work can be monotonous and often tiring, but there's comfort in this life. In knowing exactly what my day will bring.

When the end of our shift rolls around, Riley and I say our goodbyes, and he heads off to his truck. I take a minute to wash up first, cleaning the grime off my hands, arms, and out from underneath my fingernails. While I'm drying my hands, my phone rings in my back pocket. My cheeks ache with my smile when I see the name onscreen.

I answer as I head toward the door.

"Ellis?" the voice asks.

I hum, a quiet sound. A contented one.

Lucky chuckles. "It's good to hear your voice."

I shake my head. *Smartass.*

"Are you off work?" he asks.

A grunting yes.

"Good," he says, sounding as if he's settling in somewhere. Bed? "Guess where I am."

My mind spins, trying to figure out where he might be that the time difference would put him so much later than me. "Portugal?"

He makes a curious sound. "Damn, that's close. Morocco."

My hum sounds a little smug.

"How'd you figure that out?" Lucky asks, shifting again.

"Sheets," I tell him, pushing outside. The sun hits me square on, and I blink a few times before lowering my shades.

Lucky is quiet for a moment. "You can hear the sheets?" he finally asks.

"Mhm."

Another pause. "Can you hear that I'm naked, too?"

I nearly trip over my own feet, body flushing hot.

"Don't judge," Lucky says with a chuckle, as if him telling me about his nudity is no big deal. And, I guess to Lucky, it isn't. "The sheets are as soft as silk. This place must have cost the magazine a pretty penny."

I make a sound of acknowledgement, but my mind is stuck on the image of Lucky spread out naked on silky smooth sheets. My heart picks up speed, my body heats, and *there*. There it is, that intangible, magnetic force pulling me toward someone I can't even physically see.

I squeeze my eyes tight, hoping it will help white out my thoughts. Lucky is talking about the Mediterranean Sea now and the marketplace he and Dani visited earlier.

"But since neither of us speaks Darija," he's saying, "or Arabic, for that matter, we had to rely on our guide to haggle prices. I'm pretty sure Dani paid way more than necessary for a gold necklace for his sister, but honestly, he can afford it. Hey, did you get that package I sent last week?"

I nod against the phone, at my truck now. Instead of getting into the cab, I lower the tailgate and hike myself up into the bed, sitting against the hot metal near the wheel well. "Yeah," I tell him. "The...chocolate. Your mom liked that."

He chuckles softly. "I'm not surprised. And you? Which was your favorite?"

Lucky sends little care packages sometimes when he's off on his adventures. It's nice, feeling like I'm getting a small taste of whatever part of the world he's in. It makes me feel close to him, even when he's so far away.

"Liked the nuts," I admit. They were roasted cashews with a hint of star anise. I'd never had any like them before.

Lucky snickers, and it takes me a moment to realize why.

"Fuck off," I tell him slowly but firmly.

He laughs harder. "Sorry." *He's not.*

"Twelve," I tell him. He understands.

"We're all kids at heart," he says, rustling again in his silk-like sheets. I have the distinct thought that *no, we're certainly not kids anymore*, but I don't say it. I know what he means.

We hold onto the memories from our past, don't we? We cling to the pieces that made the whole of us, good or bad. Because if we don't...if we don't keep them close...we might lose that part of who we are.

"Pictures?" I ask.

"Ah, right," Lucky says, sighing long and low. I can imagine him lying in bed, hair spread across his pillow. I can *hear* the smile on his lips, and when he speaks again, there's also wonder. "Erg Chebbi."

I make a curious sound.

"It was beautiful, El," he practically whispers. "A sea of golden sand. The dunes were formed over time by the wind, and they're big. Sweeping. It was hot, too." He chuckles. "Really damn hot, but worth it. When the sun was at its peak, it was like...like the whole world was bathed in copper. Like the sun and the sand were one."

I open my eyes, not having realized I'd closed them. It's easy to picture Lucky there, in the desert. I bet his hair was as golden as the sands.

"We rode on camels," he adds, laughing a little. "I could maybe go without that experience again."

I snort, and Lucky goes on to tell me about how sore his ass got and how camels might be the worst-smelling animal he's ever encountered. It feels so normal and *good*, and even though I forget to share about Gabby and how I'm nervous for my very first official date, it's probably for the best.

How would I tell him I'm scared I might like her? How would I explain my heart doesn't know how to beat for anyone but him?

It's near dinnertime when Lucky trails off, his words apparently exhausted for today. "I should go," he says, voice soft.

Yeah.

"Talk soon?" he asks.

I hum. *As soon as you're able.*

"Yeah," he breathes. "Night, El."

I give him the two words that have never gotten easier in the three years since he's been gone. "Night, Luck." I keep the other two for myself. *Miss you.*

There's a whispered "bye" and then the line goes dead. I stay seated in the back of my truck for a minute longer, looking out over the fields and imagining golden sands instead of husk-wrapped corn. I imagine Lucky here beside me.

And I wonder if I'm even capable of letting him go.

Chapter 12

LUCKY

"What do you think?" Danil asks, holding up a forest green tunic with elaborate stitching. "Could I pull it off?"

"Honestly? Yeah, I think you could," I tell him. Danil looks good in just about anything.

He purses his lips, examining the shirt before turning toward the stall owner. It's our last morning in Morocco, and even though we don't have a guide today, Danil and I decided to stroll through one of the many marketplaces before heading to the airport.

Danil haggles using the tips he picked up earlier in the week while I step outside the stall. The narrow street we're on is bustling with activity, tourists and locals alike filling the space. The stall across the street is selling spices, each variety mounded up in large, shallow bowls. Piles of turmeric, black pepper, saffron, and cinnamon are among them. The colors remind me of the dunes. Beside that is a stall filled with brightly colored blankets, tea towels, and scarves. One scarf in particular, threaded through with green, brown, and yellow, makes me think of Ellis. Of Nebraska and corn.

Always fucking corn.

"Ready?" Danil says, at my side.

I give him a nod, and we weave our way down the cobbled street toward the exit. There's a small sandwich shop on the next street over, and we stop there, Danil getting a mint tea while I get Moroccan spiced coffee. We sip our drinks while we wait for our food.

I'm about to ask Danil what his plans are for our hop back to New York City when my phone rings. I pick it up with a smile when I see my mom's name.

"Hey, Mom. Pretty early over there, isn't it?"

"Hello to you, too," she says. "I'm doing just fine, thanks for asking."

I huff a laugh, but my mom keeps talking.

"You're heading home today, right?"

Home.

"Yeah, we'll be back in New York tonight," I answer.

She hums. "Are you getting enough rest?"

"Yes, Mom," I say dutifully. "I'm sleeping fine."

Danil's lips quirk, and I roll my eyes.

"Good, good," my mom says. I hear a muffled voice, and then, "Your dad says hi."

"Hi, Dad," I say, and my mom relays the message. "How's Mrs. Cole?"

After a small, barely there sigh, my mom says, "She's okay, Lucky, all things considered. She had her last day at the plant earlier this week, so she's at home now. I think that's for the best. She's been using her wheelchair a lot more lately, but Ellis... He's there for her."

I nod, throat tight. I have no doubt of that.

"I worry," my mom says, "about him, sometimes."

My pulse skitters. "Why's that?"

"He's such a good boy. *Man*," she corrects. "But I hate to see him put his own life on hold. At least he has a date to the corn festival this weekend."

It takes a second for her words to sink in, but once they do, I can barely breathe. "What?" I ask, my voice a hoarse whisper.

Danil goes still, watching me closely, and I look away, blinking as I try to listen past the pounding of my heart.

"A date," my mom repeats. "Nice girl he works with. I hope for his sake, it pans out. He deserves a little happiness of his own."

I can't...

Ellis has a date?

"You deserve that, too," she says. "Is there anyone you're seeing back in New York?"

I try to answer her, but my voice won't work. I have the distinct, overwhelming notion that maybe this is what Ellis feels like when his words won't come. I nearly sob with the thought, heart aching, and I slap a hand over my mouth before I can bark an ill-timed laugh. What a time to realize how very much *not over* my childhood crush I am.

Fuck.

"I, um," I manage. "No, I'm not seeing anyone. And I didn't realize...about the date, I mean. That's good. For him."

My mom says something else, but I'm distracted away from it by the arrival of our food. I thank the person before clearing my throat.

"Mom, I should get going. Danil and I need to be at the airport soon."

"Of course," she says. "Safe travels, sweetheart. And let me know the next time you'll be visiting. It's been far too long since we've seen your bright face around here."

"Yeah, Mom," I answer. "I'll, uh... Maybe soon."

I tell my mom I love her before hanging up, and then I set my shaking hand on the tabletop beside my plate.

"All right?" Danil asks, eyes creased in concern.

"I..."

How many days before we leave for Borneo? Six?

"I think I'm going to Nebraska," I tell Danil.

His eyebrows rise, but I nod, more to myself than anything. Now that I've had the thought, I know it's what I need to do. I don't even have a plan. I have no idea what I'm hoping to accomplish. But I can't fly back to New York and sit around this weekend while Ellis...while he goes on a date with some *nice girl* he works with who doesn't know him like I do. What if she hurts him? What if...what if she doesn't?

"Yeah," I say definitively. "I'm going to Nebraska."

Danil pulls out his phone. "Let's see how quickly I can get our flights changed."

"Our?" I say in surprise.

My coworker's grin is wickedly charming. "You didn't think I'd let you do this on your own, did you?"

I don't question how Danil knows what I'm doing when I don't have a clue myself. I just nod, dig into my sandwich, and hope our plane lands us in the sea of maize and green as soon as humanly possible.

"Well, this is..." Danil starts, looking around as I drive us into town. It's been a long day of travel, and that, in conjunction with the jet lag, has my body ready to give up the fight. But my mind is wired, and my fingers tap incessantly against the steering wheel as we get closer and closer to my parents' house.

"It's what?" I ask, distracted.

"There's just so much corn," Danil says.

I bark a slightly hysterical laugh. "Told you. It's an agricultural town."

"Is that a store up there?" he asks suddenly. "Can we stop?"

"Dani," I groan, failing to keep the desperation out of my voice. I need to keep moving. I need...

"Five minutes," he says. "Please, Lucky-boy. You didn't let me grab anything on the way out of the airport."

"Fine," I mutter, pulling into the small parking lot of our town's one convenience store. Danil smacks a kiss against my cheek before exiting the vehicle. Begrudgingly, I follow him inside, if nothing more than to make sure he's quick buying his smokes.

The door jingles when I walk through, and familiarity smacks me in the face. Every inch of the place is exactly like I remember. Except...

"What..." I mutter, walking over to a display in front of the street-side window. A large glass fish is set on a pedestal base and covered in a clear case, presumably so someone passing by can't touch—or break—the delicate creation. It's a good two feet across and a foot or so tall, and it's remarkable. The scales are a myriad of colors, all glass connected so seamlessly, it looks like one smoothly crafted piece. It's partially transparent, the interior is hollow, and a "sold" sign sits inside the display.

It's a parrotfish.

"Beautiful, isn't it?" someone says next to me.

I look over in surprise at Melody Shaffer, a girl I went to school with, and nod. The logo on her shirt tells me she works here now. "Yeah," I answer, at a loss for words.

"The artist drops off a new piece each month," she tells me, arms crossed loosely in front of her as she examines the glass fish. "It usually sells within an hour or two. I have a turtle at home. Want to see?"

I nod, and Melody pulls out her phone. After a moment, she turns the screen toward me. A gorgeous sea turtle sits atop what looks like a fireplace mantle. Its flippers are outstretched, and its head is bent gently to the side. The craftsmanship is breathtaking.

"He makes little baubles, too," she says. "Decorative globes and ornaments and such. They sell out just as quickly, but these"—she motions to the parrotfish—"are what folks line up on the sidewalk to see."

I'm not surprised. It's pure art.

"Who?" I ask. "Who's the artist?"

"That part's a secret," Melody says, giving me a little smile. "He prefers to remain anonymous." Before I can utter a word, she says, "Good to see you again, Lucky."

"Yeah," I reply, head reeling as she walks off.

"Ready?" Danil asks, appearing beside me with a small bag in his hand.

A flutter rolls through my stomach. "Yeah. Let's go."

It only takes another five minutes before we're pulling up to my parents'. The driveway is gravel, as it's always been, and lights are on inside the house, as well as next door. My heart feels like it's trying to fly away.

"So," Danil says slowly after a minute when I don't move. "Are we going to get out of the car?"

"Soon," I mouth, my eyes on the open shed door at the back of Ellis's property. Well, his mom's property, technically. But it's his now, too.

"What are we waiting for?" Danil asks, looking around. "Your parents' place is cute."

"Yeah," I mutter, but then there he is, coming out of the shed, worn jeans stretched tight across his thighs and a dark red t-shirt clinging to his upper body. He's a good ways away, but he's *right there* for the first time in months, and suddenly, I forget how to move oxygen through my lungs.

He doesn't see us at first. I already turned the car off, so the lights haven't alerted him. And it's the weirdest thing, but for once, I'm worried about what I'm going to say to him. I'm scared of what might come out of my mouth. Scared about why I came back here. My palms are sweating, my body feels flushed, and now that I'm finally, blessedly here after a day of rushing toward this exact point in time, I can't get myself to move a muscle.

"Ho-ly shit," Danil says from beside me, leaning forward. "Is...is *that* your Ellis?"

He sounds absolutely incredulous, and I spare him a glance. "Yeah, that's him. Why?"

And why is my heart beating so damn hard?

Danil looks at me in shock. "You never told me the man is a goddamn lumberjack-me-off-*please*. I mean, fucking hell, Lucky, he could swallow me whole." He adds a whispered, "If I were so lucky."

"Dani," I croak out, feeling an unpleasant curl of *something* in my gut that I don't want to examine too closely. "He's not a lumberjack. He's a farmer."

"As if that's the point," Danil says. "You've seriously never been on that ride?"

I turn my gaze back to Ellis, who's now shutting the shed door. "It was never... He's not like that," I try to explain.

"Not like what?" Danil asks. "Because, fuck, Lucky-boy, if I weren't concerned about you stabbing me for the suggestion, I'd be begging to join you up that mountain."

I groan, scrubbing my hands over my eyes. "Stop, please."

"See? That," he says, pointing an accusatory finger my way. "You feel some way about him."

I shake my head, not willing to get into it with Danil right now. "I'm pretty sure he's ace," I say instead. "Like, the kind of ace where sex doesn't even appeal to him."

"He told you that?" Danil asks, expression shifting.

I swallow as I watch Ellis start to make his way toward the back of his house. He still hasn't noticed the extra car parked next door.

"The last time we talked about it," I say slowly, "he said he had no interest in girls or guys. He would have told me if that had changed."

So then why is he going on a date?

"Hm," Danil says.

"It doesn't matter," I say quickly. "That's not why I'm here. I just... I just need to..."

I can't figure out a way to finish that sentence that doesn't make me a liar. So instead, I grab the handle and push open the door. Danil's soft "good luck" follows me as I step out of the car. Ellis is nearly to the back deck now, his massive frame moving fluidly. I forget, sometimes, when I can only hear his voice, exactly how big Ellis is. He *is* a mountain of a man but the gentlest soul I've ever met. And he's...

I blow out a slow breath. He's beautiful; I can't even deny that. He's lovely in the way the natural world is lovely. Imperfect but vital. Roughly hewn and uniquely himself. He's just... Ellis. He's my Ellis.

When I shut the car door, his head turns a fraction, enough for his eyes to seek me out. And it's then, when our gazes collide for the first time in half a year, that my worry fades, my tension dissipates, and I sway forward as every single part of me sings in rightness and relief.

Because finally—*finally*—I'm home.

Chapter 13

ELLIS

For a split second, I'm not sure what I'm seeing is real. But then I feel it, that crackle, that spark that lives in Lucky, and I can't move fast enough.

"Luck," I manage.

And *God*, the way he smiles.

We reach each other halfway between our houses, and my arms are around him before I've even caught up with the fact that he's here. It seems impossible. Like a dream.

But it's not a dream. The feel of Lucky tucked against my chest is enough to convince me of that. He's real. And he's here. *Here.* And I'm *shaking* with my want for him. With the need to be closer. Somehow, inexplicably closer.

Could I tie myself to him so that he'd never again be able to fly off?

"God," Lucky says, the sound nearly a sob. "It's so good to see you, El."

I grunt because no one word is enough.

"Lucky Buchanan!" comes a call. "Is that you?"

Lucky chuckles wetly, pulling back from my chest. "Hi, Mrs. Cole."

"Did my son know you were coming?" my mom asks from the back door.

"No, he did not," Lucky answers.

Mom huffs. "Well, I'm glad you're back. Come visit before you go, you hear?"

Before you go.

I force the words from my mind as Lucky tells my mom he will. She shuts the door, leaving me and Lucky alone. He looks up at me, eyes taking me in as if he's reassuring himself I'm whole. I can't say I don't do the same.

When he lets out a little breath, I bring my gaze back to his face. "I brought Dani," he says, motioning toward the car. Seemingly taking his cue, Dani exits the vehicle, waving. I lift my hand in return, trying hard to fight the way my jaw wants to clench.

"How long?" I ask Lucky, returning my attention to him.

"A few days," he answers. "We leave for Borneo on Tuesday."

I nod. It's not enough time, but I refuse to dwell on it.

"Hungry?" I ask.

He chuckles a little. "Admittedly, yeah. We didn't stop to eat. I need to say hi to my parents first, though."

I incline my head toward my house, and Lucky nods.

"Yeah," he says, squeezing my arm. "Give us ten minutes, and then we'll be over."

Us—him and Dani. I ignore that part, too, giving his hair a gentle tug. *You look good.*

He huffs a laugh. "You, too, big guy."

When Lucky turns to go, I have to remind myself he'll be right back. He's not *leaving*. Still, it doesn't feel good watching him disappear next door with Dani at his side.

My mom is waiting when I step into the house, a knowing smile on her face. "Surprise visit," she says. "Wonder what spurred that decision on."

I shake my head as I go to the fridge to grab the leftover kebabs. I have no clue.

"Hm," she says, transferring shakily from her wheelchair to the couch. I pause to watch her.

"Need anything?" I ask.

My mom shakes her head, covering her lap with a blanket before picking up the remote. "Not a thing. Go catch up with your friend."

I nod, piling beef and bell peppers onto a plate. As the food heats, I grab two, then three, beers out of the fridge. I bring everything, including a bowl of salad, out to the table on the deck. I'm too nervous to sit as I wait, so I lean against the railing, looking out over the backyard. A single firefly blinks nearby, so faint in the waning evening sun, I nearly miss it.

I hear him first, talking quietly to Dani as they approach. I force a calming breath through my body and turn.

Lucky is first up the steps, giving me a beaming smile that instantly transports me back to when we were sixteen. Or eleven or eighteen or twenty-two. It's a million memories in one, that smile, and I'm swamped by them, overcome by the history we share. There are strings connecting us, so many of them.

I don't think we could ever be unraveled.

Dani is at Lucky's heel. There's a wide smile on his face, and he doesn't hesitate to step forward with his hand outstretched. I've seen pictures of Lucky's coworker before, but this is the first time I'm meeting him face to face. He's classically handsome, tall but leanly muscled, and has this air about him I could never hope to emulate.

"Ellis," he says warmly the moment our hands clasp. He places his second overtop of mine. "So good to finally meet you."

I nod, a touch surprised by the genuine friendliness in his tone. I half-expected him to be like the rest. Like Andrew and the other guys I met while Lucky was in college.

Dani shakes his head a little before stepping back. "My God. How tall *are* you?" he asks. I have a few inches on him.

"Six-five," Lucky answers, heading over to the table as Dani whistles. I'm not sure what to make of the way he's eyeing me, but Lucky pulls my attention. "Did you make these?"

I hum my yes, chest warming at the smile Lucky gives me. He always did love grilled kebabs. When Lucky takes a seat, Dani and I follow. They both thank me as they dish up their plates, and, not hungry myself, I'm content to sip my beer and watch Lucky as he closes his eyes with his first bite of food. They flash my way when he opens them, and that warmth in my chest flows down to my stomach.

Dani clears his throat. "So, Ellis, I'm dying to know. What's Lucky's most embarrassing childhood story?"

Lucky sputters before shooting me a hard look. "Don't you dare."

"Please dare," Dani counters, grinning wickedly. I have a feeling the man is just as much trouble as Lucky is.

I only debate for a moment before telling him, "The paint."

He cocks his head as Lucky groans. "Do go on," Dani says.

"We were fourteen," I say slowly, "when Luck brought paint...to school."

Dani waits patiently while I tell the story, having to collect my words more than once before going on. He never interrupts, although I do notice him glancing at Lucky a time or two when I falter. I tell him how Lucky bought a gallon of discounted blue paint from the hardware store. How he smuggled it into school in his backpack. How, during lunch that day, he brought the paint to the bathroom with the intent of covering up some graffiti on one of the stall walls. How, when he pried open the can, it tipped, dousing Lucky and the floor in blue. How, no matter how hard he tried, Lucky couldn't get it cleaned up in time before the bell rang for the next period. And how, when he was marched to the principal's office, blue boot prints followed.

"He had...to spend the weekend cleaning up," I tell Dani, who has tears in his eyes. "Paint everywhere."

Lucky is shaking his head at me, but there's a twinkle in his eye. I wouldn't have told the story if he'd really minded.

"My God," Dani says a little breathlessly. He hiccups a laugh when he looks at Lucky. "You blue yourself."

Lucky shoves Dani's shoulder, and his coworker breaks into laughter. I can't help but join in, not minding one bit when Lucky shoves me, too.

"Assholes," he mutters, not meaning it in the least.

"What were you trying to cover up?" Dani asks before taking a sip of his beer. "On the stall, I mean."

Lucky's face falls a little, and he shoots me a glance. It doesn't bother me, but to this day, it seems to bother Lucky. He twists his beer bottle on top of the table before telling Dani, quietly, "Someone used an incredibly shitty, derogatory term to describe Ellis."

They called me a retard.

Dani is quiet for a moment, and a fox squirrel chitters nearby. "That's cruel," he finally says, voice tinged with something hard.

I shrug. "Kids."

"No," Lucky says firmly. "There's no excuse. They never would have dared say it to your face."

I smack my fist into my palm, and Lucky snorts a laugh.

"You vandalized the inside of your school for your friend's sake," Dani says softly. The smile he gives Lucky is personal—secretive—and Lucky squirms slightly in his chair. Instantly, I feel the need to defend him.

"Would've..."—it takes me a moment—"done it, too." I hope Dani understands what I mean.

His smile shifts to me. "I have no doubt."

"Well," Lucky says, beer bottle clinking softly as he sets it down, "if sharing time is over, I can show you to the guest room, Danil."

Dani snorts. "Ohh," he says to me. "He full-named me. I'm in trouble."

Lucky rolls his eyes as I frown, but Dani stands up, unperturbed.

"I'm sure your parents can show me the way," Dani tells Lucky. To me, he says, "It was truly great to meet you, Ellis. Hopefully, we can spend some time together while I'm in town."

I nod, and Dani gives me a smile before stepping away from the table. He squeezes Lucky's shoulder as he goes, but Lucky looks resolutely ahead at his empty beer bottle. I wait until Dani is gone before nudging Lucky's foot with my own.

"Okay?" I ask.

His lips twitch as he nods. "Fine. It's just... Nothing. Dani can be nosy, is all."

I shrug. He seems like he cares. I suppose I should be grateful that Lucky has another friend in his life to look out for him.

I only wish they weren't more than that, too.

I reach out and tap Lucky's beer bottle.

He shakes his head. "I'm good, thanks."

Leaning back, I prop my foot on the chair next to mine. Lucky is looking out over the backyard. The sun has set, just, and the sky is a dark, dusky blue. Crickets are chirping, every once in a while a noise from the TV drifts out through the open window, and a dog barks somewhere far off. It sounds like home.

"I always have it in my head," Lucky says, "that this place is nothing but dirt and corn. In all of my memories, I couldn't wait to get out."

I nod because I know that.

"And then..." he goes on. "Then I come back here, and it feels like..." He lets loose a breath, eyes drifting shut. "It feels *good*. And I don't understand that. I don't understand how one place"—he flicks his eyes to me—"can feel like the starting point. Like my beginning. Because I didn't grow up here. I hated coming here. But I got attached, and I miss it. I never wanted to, but I do. I miss it, and I miss you, and I don't..."

He cuts off then, shaking his head a little as he faces the yard. My heart is thudding inside my chest, and I reach over, slipping my hand over Lucky's. Without looking my way, he turns his palm up, squeezing me hard.

I almost say something. I almost open my mouth to tell him how much I miss him, too. But he knows that. I can feel it in the way his fingers clamp mine tight. So instead, I keep my hand in his so he knows I'm here. That he'll always have a place to come back home to.

It's late when Lucky's heavy eyelids win out, and he stands to head next door. He doesn't seem to want to go. "Tomorrow, we're spending the whole night together," he practically demands. "As soon as you get home from work, we'll—I don't know. We'll do something great."

I nod. Of course it will be great. It'll be with him.

Seemingly satisfied, Lucky finally shuffles off on heavy feet. I watch him walk the short distance to his parents' house before collecting our dishes and empty bottles from the table. Inside, the living room is empty, my mom having relocated to her bedroom. I clean up and then head for my own.

Before slipping into bed, I grab my laptop. I flip it open, sitting at the edge of my mattress as I start a new email to Lucky. I nearly snort, knowing he's less than a hundred paces away, and yet I'm writing to him. But my chest feels tight, my head is whirling, and I know it will help, letting some of that pressure out.

My fingers hover over the keys for a moment before I finally begin to type.

Hi, Luck. You're here, did you know that? I held your hand less than ten minutes ago, hardly able to believe the flesh and bones beneath my palm were real. Sometimes, my memories of you are so strong, I can almost feel it. The way you heat beneath my fingertips. The firmness of your body against my own. But none of my memories compare to the real thing. If I could, I'd bottle it in a jar—every glance of your hand on my arm, every small squeeze and brush of your fingers, every press of your chest to mine. I'd save them all so I could feel you when you go.

In my weakest moments, I wish you'd stay. I wish you'd hear the words I could never bring myself to give. I wish you'd know the deepest secrets in my heart and, somehow, share them in yours.

I was fifteen when I sat beside you at the top of a wind-mill, your lip split and bruised like my knuckles. It was us against the world, Luck. The two of us, always. Me and you.

We've grown. Of course we have. But still, always, I love you.

Don't stay away too long this time, my darling firefly.

When I fall into sleep, blue fills my mind, and for a moment, I can see the stars spin.

Chapter 14

LUCKY

"You love him," Danil accuses in the morning.

I brush past him out of the bathroom, my shoulder bumping his at the doorway. He turns, following me down the hall to my room. It hasn't changed much since I moved out years ago. My parents took down my posters, replacing them with framed pictures I took over the years, and they boxed up some of my trinkets, storing them in the closet. But the walls are still a light green, and the furniture is the same.

I head to my luggage, pulling clothes from within. Danil shuts the door, and I can feel his stare on my person the entire time I change. When I turn around, he's waiting with a raised brow.

"I don't know what you want me to say," I tell him. Because I can't say *no*. I can't lie. Not about that, no matter how much I try to deny it inside my own head and heart.

Danil lets out a huff, arms at his sides. "You don't *need* to tell me anything, Lucky, but I *am* here for you, you know. Just because we've fucked doesn't mean I'm not your friend first and foremost."

"I thought we were coworkers first," I mutter, taking a seat at the foot of my bed.

The look Danil gives me is unimpressed. "Semantics, you little shit. Why..." He pushes off from the door, sitting beside me. I can't quite bring myself to look his way. "Why did you lie about him?"

"I didn't," I say on autopilot.

"You did," he counters. "You said you had a crush, *once*. You belittled your feelings."

"Because it doesn't matter," I say a touch hotly. "Ellis doesn't see me that way, and I would never put pressure on him for that. I wouldn't...end our friendship just because he doesn't feel the same. I'm still his friend, first and foremost, too."

"Even though he's your *big romance*," Danil says, emphasizing the words.

I meet his eye, cheeks warm despite myself. "Ellis and I have *never* been that."

The look he gives me is smugly doubtful. "*Right*. The man—once boy—who showed up on your doorstep with two blue boutonnieres. That was prom, I assume? Surely nothing romantic about that."

I don't dare tell Danil that Ellis gave me my first kiss, too, even though that was later. I don't tell him about the times we snuck away at night to sit together in the cornfields, just him and me under the stars. I don't tell him about the thousands of quiet moments that let my feelings for Ellis grow or how, once, he carried me home in his arms because I'd broken my ankle.

I don't dare say any of that because none of it *was* romantic. It was two boys, eventually young men, who were *friends*.

Who were close. Closer than most, sure. And yes, somewhere along the way—maybe because of those two damn blue boutonnieres—my feelings grew. But that doesn't make my past with Ellis into something it never was.

"You know," Danil says slowly. "If he is, in fact, asexual, that doesn't necessarily preclude him from wanting a romantic relationship."

I hate how my heart flutters hopefully at that.

"You asked me recently why I don't date," he goes on. "I'm fairly positive I'm aromantic. I've never wanted that sort of relationship with another person, and I don't know that I ever will. Sex, on the other hand, I enjoy very much."

"I'm well aware," I mumble, my mind tumbling over.

"Yes, you are," he says, again, smugly. "But your Ellis... Is it possible he *does* want a partner? That he wants someone to share his life with?"

He's going on a date this weekend.

"I don't know," I admit. I never once thought to ask. Maybe it should have crossed my mind, but for whatever reason, I assumed he didn't want any of it. I'd hoped, on more than one occasion, that Ellis might want *me*. I asked him, directly or indirectly, so many times. I gave him plenty of chances to show me he wanted me, too. But he never did. And if he didn't want me, well... I guess I didn't want him to want *anyone*.

I still don't want him to want anyone else. Maybe that makes me an asshole, but I think I've earned the right. No one will ever know Ellis like I do.

And yet there *are* things I don't know, aren't there?

"You're having a moment," Danil says quietly.

"Yes."

"Why did you come here, Lucky?" he asks. "Why so suddenly?"

I swallow down the lump in my throat. "He has a date."

"Ah," Danil says, shifting beside me on the bed. "Are you going to stop him?"

Yes. No.

"I don't know," I admit.

"What would be the worst that could happen?"

"I'd make a fool of myself."

"Says the man who doused himself in blue paint just to protect the feelings of his...*friend*," Danil counters.

"He'd shoot me down," I say, trying another tactic.

"And then?"

"And then..." My mind whirs again.

"Would he leave you?" Danil asks. "Would he cut ties?"

"No," I whisper. I don't think he'd do that. But he'd *know*. Could I bear it?

"And what if," Danil says slowly, "he said yes? What if he wants you, too?"

I shake my head, not willing to hope. "He doesn't."

"Things change," he says softly.

"Why are you encouraging this?" I ask, turning toward him. "Why are you...pushing?"

Danil sighs, looking suddenly older than his twenty-eight years. "Lucky-boy, in the half a year I've known you, I've seen your eyes light up in front of a dormant volcano. I've seen you run with a herd of buffalo, just to get the right shot. I've seen your fearlessness worn right on your sleeve, but until last night, I'd never seen your heart. Where is your courage now? Why are you running from him?"

"I'm not—"

"You *are*," he insists, voice rising. "We came back here on a whim, but here you are, sitting in your parents' house while he's out there." He waves his arm wide, gaze imploring. "Why aren't you with him?"

"I'm scared!" I finally yell. "I can't lose him, Dani. I *can't*."

"You just said you wouldn't," he points out.

"But things might get strained between us. I might..." What? "See him less often."

"As opposed to now, when you see him a few times a year?" Danil says. "Your mom said you've been visiting less. She said in the beginning, you were here once a month."

It got too hard, saying goodbye.

"When did you talk to her about that?" I ask before shaking my head. I stand, pacing away. "Never mind. It doesn't matter. None of this matters. Could you just drop it? Please?"

Danil watches me for a fraught moment before acquiescing with a nod. "Consider it dropped. I did my duty as your loyal, intrepid friend. If you choose to continue being an idiot, that's on you."

"Jesus," I mutter, scrubbing my forehead. "I'm going to leave you here. I hope you know that."

"Never," Danil says, standing. "You'd miss me." He steps close and wraps an arm around my neck, tugging me in to kiss my cheek.

"We're not fucking here," I inform him.

"I'm not—" He makes an incredulous sound before dropping his arm. "I'm being *supportive* and *lovable*. If I were trying to get into your pants, you'd know it."

My lips twitch as I open the bedroom door.

"As if I'd even try right now," he adds, following me down the hall. "Your Ellis could rip me in half. I'm not a small guy, Lucky-boy. But that man scares me."

"He's a teddy bear," I say, mind skipping back to that day at school, when Ellis took down Brandon like it was nothing. "Mostly."

"Uh-huh," he says before falling silent. I grab my keys, waiting for Danil to catch up, but he's paused at the entrance to the foyer.

"What is it?" I ask. We're the only two in the house. My dad is at work, and my mom said she'd be heading into town for brunch with Mrs. Cole and a few other ladies they get together with from time to time.

Danil looks uncharacteristically solemn as he stands there, composing an answer. "He's...different. Isn't he?"

I bristle, and he holds up his hands placatingly.

"I don't mean that in a bad way," he says. "You just never said, and I wasn't expecting it."

I tug the front door open a little harder than necessary. "He's Ellis. That's all," I say. *It's more than enough.* "Now are you coming? I can show you around town."

Danil nods, and he doesn't say another word all morning or afternoon about Ellis or my supposed not-quite-friendship feelings.

It's just past five when Danil and I get back to the house. He tells me he has some work to get done and retreats to the guest room with his tablet, but I think he's trying to give me space with Ellis. Not that I don't appreciate it.

I walk the property line as I wait for Ellis to get home. It's hot today—Nebraska usually is in the summer—and my shirt sticks uncomfortably to my back. It doesn't help that my heart is racing and my mind is running wild.

I haven't stopped thinking about what Danil said. Haven't stopped wondering why I came here. Wondering if I could—*should*—say anything.

What am I expecting? That Ellis will feel differently than he did at seventeen, when he kissed me, only to pull back? That he'll *want* me in a way he never did before, and for once, he'll ask me to stay? Do I really think shooting my shot with my friend of fifteen years, suddenly and out of the blue, is going to end well for me?

I don't *know*. I don't know what I'm doing. Don't know what's right.

The stalks of corn wave their leaves at me as I pass. I let my fingers drift over the foliage, tracing the line of the field around the corner to where the silo sits not far off. It looks the same as ever, but when I get to the door, I realize it's padlocked. Staring at it in confusion, I give a tug, but it doesn't budge.

"Locked," a voice calls out behind me.

I turn, and there's Ellis, approaching at a steady pace. He's still wearing his dirty jeans and work shirt, the logo on his breast pocket showing a smiling piece of corn. There's a baseball hat on his head, and he gives me a smile that just about stops my heart.

Beautiful.

I stand aside as Ellis pulls out a small keychain from his pocket. He unlocks the door and then throws it wide, waving me forward. Heart thudding, I step inside the silo, only to come to an abrupt halt not two paces in.

"What..." I say.

The silo is completely transformed. Shelves curve around the entire expansive shell, atop which sits a collection of glass far more extensive than Ellis used to have. There's a big wooden table near the middle and a rack of various tools beside it. And, most notably, toward the back of the round space is what looks like a massive brick oven. A kiln, I realize, as awareness snaps into place.

"The parrotfish," I say, stepping forward. Ellis moves into the silo behind me. "You made the parrotfish."

He nods when I find the wherewithal to look back at him. There's a curious expression on his face. He's likely wondering how I knew about it in the first place. Because he never told me. He never told me about any of this.

"What...the *fuck*, El?" I snap, a little harsher than I mean to. "What is this?"

Ellis rubs the back of his neck. "Glass studio," he finally says.

"How..." My voice fails me. "How long has this been here?"

He holds up two fingers and then three.

Between two and three years. He's been crafting glass art for *years*, and he never said a word about it. What the *hell*?

And why didn't I notice? Have I really been that absent?

"Why didn't you tell me about this?" I ask, voice hoarse.

He shrugs, and *oh*, that rankles.

"I thought we didn't have secrets," I say, even though I know we're not kids anymore, back when a pinky promise meant more than anything. Even though I *know* I have no right to feel this hurt.

Ellis's eyes drag up to me slowly. "You and Dani," he says simply.

It feels like a sucker punch. "You and the girl from work," I spit.

Ellis flinches.

"*Fuck*," I mutter, turning away. I rake my hair back, eyes prickling.

Why did he keep this from me?

"We're...not what we once were," Ellis says from behind me, closer than I expect him to be.

I shake my head quickly because no. We're not. And I didn't realize until right this moment exactly how much we've changed. How much we've *allowed* to change.

"But we're still..." he says.

And I nod. *Yeah.* "Me and you," I answer.

Except if neither of us are what we once were, what does that make *us*?

Chapter 15

ELLIS

"Luck," I say quietly.

He doesn't turn around, so I remove my hat, slipping it in my back pocket, and, taking a chance, I step forward. Lucky's arms are around his stomach, and I wrap mine slowly over his, bending my head and resting my forehead against his hair. He smells faintly of oranges, and I wonder if he uses the same shampoo he used to.

"I'm sorry," I tell him. *For lying. For keeping pieces of myself from you. For whatever it is making you hurt.*

"Why didn't you tell me?" he asks again.

"Which?" I ask. *The glass or Gabby?*

"Either," he answers. "Both."

I blow out a slow breath, burying my nose in his hair. "This...the glass...was supposed to be..." I shrug a little, my arms brushing his shoulders. "Mine."

My way to keep Lucky close. My way to keep him here with me, even when he was in New York or halfway around the world. It was—*is*—my coping mechanism.

But it's more than that, too. It's my heart. A love letter I was too afraid to show Lucky. It was safer, keeping it to myself. Just like all those emails littering my drafts folder.

Self-preservation is a strong motivator.

"And..." he says, swallowing. "The girl?"

"Gabby," I tell him. He shudders a little. "New."

His nod is small, a brush of hair against my face. When he steps away, I let go, even as I hate it. Lucky wipes at his face before turning around, but even then, he barely meets my eye. His gaze swings around the silo, seeing the glass on the shelves or who knows what else.

"You knew about Dani," he says.

I nod. Of course I knew they were fucking. I figured he didn't say anything because it was *more*. The start of something, maybe. And truthfully, I didn't want to know.

I don't think it's that now, not having seen them together. But for whatever reason, Lucky kept it from me. Just like I've kept things from him.

"What the fuck happened?" he asks, looking at me then, asking for answers I'm not sure I have.

We grew up? Grew apart, just a little, in the years since he's been gone? We moved forward, but we did it in different places?

"Life," I answer.

Lucky looks up, blinking several times. He goes still when he sees the lights overhead, and then his head is on a swivel. "El..."

Taking a few steps away, I flick on the power. The electricity is new since Lucky was last in here. He gasps when the glass fireflies light up, two dozen of them hanging suspended thirty feet above our heads. Each is the size of a baseball—but they look smaller than that from down here—and they glow a gentle yellow with the LED lighting that's piped into their center. It took me a long time to position them just so, but now, they appear to be floating without strings. Flying. If you hold up your hand, it's almost as if you could touch them.

Lucky's gaze lowers to me slowly. "They're beautiful."

They're you. The closest I could ever come to capturing you.

He doesn't say anything for the longest time, his blue eyes blinking at me in the soft light. I don't know what's running through his head, have no idea if he's mad at me or if I've been forgiven by default, but I can't bring myself to ask.

Finally, he looks away. "I should get back," he says, voice rough around the edges. "I left Dani alone."

I nod, even as my insides tremble. Even as I want to remind him it was supposed to be *us* tonight. Lucky takes a step, but I can't...

"Luck."

He stops, looking back.

"Okay?" I ask.

He nods slowly, but his eyes are sad. "Yeah, El. We'll always be okay."

With that, he goes, and I can't help but feel like my world has cracked just a little, sending us further apart.

I wait for a long time before I head inside to get dinner ready. But before I go, I pull my phone from my pocket. Confronted with the truth of my feelings—*still, always*—I text Gabby and call off our date.

Lucky doesn't come back that evening. And I don't see him the next morning. He and Dani stay away from the house, and I stay away from the corn festival where I was supposed to be with Gabby. I spend some time in the silo, breaking glass in preparation for a new piece. The shards will be melted down and reformed. Reshaped. Made into something greater.

It took months to learn the process. Most was self-taught, watching videos and then spending hours in the heat of the silo, carefully blowing and shaping the glass. But I also attended a week-long workshop a few hours from here, learning the finer points from an expert.

Now, the techniques are second nature, although I never did care whether or not it looks perfect in the end. It's more about the catharsis of it. Taking the pictures Lucky paints in my head and bringing them to life. The extra income doesn't hurt, either. I didn't expect people in town to be so excited about the glasswork, even the smaller pieces I make to keep my hands and mind busy, but they sell out faster than I can produce them.

It's late afternoon, and I'm on the back deck, having just showered, when Lucky and Dani return from wherever they were. The car crunches down the gravel drive before stopping, and both men get out. Dani heads into the house next door, but Lucky beelines my way, his hands deep in his pockets. He looks young again. Vulnerable.

"Hey," he says once close.

I set down the large glass jar I'd brought outside, and Lucky quirks a smile.

"Making sun tea?" he asks.

I nod. I always did like it better this way, rather than heating the water on the stove. I used some of the tea bags Lucky sent months ago and added a bit of lemon. It'll be delicious once it's steeped in the sun.

Lucky sighs a little, his smile faltering. "I'm sorry, El. I shouldn't have left yesterday."

I shrug, not wanting him to feel bad about it. It's not often the pair of us fight, but Lucky's not to blame. I *did* keep things from him, and that's on me. I don't fault him for being upset.

"Did you..." He peters out. "Did you have a good day?"

I think that over before nodding. It was fine.

Lucky swallows, nodding, too. He looks a little uncomfortable, although I'm not sure why. "Yeah, okay," he says. "Um... Could we do something tonight? Just the two of us?"

My smile is immediate, and Lucky's face softens, expression smoothing out.

"Yeah, yeah," he says, chuckling. "Like I have to ask. Are you ready now?"

I nod, holding up a finger. Lucky waits as I grab my phone from inside. Mom is in the living room, running through a few exercises that are supposed to help with her muscle cramps. She does them from her chair now.

"Heading out?" she asks, eyes trailing to Lucky out on the deck.

I nod. "Need anything?"

"No, baby. Have a good time tonight."

She motions me forward, however, so I step around the couch to give her a kiss on the cheek. She pats mine afterward.

Outside, I hold up my keys, and Lucky grins. "Hell yeah," he says. "I've missed the truck."

I snort, but there's a lightness to Lucky's steps as we head around to the front of the house, and it settles me down to my marrow.

Lucky slaps the open window once I climb inside the cab a second after him. "Drive on, Ellis. Show me the world."

I give a salute, and he laughs.

Sitting inside my truck with my best friend as we bump down the dirt roads is like a blast from the past. He shoots me an exasperated smile as we pass the school and mouths *clams* with wide eyes as we drive in front of Maisy's Diner, and every moment is one I soak up. It feels good. Like us again, that easily.

We're about five minutes outside the town center when Lucky says, "So where are we going, anyways?"

I shoot him a look, even though I'm the one driving. *How should I know? You invited me.*

He laughs. "Guess we didn't really think that through, huh?"

I let out a sigh, barely able to hold back my smile. In the end, we turn around and drive to the grocery store, grabbing a few easy to-go food options and a case of beer. Then I lead us out to the edge of town to a property I know will be deserted. I drive my truck right onto the flat land in front of the corn rows before turning off the engine. Grabbing an old blanket from the back of the cab, I motion for Lucky to follow. He looks out over the land for a moment, as if he hasn't seen corn a million times before, and then, once he turns around, he smiles.

"What are you doing?" he asks, following me up into the bed of the truck. I already laid out the blanket, and now I'm pulling food out of our plastic grocery bag.

"Picnic," I grunt, as if it isn't obvious.

"God, El," Lucky says quietly, shaking his head. His expression is soft and fond, but then it turns a little mischievous as he eyes the beer. "If we get drunk and neither of us can drive, you're carrying me home."

I grin, and before Lucky can react, I pull him off his feet into a fireman's carry.

He shouts. "Fucking hell, Ellis! What are you—"

He goes silent when I swat his ass, and in the starkly quiet aftermath, my heart starts to pound. I set him down quickly, turning away and fiddling with the beer. My cheeks feel hot. I don't know what I was thinking.

"You," Lucky says, a hoarse sort of chuckle in his voice, "are trouble."

I shake my head, clearing my throat. "That's you."

He huffs. "Well, I think you're catching up."

"Uh-oh," I deadpan.

Lucky laughs again, gentler this time, and my tension starts to flee. When we settle side by side on the blanket, it's only five-thirty, but we start in on our dinner. Lucky pops grapes into his mouth while I make a quick sandwich with a loaf of crusty bread and sliced roast beef. I hand half of it to Lucky, and he passes me an open beer.

"You know, nowhere on Earth smells like this place," Lucky says.

No?

"No," he says. "It used to bug me. The way the smell would change over the season. How, no matter what time of year, I couldn't escape the corn."

His chuckle is rueful.

"And now," he goes on, "if I'm not here, I can't find that smell anywhere. And *that* bugs me."

I bump his shoulder with mine. "Home," I say, a simplification of what I mean. This place grew on him. He said so himself the other day.

His swallow is rough, and he chases it with a sip of beer. His eyes flick to me when he says, "Guess so."

"Luck," I say, setting down the remnants of my sandwich. "I'm sorry. About...the glass. I..."

Lucky waits while I compose my thoughts into words. The sun sits behind him, lighting the wisps of hair at the front of his face. They look like strands of swirling gold, and for a moment, I get caught up in them.

Finally, I say, "When you're...gone, you... You share your life. With me. Your adventures and... And your joy." I set my gaze on the corn as I go on. "It means the world to me, Luck. To be a part of that. I... Please don't stop just...just because I was..."

Scared, I can't say. I can't.

I let out a small breath before continuing. "I don't ever want to lose...the place I have in your world."

Lucky looks at me for the longest time. I can feel his gaze on the side of my head, and when I finally meet his eye, he doesn't look away. "You say so little," he nearly whispers. "But then, sometimes..."

He grabs my hand, and I swallow, tingles chasing one another up my arm.

"You won't lose me, El," he says. "Not ever."

I nod in a fierce jerk, and Lucky and I finish our meal. We spend a good few hours on the blanket in the back of my truck, swapping stories and watching the sky turn dark. And despite the prior tension, I believe him. He said it before, after all.

"We'll never be done. Me and you, we don't have an ending."

Chapter 16

LUCKY

"You're moping," Danil notes.

"I'm not," I counter.

"Are too."

"What are you, five?"

He sticks his tongue out at me, and I toss a shirt at his face. It helps for a second, until I go back to packing.

"I still think you should say something," Danil says.

"I thought you said you'd drop it."

"Dropped," he replies quickly, sealing his lips. He refolds my shirt before walking over and setting it inside my suitcase. "We need to go soon."

The reminder is gentle, but I can't bring myself to speed up. I know I'm putting off the inevitable, but I'm not ready to get on that plane. My insides are rolling, every inch of me uneasy.

"If we miss our flight, you get to talk to Chelsea," he says. *Our boss.* With that, he slaps my shoulder and leaves the room.

I procrastinate as long as possible, but finally, I finish packing and zip up my luggage. When I go looking for my mom, I find her in my parents' bedroom. She's sitting at the computer, her reading glasses on.

"Hi, sweetheart," she says, sitting back. "Ready to go?"

No. "Yes."

She nods, coming over to give me a hug. "Be safe, all right? We like you in one piece."

"I will," I say with a chuckle. My eyes catch on the dresser when we step apart. "Is that..."

"Oh," my mom says, smiling. "One of Ellis's. Isn't it beautiful?"

I walk over to the dresser, atop which sits a glass sailboat. It's a little smaller than the parrotfish, but not by much. The base of the vessel is opaque white, but the sails are a blend of yellows and oranges, almost like a sunrise. It's simplistically made—not an extra piece or frill on it—but it's intricate. Delicate.

"I didn't know he did this," I tell her, tracing my finger over the smaller sail. "I just found out."

She hums. "I wonder why he didn't tell you."

I'm still not sure of that myself. He seemed almost embarrassed by it, like he was scared of my reaction. Did he think I wouldn't support him?

The thought stings.

"When did he make this one?" I ask, having a feeling I know the answer.

My mom thinks it over. "A year and a half ago?"

After my trip to the Grenadines. Geoff, my first partner, and I spent three days sailing, hopping islands and exploring some of the lesser-known beaches in the area. I remember recounting the details to Ellis, like I always do. The white sands. The salty air. The feeling of soaring over the water as if I were a bird. The sunrise I enjoyed alongside Geoff as we sipped espresso aboard the boat. And the yellows and oranges that crested over the water as if the sun were bleeding up into the sky.

He brought it to life. Ellis brought it to life.

I let my hand fall away from the glass. "I should get going," I tell my mom.

She gives my shoulder a squeeze. "Of course. Let me know when you land."

After one more hug, I find Danil waiting for me in the living room.

He stands and pops his phone into his pocket. "Ready?"

Why does everyone keep asking me that?

I nod, and luggage in tow, we head out to the rental car. I already said goodbye to my dad early this morning before he left for the paper mill. And all of us—me, Danil, my parents, Mrs. Cole, and Ellis—spent the entirety of Sunday together, grilling and catching up. I said my goodbyes to Ellis's mom then.

All that's left is Ellis himself.

On our way through town, I pull up in front of the convenience store. "Just have to make a quick pit stop," I tell Danil.

He nods, staying in the car as I head inside the building. I find Melody near the checkout counter, and she gives me a surprised sort of smile.

"Hey, Melody."

"Lucky," she says. "Still in town?"

"On my way out, actually. I just..." I glance over at the parrotfish, displayed proudly at the front of the store. "Why's it still here?"

Melody kicks her hip against the counter. "Well, the first few that sold went home with people right away, but once folks in town started hearing about them, I got asked a good hundred times if the pieces could be displayed first. Not like we have an art gallery here."

I nod. That, we do not.

"So now we have a rule where they stay here for three weeks so people can come see them," she says. "After that, they go to their new home, and the artist brings in a new piece."

I pull my wallet out, slipping a business card free that I pass to Melody. "Do me a favor? If there's ever one that *doesn't* sell out in a few hours, give me a call? I'll buy it."

Melody huffs a small laugh, accepting the card. "I'll do that, but I wouldn't hold your breath."

"Thanks," I tell her regardless. I turn to go but stop at the last minute. "Hey, Melody? How's Jace?"

She rolls her eyes. "My brother is up in Minnesota now, did you know that? He and his boyfriend got a place right near the Canadian border."

"His boyfriend?" I ask in surprise. Last I knew, the Jace who propositioned me beneath the bleachers was still *far* in the closet.

She nods. "They've been together for two years now."

"I had no clue," I tell her. *Good for him.* "Well, thanks again. Take care."

"You, too, Lucky," she says, giving me a wave as her focus shifts to a customer coming up to the counter.

Danil raises a brow when I get into the car. "All good?" he asks.

"Yeah, let's go."

It only takes another ten minutes to get to the facility where Ellis works. He told me he'd be onsite this morning, so once I park, I shoot him a text, and he says he'll meet me outside.

I wait near the shade of a maple tree as a few other employees come and go. One heads off on a tractor. Another is leaning against the outside of the building, spitting sunflower seed shells onto the ground. Not far off, one of the town's many processing plants sits, its smoke stacks rising high into the air.

Ellis steps out of the door before long, the morning sun causing him to squint. He spots me almost immediately and heads my way. I can't quite get my heart to stop pounding as he nears, and that rolling inside my gut returns tenfold.

I feel the same way I did before I jumped out of a plane for the first time, a parachute securely on my back. A little scared. A lot determined.

"Hey," I greet before Ellis has even come to a stop. He steps under the shade of the tree with me, a sad smile on his face.

"Luck," he says simply.

It's all I can do not to whimper.

"I, uh... We're heading out," I say, even though he knows as much.

Ellis nods.

"I..." *Fuck, come on.* "Can I ask you something?"

"Always," he answers.

I lick my lips, as if it will help the sudden dryness of my mouth. "Do you want a partner? A, uh, romantic relationship, I mean. Is that something you want?"

Ellis's brow furrows slightly, and I'm not surprised. My question is coming out of nowhere.

After a moment, he answers, "With the right person."

I nod, feeling a little lightheaded. "And, um. Have you...ever had sex?"

His brows fly up, and he shakes his head, completely un-abashed by that fact. That's something I've always loved about Ellis. He doesn't care about what's considered *normal*. It doesn't bother him that most people would look at a twen-ty-five-year-old virgin as an oddity. It's not a concern to him. He's only ever wanted to be himself.

I hope that never changes.

I'm relieved by his answer, if only because it means he hasn't kept something that big from me. But still, it's been years since we've talked about this outright, and like Danil said, sometimes things change.

Swallowing, I force my next question. "Do you want to?"

If Ellis is wondering why I'm asking whether or not he wants to have sex, he doesn't show it. "Right person," he answers again.

My pulse thunders. "And has there been anyone recently?" I ask, voice nearly a whisper. "Anyone who's caught your eye?"

Ellis doesn't once look away, even as it takes him a moment to respond. "One," he finally says. "One person."

Gabby.

It takes everything in me not to react. To keep my emotions locked down tight. I wish I had a parachute now because *fuck*, does the ground hurt.

"Right," I say, forcing a tremulous smile. "Well, Dani and I need to get to the airport, so—"

"Why?" Ellis interrupts.

"Why what?" I ask, sticking my shaking hands in my pockets.

"Why ask?"

My sigh is small, but my whole chest deflates as I step forward and wrap my arms around Ellis. "Because you're my closest friend," I tell him, hiding the truth of it against his shirt. "I just want you to be happy."

His arms come around me slowly, but it's the most natural thing, the way we fit together. I hate that, for a brief moment, I allowed myself to hope. But if Ellis likes Gabby, if she's the first person he's been attracted to, possibly *ever*, I won't stand in the way of that. How could I?

I refuse to be that petty, even as every part of me wants to demand he look again. That he see *me*. *God*, just *see me*.

Instead, I let him go. His expression is downcast, and I wonder if this is as hard for him as it is for me, these goodbyes.

I clear my throat. "I'll call when I can," I tell him. He knows that, though.

Still, he nods. "Better."

I huff a pained laugh. "I love you, El. Just be happy, okay?"

He nods, brows drawn.

I can't quite stop myself from giving him one last hug. I hold on a little too long, soaking up his presence and the solid feel of him against my cheek. I remember, without my permission, the feel of his skin underneath my palms when we were seventeen. When Ellis kissed me beneath a waterfall. My first kiss.

My first love.

Eyes stinging, I step back. "Bye, El," I say quickly, turning away.

His "Bye, Luck" trails after me.

Danil is frowning when I get back to the car. I give him a swift shake of my head, and he nods. Ellis is still by the maple when I pull the car around, and I watch him from the rearview until I can't see him anymore.

So much for hope.

Chapter 17

ELLIS

"It's been harder at night," my mom tells the doctor.

He nods, not looking particularly surprised by that. "We can adjust your medication, and that should help the night-time muscle stiffness some. But I'll also give you a sheet with stretches you can do in bed. Your physical therapist can aid you with this, as well."

My mom nods, going through the stretches with the doctor before he checks her vitals, performs some routine tests, and writes a new prescription. It's an average visit, all things considered, but for whatever reason, it hits me harder today. My mom looks older, weaker than she did seven years ago when she got her diagnosis. Some days, weeks, months, the change is so minimal I can barely see it. And then other times, it's impossible to ignore how very much has changed.

Reminds me of something else in my life.

Before we go, the doctor recommends a few ways I can help my mom when the muscle spasms are particularly bad. I listen attentively, thanking him when he's done.

"We should go to the pharmacy on the way home," my mom says as I help her into the truck. Her hand shakes as she tries to buckle herself in, so I take the seatbelt from her gently, clicking it into place. She waits until I'm in the vehicle before going on. "We can run into the store, too. Get something special for dinner tonight."

I shoot a quick glance her way.

"Why not?" she says with a shrug. "Life's too short not to treat yourself every once in a while. And I don't know about you, but I could go for some steak."

My smile is wobbly, but I nod, turning out onto the road.

"Potatoes, too," she says. "Baked. With sour cream and chives. *Oh*, yes." She hums. "That'll hit the spot."

I park in front of the grocery store, and while my mom starts shopping with the use of a motorized cart, I jog across the street to the pharmacy. My phone buzzes on my way back, and I stop in front of the store, pulling it free.

The smile on my face slips when I realize it's not an email from Lucky but rather...my *dad*.

My fingers shake as I click it open. Three simple sentences stare back at me.

Hi, Ellis. I hope you don't mind, but I got your email from Sandra. Can we talk?

The first time I hear from the man in over fifteen years, and that's it? *Can we talk?* No *I hope you're well.* No *I shouldn't have left you and your mother like that.* No *I'm sorry.* Three impersonal sentences; that's all I get.

I barely spare a thought for my mom's friend, Sandra. I just shove my phone back in my pocket and turn toward the door.

I find my mom near the refrigerated cheese section, debating between cheddar and Colby-Jack.

"Which one?" she asks me.

I point to the cheddar, and she nods, putting it in the cart. I don't move at first when she drives onward, but once I catch up with her near the milk, she looks at me oddly.

"Something wrong?" she asks.

I shake my head. No use in worrying my mom over an email I'm surely not going to respond to. What would be the point?

She hums. "Do we have sour cream?"

I nod, and we head toward the produce.

"How's Lucky?" she asks. She's fishing, I think. Trying to figure out what's on my mind. I can't fault her for caring.

"Good," I tell her, and as far as I know, that's true. Our conversations have been a little more stilted over the past two months, ever since he left. I hate it, but I don't know how to *fix* it. I debated, ever briefly, flying out to New York to see him, but the idea of leaving my mom alone fills me with dread. What if she needed me while I was gone?

Lucky and I will find our way back to one another. We have to. Right?

"Why don't you grab the potatoes?" my mom says. "I'll get the chives."

I nod, and we split up. I'm debating between russet or Yukon gold when I hear my name.

"Hey, Ellis."

Turning, I find Riley, a small shopping basket in his hand. I give him a nod.

"Watching the game tonight?" he asks, grabbing a couple onions.

Considering I don't know what game—or sport—he's talking about, I shake my head.

He nods, seemingly expecting as much. Thankfully, Riley has never been one to push me into small talk. "See ya Monday?"

Yep.

He takes a step away before pausing. "Hey, Ellis? If you ever wanna hang out, me and a few friends go to the bar most Fridays." He doesn't need to clarify which bar. We only have one in town. "Show up if you want. Or you can always text me. You have my number."

A little surprised by the offer, I nod, and Riley shoots me a smile before walking off.

"Got the potatoes?" my mom asks, nearly bumping into my calf with her motorized cart.

I drop them into the basket, and we head toward the checkout.

"Was that Riley Evans I saw?" she says once we're outside.

I grunt a yes.

"He seems like such a nice young man. Did you know he's on the volunteer firefighting team?"

I nod as I load our groceries into the truck, and my mom launches into a story about her friend Lydia and the time her cat got stuck on the roof. Apparently, Riley was the one who got the feline down. My mom pauses her retelling as I run across the street to pick up her filled prescription, but as soon as I'm in the driver's seat, she goes on.

I listen, but my gaze strays out the window. The once summer-green corn has turned a harvest-ready brown, but that's not what catches my attention. There are storm clouds gathering in the distance, gray and ominous. The sky below them is dimmed, as if the color has been leached away. Looks like rain is coming.

When we get home, I heat the grill as my mom washes potatoes. With the temperatures dropping, we won't be able to grill for much longer. Lucky's dad pulls up while I'm still out on the deck. He gives me a wave on his way inside, and I hold up my hand in return, thoughts drifting to the email in my inbox.

What could my dad possibly want to talk to me about after all this time? Do I even care? He left. He left me, my mom, the house he grew up in. He packed up his belongings like it was the easiest thing and loaded up a moving truck as I sat inside and watched.

He waved when he backed out of the driveway. I'll never forget that. I haven't heard from him since. Not until today.

My mom has the news on when I get back inside. The potatoes are in the oven, baking, and the steaks are waiting on a plate. "Storm's coming in," she informs me, nodding toward the TV. The next couple days are forecasting rain and thunderstorms, and a banner along the bottom warns of possible tornadoes.

"Prepared," I say.

As soon as my mom started using her wheelchair, I had a battery-operated lift installed in the storm shelter. That was years ago now, although we've only had to use it once.

She nods, giving me a smile. "Yes, we are. We'll be fine."

As the grill heats, I grab my laptop, sitting at the kitchen table. The low hum of the TV is white noise as I bring up my email. I ignore the one from my dad, instead opening up the last one I received from Lucky. He's on his way to Greece, and although the tone of the message is excited—he's never been there before—it's perfunctory and *quiet*. Lucky has never been quiet. Not with me.

I click out and open up a new thread.

Luck. Hey. I don't like this. There's a distance between us that never used to be there. What can I say to bring you back? What can I do? I was foolish, I think, taking our friendship for granted. Assuming there was nothing I could do that would fuck us up. I assumed I couldn't hurt you, but I was wrong. I forget, sometimes, that you're not invincible. That you bleed just like me. You've always been larger than life. A force. But your heart is big, and I bruised it, didn't I?

I wish I could say I'll never keep anything from you again, but I know that's not the truth. I'm keeping the biggest thing from you. If I told you, would it fix this? If you knew how I love you, would you understand? Or would it only drive another wedge?

I was seventeen when I kissed you at Smith Falls. I didn't understand then what I was feeling, but I knew, in a way I hadn't before, that I wanted to follow you. I wanted to go with you. It would have been worth it just to be near. Me and you, we could take on anything.

Things didn't work out that way. You know that. The world isn't always kind, and circumstances change. My mom... I couldn't leave her. Not like that. Not like he did. But it meant, in a way, I left you. So maybe I started this.

If that's the case, I'm sorry. I'm sorry for a lot of things. Please forgive me. Please. Please.

I miss you, my precious firefly.

I close out the email when I'm done and reopen the one from Lucky. This time, my message is meant to be read.

Hey, Luck. I hope you arrived safe in Greece. Can't wait to hear what you get up to.

I know I said it before, but I'm sorry about the glass. It was never my intention to hurt you, and if I could go back, I'd do things differently. I wouldn't keep it from you. As for Gabby, well, it had only just happened. I would have told you, but then you were here, and now... Now, we're here. But I suppose, in the end, intentions only stretch so far.

I'm sorry, okay? I've been a shitty friend. I'll do better, I promise. Please believe me.

Ellis

With a deep breath, I hit send. I can only hope it helps, at least a little.

"Don't forget the steaks, baby," my mom says.

I grab the plate and head outside. As I'm loading our steaks onto the grill, the first drops of rain hit my arm. They're big, fat, and they splatter against me like paint on a canvas. I hustle inside before they start coming down in earnest.

Storm's coming. Feels fitting.

Before I put my laptop away, I click open the email from my dad and type out a quick response. He wants to know if we can talk?

No.

I hit send and put it out of my mind.

Chapter 18

LUCKY

"I can't believe I'm saying this, but this is a bad idea, Lucky-boy."

I scoff, tugging Danil's shirt up higher and bending to lick his nipple.

He hisses, arching toward me, even as his hands make like they're going to push me away. "Anyone could see us."

"And that's a problem, why?" I counter, scraping my thumb across the bud as I bring my lips to his neck.

His head thunks against the wall. "Because we're in a foreign country, *far* from home and legal representation, and I don't want us getting arrested for indecent exposure in the back hall of a *family restaurant*."

I huff against his neck, pulling back as someone walks past us toward the bathroom. "Since when are you the voice of reason?" I ask, tugging his shirt down.

He brushes his hair into place with both hands, chest rising and falling and jeans tented. "Oh, I don't know," he snarks.

"Since about two months ago when you decided getting past a broken heart meant diving headfirst into any and all potential danger?"

Irritated, I turn and walk away, but Danil catches up to me quickly. His hand curls around my wrist, grip loose.

"Lucky, if you want me to blow you back at the hotel, I'm all for it. You know that. But this isn't like you. I'm worried."

I pull from his grip, hackles up. "I don't want your pity."

"It's not *pity*," he says, stepping with me onto the street. "It's caring. If you want to use me as a distraction, fine. I have no problem with it. But you've been...off, ever since we left Nebraska. It's like you're courting danger. Taking risks you never used to."

I hold up my hand for a taxi, shaking my head. "We both take risks for our job."

"That's not what I mean, and you know it," he snaps. "This isn't you swimming with sharks. This is you being reckless. This is you drowning and not giving a shit."

"Come on, Dani. You're making a bigger deal—"

"Oh, no, no," he says, not to be dissuaded. "You're *drunk* tonight, Lucky. Sloppy drunk. It's the third time this month. You didn't drink like this before."

I huff, but he's not wrong.

"And last month?" he goes on. "You went off-trail minutes after our guide told us not to because of the high probability of crocs in the area. We couldn't find you for five minutes, Lucky. Do you know how terrified I was?"

My frustration dissipates in an instant, and I curse. "I'm sorry," I mumble, rubbing my forehead.

"I know," Danil says gently. "Just...talk to me. Stop shutting me out."

Again with that phrase.

I work my jaw as a cab pulls to the curb. Danil and I get in the back, and he gives the driver our hotel address. My head swims a little as we pull into traffic, so I close my eyes, trying to ride the wave.

"He thinks I'm mad at him," I finally say, my mind running over Ellis's email. *"I'm sorry, okay? I've been a shitty friend. I'll do better, I promise. Please believe me."*

I scrub my hands over my face as guilt flares, bright and hot.

"What do you mean?" Danil asks.

"I've been..."

"Hurting?" he fills in when I trail off.

I nod, accepting the simplification. "Yes. And it's not his fault I'm so..." I wave a hand over my chest. Over my heart. "But it's been hard, harder than normal, talking to him. And he thinks I'm mad because of it. Which in turn makes me feel like shit."

"Maybe explain it to him?" Danil suggests, as if it's that easy.

"How?" I ask, meeting his dark gaze. "I'm honestly asking, Dani, 'cause I don't know how. I can't tell him I'm...heartbroken. I can't tell him I've been secretly wishing, all these years, that he and I could... That we could be..."

"Maybe you need some space," Danil says.

"No," I reply immediately, shaking my head. When my vision swims, I stop and breathe through it. "I can't do that."

"You still want to be his friend?" he asks, voice soft.

"Yes. Always."

"Okay," Danil says thoughtfully. "Then you need to get over it."

I bark a laugh. "Just like that?"

Danil shrugs. "What you're doing—this whole outrun your feelings thing—clearly isn't working. So yes, do what you need to do to accept the state of things and move on."

"Have you ever wanted someone so much," I say slowly, "that it feels like your atoms are vibrating when you're away from them? Like you're half of a whole, and your body knows it. And until you're in their arms again, every single piece of you is straining toward them because...because they're your home. They're part of you. Your beginning and your never-ending. How? How do I move on from that?"

"Lucky," Danil says softly, his face mired in sadness.

"But I have to, don't I? I have to figure it out. I will."

He squeezes my leg as the driver pulls around to the entrance of our hotel. Danil pays, and we head inside. Once in the privacy of our shared room, Danil starts unbuttoning his shirt. I grab a bottle of water before turning right back around.

"I'm gonna step outside," I let Danil know.

He gives me a nod and spreads out atop his bed. I know he'd make good on his offer from earlier if I asked, but I'm not in the mood anymore. And, frankly, Danil deserves better than playing the part of my distraction.

Out on the veranda, I drink half of my water in one go before leaning against the railing that overlooks a beautiful, sloping hill. It's dark now, but some light from the hotel illuminates the grounds where manicured olive trees stand like little soldiers. I breathe in the cool evening air as I drum up the willpower to pull out my phone.

Once I make the call, Ellis answers quickly.

"Hey," I say, my voice sounding loud in the still night air. "How are you doing?"

Ellis is quiet for a moment, and I cringe. *How are you doing? Really?*

"Good," he finally says. "You?"

I nearly smack my forehead against the tile pillar nearby. "I'm good, El. It's good to hear you."

He hums, and I force a slow breath through my body. This is Ellis. Still my Ellis. Always.

"Dani and I are in Crete," I say, figuring the quickest way past this awkwardness is just to dive in. "The island is gorgeous, and the people here have been so welcoming. We visited the Palace of Knossos yesterday."

He makes a curious sound.

"It was fascinating," I admit, settling against the rail. "Haunting, too. So much of it is just rubble now, but it's like...you could see what it used to be, you know? The grandeur of it. Legend has it the Minotaur was kept in Knossos in an underground labyrinth."

He hums, and I smile.

"Yeah, can you imagine? We'll be hiking the Samaria Gorge the day after tomorrow. It's about ten miles down on foot, but they shuttle you back to town afterward, so you don't have to make the climb back up. Probably a good thing. I've heard the views are gorgeous. I bet I'll be snapping pictures the entire way."

Ellis makes another soft sound, and it's so comforting and familiar that my eyes slip shut.

"I'm sorry," I whisper. He doesn't reply right away, so I keep going. "El, I'm *sorry*. I know things have been...weird, but it's not your fault, okay? I'm just... I guess I've just been going through some stuff."

"What can I do?" he asks slowly.

God. *God.*

"Nothing," I tell him, voice hoarse. "Just...keep being you. That helps."

"I can do that," he says, and I huff a small laugh.

"How, um... How are things going with Gabby?"

I haven't been able to bring myself to ask before now. I didn't want to know, but I can't keep sticking my head in the sand. If I want to repair this, I have to make an effort to be the friend Ellis deserves.

He makes a curious sound, one I'm not quite sure how to decipher.

"Good?" I ask. "Not good?"

"We're..."

The silence stretches. "What?" *Madly in love and planning the wedding? Fucking like bunnies? Getting matching tattoos?*

I cut that line of thinking off at the head.

"Not together," he finishes.

"Wh-what?" I ask, a little stilted. "It didn't work out?"

I shouldn't be happy about that. I *know* I shouldn't. But I can't help the utter relief that rushes through me at hearing those words. Guilt follows quickly on its heels.

"Never together," Ellis says.

I blink out past the veranda, his meaning not computing. "Wait, what? You just had the one date?"

"No date," he answers.

My mouth opens.

"Didn't go," he adds. "Thought you...knew that."

Suddenly, I can barely breathe. He didn't—what? He never went to the festival with Gabby? But I thought...

"You said... You said you were into her," I point out.

There's a pause. "Didn't."

"Then who—" I cut off, chest rising and falling with my heavy breath, a million little pieces tumbling into place. I can practically hear the click of them inside my mind, each one slotting together to make a whole. "Ellis," I say roughly, clutching the railing in front of me. "What did you mean when you said *one person*? That there was one person. Who?"

Silence greets my ears, apart from the pounding of my own heart, and then there's a *boom* on the other end of the line.

"El?" I ask, alarmed.

"Storm," he answers. A beeping follows, like a weather alert on TV.

"Is that a tornado warning?" I ask, heart pounding somewhere in the vicinity of my feet.

"Watch," he amends, which is better than a warning. It means one hasn't been sighted, but the conditions are right.

"El," I croak again, wanting to tell him to be careful. Wanting to demand he answer my question. Wanting to—I don't *know*.

But before I can say anything, another boom shatters the silence, and I hear Mrs. Cole in the background.

"Have to go," Ellis says, and then he's gone.

I stand there for a long minute, my pulse racing like a rabbit's. And then, like a shot, I'm off. Danil looks up in surprise when I all but burst into the room.

"What's going on?" he asks, sitting up quickly as I rush to my bag, tossing clothes inside. "What are you—"

"I'm an idiot," I tell him, grabbing my extra pair of shoes from beside the bed. They go into my bag, the contents a haphazard mess. I grab my toiletries from the bathroom, check to make sure I have my passport, and then zip up my bag.

"Lucky," Danil says, at my side now, alarm in his voice. "What's going on? Where are you going?"

I spare my friend a glance, heart pounding like a drum. "Home."

Part III: Waxing

Chapter 19

ELLIS

The storm lasts all day and night, rattling the windows, thunder shaking the ground. No tornadoes touch down, but the watch stays in effect until the early morning hours. It's around ten that I get a call from Gabby, panicked about her missing dog. Apparently, Toodles took off in the middle of the night, and Gabby hasn't been able to find her.

I join the search as the sky sends down drizzling rain. The day is gray and overcast—miserable, really—but I'm grateful for the distraction. It keeps me from obsessing over my phone call with Lucky. He hasn't called back, but I know it's only a matter of time.

What do I say when he does? What do I tell him? That *he's* the only one I've ever wanted? The only one I've ever thought of in my life, in my arms, in my bed? How could I?

He was already caught off guard; that much was clear. I upset him, once again, because I left out information about

Gabby. It feels like a giant step backwards, but I thought he *knew*. He was in town when I skipped the date, after all.

So stupid. Such a careless mistake.

I don't know what I'm going to say when I talk to him again. When he pushes—because he will—I might not have a choice but to give him the truth.

I have a small baggie of treats in my pocket as I scour the fields for a lost Lhasa Apso. Gabby has shown me enough pictures that I know what she looks like: small and cream-colored, with some darker fur around her face and ears. But no matter how much I whistle, no dogs appear through the slate-gray gloom.

It's well past lunchtime, nearly two o'clock, when I get a call. The rain has been spitting steadily all day, and while my hat keeps it from my eyes, it doesn't stop spots from forming on my screen as I stare down at Lucky's name. I answer on the fourth ring, pulse kicking.

"Ellis," Lucky says immediately, his tone almost harsh. "Where are you?"

Not the question I was expecting. "Dog," I say. "Looking for a dog."

"*Where?*"

I fumble for a moment. "Field near...Miner and Fourth." I've barely finished listing the street names when the line goes dead.

For a moment, I wonder if... But, no. Surely not.

I stick my phone back in my pocket and resume the search. I'm almost done with this area when there's a loud honk that nearly sends me out of my skin. It persists for a good seven seconds before I'm able to get myself into gear and move my feet toward the noise. The honking doesn't stop. There's a tap, followed by another, someone clearly trying to get my—or another's—attention. I tell myself it's not him—there's no way it's him—but I think I know, even before I've cleared the field.

It is him. Lucky. Standing beside a beige car with his arm reaching through the driver's side door. He stops honking the horn when I step into the clearing, and then he stands up straight. He's wet, same as me, the rain coming down between us like a blanket of mist.

I can't take another step as Lucky shuts the car door and tromps my way. I feel rooted. Stuck. Completely immobilized.

"What did you mean?" he calls once he's close enough. My heart thuds. "*Who?* Who did you mean?"

I can't get my voice to work. Don't even want to.

"Ellis," he yells, stopping right in front of me. I don't think I've ever seen him look so determined. No, that's not true. He was wearing a similar face that day he snuck paint into school. But what I don't understand is *why?* Why is he here? Is he *that* angry with me?

"How..." I start, waving to him.

"Not glad to see me?" he counters, hands on his hips.

I glower.

"Answer the question," he says.

I know which one he means.

"Why?" I say, stalling. "Why are you..."—I huff out a breath—"back so soon?"

Lucky steps forward, putting us toe to toe. For the briefest of moments, something akin to fear flashes in his eyes. But then it's gone, and Lucky is answering the question. "To do what I should have done the last time I was here."

I don't have time to unwrap those words before Lucky is going up on his toes, tugging me in by the back of the neck, and pressing his lips to mine.

I freeze. For a split second, I freeze, completely caught unawares and unable to make sense of what's happening. But when Lucky's mouth urges against my own, demanding something—*anything*—I snap.

I kiss him back, my hands threading into his hair, my lungs infiltrated with the heady scent of citrus as everything in me sparks to attention like the quick snap of a lightning strike. I almost expect to hear a boom of thunder, but there's only Lucky's sound of desperation and the feel of his lips on mine. Like softness. Like surrender. Like every whisper of home I've ever heard.

For a moment, I float in it. My heart beats, my head sings, and my hands grip tight, not wanting to let go. But when Lucky's hand trails down my stomach, his touch sure, fingers snaking under my shirt and landing like a brand against my skin, I pull back. He looks surprised, eyes snapping open and pinging between my own. But neither of us has a chance to say a word before a tornado siren pierces the air.

Lucky curses, his eyes wide. "We have to go."

I nod, grabbing Lucky's arm and pointing to the east. I passed an old farmhouse only 300 feet from here with an underground hatch that likely leads down to cold storage. I have no clue how close the tornado touched down, but I'm not about to wait and find out, and driving fifteen minutes back home isn't a safe option.

Lucky doesn't question me. He gives me a swift nod and follows as I jog along the edge of the field toward the farmhouse.

"Your mom?" he yells over the rain that's now pelting our faces.

"Okay," I manage. Even if the Buchanans aren't there, my mom will be able to lower herself into the shelter on her own. The door is rigged to close from a push button at the bottom.

It doesn't take long to reach the old farmhouse. No one appears to be home—there are no cars in the driveway, no people emerging from the house—so I don't hesitate to head straight for the hatch and give it a tug. Thankfully, it opens with ease, showing steps that lead down under the house. I urge Lucky in first before glancing back at the skyline. I can't see any tornadoes, but the rain is coming down with force now, and the clouds above are dark and foreboding.

I shut the door before heading down the stone steps, my breaths ragged. Lucky sounds equally winded, his shirt sticking to his skin, his hair a mess around his head. There's a lantern-radio combo sitting on a shelf next to a whole collection of various canned goods, and after confirming cell service is nonexistent down here, I make my way over to it. The radio crackles to life as Lucky steps up beside me.

"Okay?" he asks quietly.

I nod, giving him a questioning look.

"Fine," he answers.

We're both quiet for a moment as I find news about the storm. We'll have to wait for the tornado warning to pass before we leave the shelter. They cautioned about the storm system on the news, of course, but it's never easy to tell when the tornadoes will come. They're unpredictable. Wild flights of nature. There's no stopping them, only running.

"I can't say I missed this part," Lucky says, leaning against the cobblestone wall and crossing his arms. The floor in here is packed dirt, and cobwebs hang in the corners of the room, but at least there's a working light.

"Thirteen years old," I point out.

Lucky rolls his eyes, but he's fighting a smile. "You're never going to let me live that down, are you?"

I shake my head.

"Well, don't worry," Lucky says, "I have no plans to take up tornado chasing."

Good to know, but it doesn't stop the tornadoes from chasing *us*.

Lucky lets out a little breath, his expression turning serious. He eyes me closely, and my pulse kicks back up. "We're going to talk about it."

There's no use asking *about what?*

Lucky pushes off from the wall, taking a step forward. "I kissed you."

I nod, breathing through my nose as he slowly closes the distance between us, stalking me, it would seem. I sure feel like prey.

"Ellis," he says, less than a foot away now. "You kissed me back."

No denying it. I incline my head again.

His eyes slip closed for a breath in time, and then they're opening, a slow-blossoming smile on his face as he reaches for me.

"Luck," I croak out, tensing as he removes my hat. His fingers rake through my hair, and I nearly groan. "Don't."

He goes stock-still at the one word, his gaze flashing to mine. "What?" he asks, like he's not sure he heard me right.

"Don't," I repeat, closing my eyes. *Please.* "I can't..."

His touch feathers away, and it feels like the worst thing. "Why?" he asks, clearly confused.

I keep my eyes shut because I'm afraid to see his face. Afraid to see if I'm disappointing him.

"You said there was only one person you wanted," he repeats.

I nod, my eyes welling.

"Me?" he asks, like he's suddenly unsure. Like he's suddenly doubting, when I know for a fact he figured it out. I don't know *how*, but he did. His lips crashing into mine made that abundantly clear.

But I don't know what this means for *him*. And if this is some flippant, passing thing or, hell, a *favor* to knock sex off my bucket list, I don't want it. I wouldn't be able to *bear* it. I can't start something with Lucky only to lose him. Not like that. It would destroy me.

I nod slowly in answer, my heart in my throat. *Yes, you.*

He makes a small, wounded sound. "Then why... Why can't we..."

I force my eyes open as the door rattles above us. The radio continues its stream of information— *"Tornado spotted off Summit Street, heading west toward Baker"*—but my attention is on Lucky.

"Can't if... I... Y-you..." I have to pause, my words getting all jumbled. But no matter how hard I try, I can't get them to come out right. "Meaningless. *Can't.*"

Lucky's face falls for the briefest of moments before he shudders out a breath. "El," he says, almost in relief. He steps in close again, hand hovering near me but not touching. "Do you really think anything between me and you could be meaningless?"

My swallow is heavy.

"Do you think," he goes on, foot bumping mine as his hand lands on my abdomen, "that I would fly halfway around the world and drive into town during a tornado watch just to kiss you if it meant *nothing?*"

My pulse is feathering so quickly I can feel it in my neck.

"Well?" he asks, leaning close. His eyes drop to my lips, and I can hardly control my breathing. "Do you?"

I shake my head slowly. When he puts it that way, no, I don't think he would do that. But I've spent years, since the moment we first kissed, really, assuming my longing was fruitless, and I'm having a hard time reconciling that this is real. That Lucky is in front of me, somehow telling me he wants me, too.

Since when?

"No," Lucky says, hand curling against my jaw. "No, I wouldn't do that. You're not *nothing*, El. You're the person I know most in this world. This"—he presses his lips softly to the corner of mine—"isn't meaningless."

I don't move. Can't, apart from the shaking of my body.

"You want me," he whispers, hand twisting in my shirt as his other cradles my face.

"Yes," I croak.

"*Only. Me.*"

A nod.

His exhale is near tortured. "Then kiss me, Ellis."

I'm scared. So goddamn scared.

This is Lucky. *Lucky.* I've kept my feelings for him carefully leashed for so very long, afraid of the potential fallout. It's ingrained in me to push those thoughts away. To deny those urges. How do I come to terms with the fact that I'm not alone in them? What if this ruins us? There are countless ways it could go wrong. What if I lose him? What if—

"Ellis," Lucky practically growls. The light flickers above us, the radio crackling. "I didn't see it before, but I do now. And I'm here. I'm here, okay? So kiss me. Kiss me, *please*, or I swear to God—"

As a tornado rages somewhere overhead, that leash around my heart snaps, and I give in to the thing I want above all else.

I lunge forward and kiss my best friend.

Chapter 20

LUCKY

If pressed to come up with a single word to describe the onslaught that hits me the moment Ellis's lips crash into mine, I would pick *landslide*.

Have you ever seen a mountain give way? Seen the rock face sheer off in the force of nature's demand, trees and dirt and tons of once-steady terrain rushing toward the ground, unable to fight the tide of gravity?

That would describe this moment. Sweeping. Earth-shattering. Destructive in the best possible way.

Unstoppable.

Ellis's teeth snag my bottom lip as he kisses me hungrily. My back hits the wall, and he follows me into it, his weight securing me in place. I nearly laugh, nearly shout with joy, but no sound escapes except a moan.

Ellis.

My Ellis is kissing me. And this isn't a seventeen-year-old's tentative first time. It's urgent and consuming and filled with intent. The type of intent that has my mind spinning because part of me wasn't convinced I got it right. Even though I knew—I *knew*—there was still a niggle of doubt telling me I was wrong.

But then I remembered the waterfall. The looks Ellis would give the guys I was with. The easy affection and nervous blushes. The way he was *broken* that day I got the job at the magazine, even though he tried so hard to hide it. How sad he was when I finally left town. How *happy* he always is to hear from me, same as I am with him. The parrotfish. The glass sailboat. *Fuck*, the picnics in the back of his truck. Nights under the stars. Our windmill.

I remembered our history in a series of snapshots, but I saw it under a different lens. And I *knew*.

And now, here with Ellis's lips pressed against mine, there's no question or doubt—he wants me. He has *feelings* for me that extend beyond the bounds of our friendship.

I feel like an idiot that it took me this long to see it. But I'm not about to waste any more time away from the one person who has always felt like my port. The person I return to, time and time again. The one I come home to.

Because he is. Ellis is home to me.

His hands tangle in my hair as he kisses me. Once, twice, longer. He doesn't stop. His mouth is persistent and hot and *familiar*, even though this is entirely new. He kisses me as if he's trying to memorize me by touch, his lips mapping my own. He kisses as if he wants to *consume*. He kisses with all the energy I saw that day he punched Brandon square in the nose.

He's unrestrained, finally, *blessedly*, and I match every ounce of what he's giving me because I don't have another choice. I'm undone. Completely unraveled. And I don't think I could ever be put back together the same way again. Not after this.

Ellis pulls away to take a breath. It's only an inch, only a second, but I can't let him go. I *can't*. So I chase, tugging against the back of his neck, trying to bring him closer. He meets me eagerly, and I scramble, pulling myself up, wrapping my legs around his waist so there's no chance of him getting away. His grip adjusts in an instant, hands dropping to my thighs as his body bumps me back into the wall. The span of his fingers and the sheer breadth of him—the unwavering strength—has my cock jerking against the inside of my jeans. I couldn't care less about the unforgiving surface at my back or the dirt and grime or the fact that I'm still soaking wet. All I care about, all I know, is *Ellis*.

His lips take me apart systematically, and with anyone else, I might be embarrassed about the sounds coming out of my mouth. The moans and—*fuck*—whimpers. But each one fuels Ellis, tightening his fingers against my thighs and spurring the hungry movements of his mouth, so I don't dare stop. I let him hear every way in which he affects me. I don't hold a single thing back.

I don't think I could even if I tried.

Ellis is quiet, apart from his panting breaths, but his body tells me everything I need to know. He's always preferred physical communication anyway, and I'm not about to ask him to change, not when his hands are holding me as if I'm precious cargo. Not when his lips are telling me I'm the very air he needs to breathe.

How could I have missed this? *How?*

When Ellis starts moving against me, shifting and *rutting*, my gasp is more than a little surprised.

"El," I breathe.

He grunts, lips trailing to my jaw. My chest heaves in and out as he kisses down to my neck. Lower. The sensitive skin at the crook of my shoulder.

Oh God.

"Ellis," I groan, head thunking back against the stones. I turn, baring myself to him, giving him more space.

He makes use of it, kissing up and down the column of my neck, tongue tasting, his stubble scraping my skin. My breaths are more than a little ragged, and my body feels electrified, as if the storm is right here inside this cellar, not raging outside these walls. I barely register the ongoing news from the radio— *"Storm system heading east toward Fourth"*—or the rattling of the door above from the harsh, circling winds. There's only Ellis's mouth blazing a path across my skin.

Yours. I'm yours.

When Ellis brings his lips back to mine, letting my body drop a couple inches so his cock is pressed up beside my own, my entire body flushes in a cascade of heat and bubbling anticipation. I'm not even sure if he's consciously aware of what he's doing or guided only by instinct, but his hips roll against me again and again, the pressure exquisite, and it's all I can do to hang on, desperate for anything—*everything*—he'll give me.

I should have known kissing Ellis would rearrange my world.

"Luck," he croaks, breaking from me at last. He drops his head beside mine, lips at my cheek as his breath stutters. His fingers dig against me almost painfully, and he gasps, hips stuttering.

Holy fuck. Is he... Is he about to come?

"Yeah, El," I encourage, pressing my heels against his ass to meet his movements. The feel of his cock rubbing against me through our clothes is enough to have me mindless. "That's right. Just like that. It's okay to let go, baby. Let go for me."

His mouth meets mine with bruising force, the muscles in his back bunching beneath my palms. My desire for him to come is overwhelming. It's a *need*, visceral and embedded down to my very bones. I want him to splinter apart in my arms. I want to give him what he needs, want to *be* what he needs, what he wants, what he craves with every fiber of his being because he's that for me. He's not just a crush. He never was.

He's the man no one else has ever measured up to.

When Ellis jerks against me, a guttural noise leaving his lips, I nearly come right along with him. He drives against me, chasing pressure against his dick, and my soul sings, a lightness inside that makes me nearly giddy.

No, this isn't meaningless. It never could be.

I bring my hands to Ellis's cheeks, kissing over his face as he shudders and comes down from his high. It's the first time he's come with another person, and I know that might be hitting him hard. But Ellis surprises me. He doesn't look shaken or remotely self-conscious. He leans back enough for his eyes to find mine, and he watches me intently.

"Luck," he says, the one word filled with so much meaning.

"Yeah," I answer, my small laugh sounding like a sigh. "Yeah, El."

He tucks his face against my neck, holding on to me tightly. For a moment, he shivers. An aftershock. But then he's calm. My mountain of a man, breathing me in, his lips pressed lightly to my skin.

I close my eyes, the sounds of whipping wind and heavy rain above us at odds with the utter peace I feel inside. I could stay here forever, tucked against Ellis's chest, him against mine. Just the two of us. Him and me.

But Ellis seems to have other plans. In an easy move, he steps back, me in his arms, and turns.

"What are you..."

My question peters out when Ellis lowers me to the dirt, his body draped over mine. My heart beats heavily as his palm snakes under my shirt, heated skin holding tight to my hip. He catches my eye.

"Luck."

It's a question, and I nod, breath hitching as Ellis brushes his lips against my own. My eyes slip shut as he kisses me slowly, a drugging press of his mouth against mine, each movement so much more careful and precise than before. His tongue swipes at my lips, a tease, and I realize what's happening. Ellis is *seducing* me. Savoring me.

I nearly laugh at the abrupt switch in our positions, but my amusement dies when Ellis drops his face to my neck and nips at my skin. My cock jumps, not having softened in the least since the moment Ellis first shoved me up against the wall.

"El," I moan, shifting against him restlessly.

I swear I can feel his smile.

He takes his time, fingers toying with my hip as his lips drag a slow path down my neck, to my collarbone, the hollow of my throat. They feather over my shirt, along my chest. My pulse is heavy in my ears as Ellis's mouth pauses, brushing achingly lightly over my nipple. The heat of his breath through the fabric is near torture, and I don't even feel bad when I grab Ellis's hair and tug. He chuckles hoarsely.

"Ellis," I warn.

He nuzzles against me and then nips. I curse, my hips hitching as lightning snaps along my spine. I'm so focused on Ellis's slow descent down my body that it takes me a moment to register what I'm hearing.

"El," I say, freezing.

He hums, his fingers inching up my shirt. His lips land on my stomach, near my belly button, and my core clenches tight.

The thundering recaptures my attention.

"Ellis, do you hear that?"

He pauses, his face poised directly over my crotch, eyes meeting mine. He's still for a moment, registering the same thing I am, and then his eyes flare wide. The door rattles dangerously on its hinges, a loud crash making me jolt, and then Ellis sets into motion. Before I can comprehend what he's doing, Ellis is up over my body, rolling the both of us toward the wall. My breath whooshes out of me as I topple over him, only to end up returned to my back, my shoulder pressed against stone. Ellis sinks over me, his arm around my head as the very ground begins to shake.

I think Ellis is saying something against my ear, but I can't hear it. It sounds like an airplane is landing on the house. Feels like it, too. Every muscle in my body is tensed, my teeth clenched together and rattling, as an earth-shaking groan bellows from above and dust rains down over us like sugar shaken from a sieve. There's an ungodly crash, a tearing like nails on chalkboard, and then the vibration of a thud as the broken remnants of a beam land less than five feet away.

Ellis shouts something as the overhead light flickers out, his grip on me tightening, but I don't need to hear him to understand exactly what's happening.

The tornado is directly overhead.

Chapter 21

ELLIS

It only lasts seconds, but it's the most terrifying few seconds of my life. Through the dim light from the lantern radio, I watch the dust float down as the house stops rattling, my head tucked against the side of Lucky's. That wooden beam landed right where we were lying.

Lucky's hands are wrapped around my arms, his body shaking below me in little bursts. I wait for the longest time as the tornado moves on, its deep roar like a departing train. My ears ring in the aftermath, popping when I swallow, but eventually, the noise quiets enough for me to hear Lucky's breathing. There's a boom of thunder, but it's distant.

"Holy shit," Lucky finally mutters.

I unwrap my arm from around his head slowly, leaning back so I'm no longer crushing him. "Okay?" I manage, surprised I have words at all right now.

Lucky looks up at me with an expression I'm not sure I've ever seen on his face. Genuine fear. He blinks several times, his mouth opening but no sound coming out.

"Gone," I assure him, brushing his dirt-ridden hair back from his face.

He nods slowly, swallowing, before snapping into action. His hands run over my back quickly, and his eyes flit across my face. "Are *you* okay?" he asks, palms moving to my cheeks and then my shoulders.

I nod.

"Did you get hurt?" he persists, voice frantic. "Did...did anything fall on you?"

His hands are on my back again, roaming. He won't find anything but dust and dirt.

"Fine," I say softly, knuckles grazing his cheek. I have the briefest pulse of *awe* rush through me at being able to touch him this way, but I push it aside. Not the time. Sitting up, I hold out my hand and pull Lucky with me.

"Fuck," he says, settling his back against the wall. He rubs his palms over his face, hands shaking.

"Need to check," I say, pointing out from our position, and Lucky nods. He eyes the ceiling, as do I. But considering there's not a thing I can do about the structural integrity of the house, I do my best to ignore that potential danger as I go to the toppled radio. The volume got lowered when it fell off the shelf, so I turn it back up, grateful for the light that lets me see the controls.

"Second tornado has touched down near Webster. All residents advised to seek cover immediately."

"Jesus," Lucky says, scrubbing his hands through his hair.

I head back his way with the radio, setting it in front of us as I take a seat next to Lucky, shoulder pressed to his. He grabs my arm, and I nudge a kiss against the side of his head, breathing him in as my heart rate returns to normal. I don't like sitting down here, knowing the danger that lurks above, but it would be even less safe for us to be out in the open right now. I just pray our ceiling will hold for as long as we need it to.

"Could've...been in Crete," I say, hoping to lighten the mood.

I should have expected Lucky's shove. "Stop that," he says, voice hard. "There's nowhere I'd rather be right now, Ellis. Thinking of you here alone..."

He doesn't finish his thought, but he looks haunted. Even more so in the dark shadows playing across the room.

"Wish you were safe," I tell him.

"I am," he says. "I'm always safe with you."

My pulse kicks up at that, and I don't know what to say.

"Parents," I realize aloud, pulling my phone from my pocket as Lucky does the same. The tornadoes are nowhere near them, but still.

"Do you have any service?" he asks.

I shake my head.

"Me neither, but if we send a text, it should go through if we get a bar."

I nod, and we both type out messages. I imagine my mom is worried sick, not knowing if I'm safe.

Lucky drops his phone beside him when he's done. His foot taps the ground, and his fingers drift through his tangled hair. I grab his hand, holding it between my own, and he offers me a wan smile.

"What a fucking day," he says.

I bring his palm up to my lips, kissing it gently, and his expression softens.

"Silver linings and all, huh?" he says, gaze on my mouth before it lifts slowly to mine. "Ellis."

My throat feels hoarse. "Luck."

"How long?" he asks quietly.

I swallow, looking down at his hand tucked between my own. In the end, I shrug because I'm not entirely sure when the turning point was or if I was always on a slow path toward falling in love with Lucky. Not that he's asking about love, exactly. But it was always love when it came to him. That I know for certain.

His lips twitch a little, and he resituates against the wall, letting his knee bump into my leg. "We're going to date," he says simply. Bluntly. "We're not skipping that part."

I nod, pulse jumping.

"And we're going to do *that* a lot," he adds, nodding down toward my crotch, where the sticky evidence of my orgasm is hidden away. I can feel my cheeks heat, but Lucky's smile has my chest warming, too. "No more holding back, okay, El? Not for either of us."

I nod in a sharp jerk.

"We've been such idiots," he says, head leaned against the stone wall. His eyes sweep over my face, but there's a softness on his. A gentle sort of happiness, despite his words. His voice, when he speaks again, is a whisper. "I've wanted you for such a long time."

My breath quickens. I'm still having a hard time believing that. That this brilliant man in front of me wants me as—what? A boyfriend? A partner? As more? It's almost too much, and I think it's going to take me some time to catch up. To truly wrap my head around it.

But one thing I know for sure. "You have me."

He inhales a deep, slow breath, squeezing my hand. But then he stills. "Hear that?"

"—*diminishing as the storm front moves east. Threat level has been returned to a watch, but residents are recommended to stay indoors until the system has passed. First responders have been dispatched. If you need immediate medical attention, please dial 911.*"

The broadcast continues, but that's all I need to hear. The tornadoes are gone, which means Lucky and I should get out of here before the house comes tumbling down.

I notch my head toward the door, and Lucky nods, grabbing his phone before standing with me. I pick up the radio, and, carefully, we move across the cellar, making a wide arc around the area where the beam broke. There's a large crack in the ceiling that I don't want to step foot under.

The air feels muggy as we ascend the stairs, but it sounds like the rain has stopped. Ready to get out of here, I give the hatch a shove.

It doesn't budge.

"What's going on?" Lucky asks from a step behind me.

I set down the radio and try again, using both hands to push at the door. It doesn't move in the least, and when I knock on the wood with my fist, the sound is muffled. I close my eyes briefly, refusing to panic. Taking a breath, I turn back to Lucky, whose eyes are wide.

"Blocked," I tell him.

He inhales sharply, immediately reaching for his phone. His face pales when he looks at the screen. "Shit. Ellis, we're in a dead zone. There's no signal, not even for emergency calls." Even as he says it, he dials 911, but the call doesn't connect.

Lucky's hand returns to his hair, fingers dragging through the strands. He starts to pant in short bursts, and I reach for him, cupping the side of his neck. "Okay," I assure him, pointing to the radio. "Responders."

"Right," Lucky says, nodding and clenching his phone tight. "Yeah, you're right. Police and ambulances are out. They'll find us."

He doesn't sound so sure, though, and he curses again before sinking down to the stone steps. I follow, sitting beside him and tucking him against my body, doing what I can to soothe his worry. Despite the circumstances, he feels perfect in my arms.

"This is so fucked," he says, shaking his head before setting it against my shoulder.

I turn to press my lips to his hair, not disagreeing.

"We're stuck in some basement—no, not even a basement," Lucky says, voice muffled against my neck. "A cellar. We're stuck in a goddamn cellar because a tornado razed the house above us. Because that's what happened, right? I mean, we both heard it. The house..." He jolts. "*Shit*, are...are we *buried* down here? Is that why the door's stuck? How are they going to find us, El? No one even knows we're here. We could be stuck down here for days, or—"

I shush Lucky's ramblings, tugging his face around. He grabs my wrists, and I bring my lips to his. He goes quiet, and after a moment, the tension leaves his body. It's not so much a kiss as a reassurance, but it snakes inside me like a wild, living thing regardless, taking up camp. A vein of lightning, leaving behind a permanent, welcome scar.

When I pull back, Lucky looks calmer. His eyes are dark in the dim light, but they're no less familiar to me. I've seen those eyes in every color, every shade. I've seen them happy, sad, overjoyed, and, like now, worried.

I brush my thumb over his cheekbone. "Okay," I say again. We will be; I know it. My mom and Gabby both know I'm somewhere out here.

Lucky nods, and letting go, I pull out my phone. He understands my intent when I brandish it.

"Yeah, we should keep trying," Lucky says, making another fruitless attempt to call 911. "Still nothing. You?"

I shake my head.

"Do you think the tornado took out the cell tower?" he asks.

I shrug. It's entirely possible, but this area got poor service to begin with, and we're underground. It might be enough to block the signal. Either way, I compile another handful of messages with our location and the fact that we're uninjured but trapped. None of my texts have gone through, and a quick glance at Lucky's phone shows the same.

Lucky sighs. "I didn't plan on pissing in jars today."

I can't help but snort, and Lucky gives me a small smile. He grabs my hand, toying with my fingers, and the feel of his smooth skin tracing along the digits is so distracting I almost miss his question.

"Do you think it's safe here or should we head back down?"

I consider that, not entirely sure. If the house is toppled above the hatch, the foundation could very well be more compromised over the stairs. But it's impossible to know for certain from down here. The entire upper portion of the house could be crumpled, for all we know. It might not be safe anywhere.

Getting up, I give Lucky's hand a squeeze before heading down the steps. Walking around the perimeter with the light from the radio, I take a closer look at the ceiling. The crack that leads to the broken beam runs along one end of the room. There's a portion of the ceiling that looks bowed, and

I stay far away. But the other side looks fairly unmarred and possibly sturdy. There's not much in the space we could use as protection. A large rack with canned goods. An old washing machine.

Coming up with an idea, I wave Lucky down.

"I'm going to leave my phone here," he says, setting it on the top step. "Just in case it gets service. We can keep yours with us."

Good idea.

Lucky joins me back on the dirt floor, his hand running a trail along my back. "Got a plan, big guy?"

I nod, and the two of us set to work creating a temporary shelter beneath the tornado-ravaged house. After that, all we can do is wait.

Chapter 22

LUCKY

"Peaches or beans?" Ellis asks, holding out two mason jars. We're hunkered down under the storage shelf we're using as a barrier. After removing all the jars, we dragged it over to the corner of the room deemed most stable. Using the washing machine as a prop on one end, we wedged the shelf against the wall and laid it at a forty-five degree angle, giving us a small space to hide beneath. If the ceiling *does* fall, hopefully, the shelf will protect us from large debris.

I'm trying not to focus too heavily on the *hopefully* part of the plan.

"Peaches," I answer, accepting the opened jar. At least the homeowners had some canned goods down here. I'd feel bad about eating their food, except I think they're going to have bigger fish to fry than a few missing jars of produce.

Ellis snaps a bean off in his mouth before leaning his head back against the washing machine. The poor guy is stretched down so low, his back is bent like a C, and his knees are spread wide so that he fits beneath the shelf. It's easier for me, but I do admit my eyes have strayed more than once to that wide open space between Ellis's legs.

The radio is still on, but at this point, it's cycling information we already know. Without a way to contact the outside world, we don't have any option but to wait for someone to come find us. It's been three hours so far and nothing.

I eat a few peaches before setting the jar aside. I don't have much of an appetite.

"El?"

He grunts.

"How are you feeling about all this?" I ask gently.

He turns his head to look at me, brows furrowed a little.

"Us," I clarify. We've been rightfully preoccupied by the aftereffects of the tornado, but it's a question that hasn't left my mind.

He doesn't answer for the longest time, but his hand comes up to toy with a piece of my hair. It's such a simple gesture, but it's something I'm not sure he would have allowed himself to do so casually before.

"Scared," he finally says.

My breath catches. "Why?"

"Can't lose you, Luck," he answers, voice a whisper.

"You won't," I breathe.

"When..." he starts, pausing a moment. "Do you go?"

My heart sinks, but I don't have time to answer him before there's a shout from above. I jerk, as does Ellis.

"Down here!" I yell.

It's hard to make out whatever they're saying, but I think I hear something about staying back from the door. I grab Ellis's hand, my heart pounding. We're going to be okay.

Ellis and I are still and quiet as we listen to whoever is above ground trying to clear a path. It's impossible to tell how many people there are or even what they're doing. But there's a bunch of muffled sounds—scraping, thunks, what might be a saw—and every once in a while, more dust rains down into the cellar. I grip Ellis's hand a little tighter each time that happens.

Eventually, after a half hour or so, the noises become more distinct. And then there's a voice.

"Hello?"

"Yeah," I call back, my relief nearly bowling me over. "We're down here."

"Who am I speaking to?" the person asks.

Ellis gives me a nudge and nods toward the hatch door. "Riley."

"That's Riley Evans?" I ask him.

He nods.

"Riley, it's Lucky Buchanan," I yell. "I'm with Ellis Cole."

He's quiet for a beat. "Lucky, I didn't... We've been looking for Ellis, but I didn't realize you were here. Hang tight, okay? We're nearly through the rubble. We'll have the door open shortly."

"Thank you," I manage to get out, my throat tight.

The sounds from above continue, and Ellis gives my hand a squeeze.

"My parents are going to kill me," I mutter.

Ellis huffs what sounds like disagreement, but they didn't even know I was here. No one did, apart from Danil. And, well, Ellis. I can't imagine my mom and dad are going to be thrilled to find out I ended up in the path of a tornado. At least they weren't worried about me this whole time. One positive, I suppose.

I allow myself a moment to take in the fact that we'll be out of here shortly. Ellis has his eyes closed beside me, and I wonder if he's doing the same.

"You're really good at this, you know," I tell him.

He opens his eyes, a question there.

"Staying calm in a crisis," I explain.

Not that I'm surprised. Ellis has always had that sort of steady presence about him. That unwavering dependability. I can count on one hand the number of times he's lost his cool.

"Thank you for keeping me calm, too," I add.

He sets his head against the washing machine, eyes raking over my face. His gaze feels focused yet distant all at once, and not for the first time, I get the feeling he's aware of something I'm not.

"What do you see?" I ask quietly. I'm not even sure if he's going to answer me, but he's been surprisingly open since we kissed.

"Gold," he says, reaching up and twining a piece of my hair around his finger. His touch is gentle, voice soft. "Sands and...sun. Light. Camels."

The last is said with a smirk, and I huff a somewhat disbelieving laugh. "Is that all?"

"Here," he says, touching the corner of my eye, his focus absolute. "Ocean. Sky and sea. Smith Falls. Great...Blue Hole."

I snort, and his lips curl into a smile, but his gaze never wavers. His thumb travels down, brushing over my top lip. My breath hitches.

"Sails," he says, tracing the two arches of my lip. "Birds in flight. Palaces and...windmills."

My pulse skitters as Ellis's eyes travel back to my own.

"All the life in you," he says simply. "That's what I see."

"El..."

I jolt as a thunk comes from above. A second later, there's a large creak, and light floods into the cellar.

"Lucky?" Riley calls. "Ellis?"

"Shit," I say, an overwhelming rush of relief, happiness, and lingering fear rushing through me. My eyes prickle as I scoot out from under the shelf. Ellis follows, and once he unfolds his large body and I help him to his feet, I step forward and look up the length of the steps. Riley Evans is standing at the top, his body silhouetted in light.

"Are you guys all right?" he calls down. "Are you hurt?"

"No," I rasp, holding Ellis's hand tight as I rush for the stairs. "We're okay."

"Thank goodness for that," Riley says, stepping back as we reach the surface. I have to cover my eyes for a moment as the sun assaults me, so much brighter than it was when we first went down into the cellar. When I turn around, I stop dead.

Half of the farmhouse is missing. Well, maybe missing isn't the right word. I can see great heaps of it piled on what was once the first level of the home but now looks more like a post-demolition site. And the rest of it is scattered up to hundreds of feet away, pieces of wood and plaster and even broken furniture strewn over the ground amidst flattened corn and unidentifiable, smaller debris.

But the house—the part that remains—stands like a torn, jagged skeleton, insides opened to the air. The tornado swept the rest of it away as if it were nothing. Inconsequential. And Ellis and I were less than twenty feet below.

"God," I rasp.

Ellis's palm lands on my back, running soothing circles over my shirt. Distantly, I register a few men moving about, more than just Riley, and one comes over to us, asking how we're doing. He has bottles of water he hands us, and I take a few drinks, but I can't look away from the destruction spread in front of us. Despite the almost macabre horror of the situation, the sun is out, scattering light on the dew-damp ground, making the entire scene glitter. It looks so disparate—death and light—and I can't help but wish I had my camera, if for no other reason than to remember this day for what it was. For what I could have lost.

A tap on my arm has me looking over. Ellis is holding out my phone, camera app open, as if he read my mind.

"Thank you," I say quietly before squatting down and snapping a few pics.

"Are you sure you guys are all right?" I hear Riley ask. Ellis doesn't respond, but I assume he nodded because Riley says, "Okay. But if either of you are suddenly clammy, have trouble breathing, feel heart palpitations, or are vomiting, you could be in shock. Don't hesitate to call 911."

"We will," Ellis says.

I look over in time to see Riley clapping Ellis on the shoulder. "I'm glad you're both okay, Ellis. Maybe take a few days off, yeah? I'm sure Marcus would understand."

Ellis grunts his assent, and Riley nods my way before walking off. I'm not all that surprised when my phone starts to ring now that we're above ground, but I am surprised by the caller.

"Dani," I say, standing back up.

"Took you long enough," he says. "Before you ask, I already talked to Chelsea. She wasn't happy, but she agreed to extend our trip out half a week, and I was able to push back our visit to Samaria Gorge until Friday. So, if you can get back before then, we'll still be able to complete our assignment."

"Yeah," I breathe. "I can do that."

"Now why the hell weren't you taking my calls?" Danil asks, sounding put out. "If the answer is anything but ravaging the love of your life, I won't accept it."

I huff a small laugh. "I was in a tornado."

Silence greets my ears.

"Well, under it," I amend.

"Lucky," Danil says, tone hard. "*What?*"

I brush my hair back, pacing a little ways away from the house. The nearby field is in shambles, stalks bent and broken. Some pulled from the ground.

"There was a tornado," I say, glancing back at Ellis. My heart trips. If anything had happened to him... "Ellis and I got underground, but we were right in its path. We're okay. Safe."

"Holy fuck. I..." Danil growls. "Damn it, now I feel like a dick."

I can't help but laugh. "And this is an unusual occurrence?"

"Oh, fuck off, Lucky-boy," he shoots back. "I'm glad you're safe, but I still want to kick your ass. You can't scare me like that."

"You realize we do dangerous things all the time?"

"It's different," he says. "Those are calculated risks. Getting caught in a tornado..."

He doesn't need to finish his sentence because I know. It was terrifying.

"Yeah, well, all good," I assure him, puffing out a breath. I'm sure I'll spend some time processing it, but I'm uninjured, as is Ellis, and that's all that matters.

"And Ellis?" Danil asks, mind going to the same place as mine. "He's there with you?"

"He is."

"Does that mean you two talked?" he asks.

"We did."

A pause. "Are you going to make me beg for it?"

I refrain from making a joke. "We're...good," I say, gaze still trained on Ellis. He's nodding at one of the men who found us as the crew packs up, presumably to go help others in town. "We kissed." *And such.*

Danil hums. It's a happy sound. "And now?"

A slow smile spreads over my face as I remember the press of Ellis's lips against mine. "And now... We start something new."

Chapter 23

ELLIS

"Do you boys need a ride?" one of our rescuers asks, an older man I don't know.

I shake my head, pointing to the familiar van I see approaching down the dirt road. It pulls onto the grass in front of the destroyed farmhouse, coming to an abrupt stop.

"All right, then," he says, giving my shoulder a pat. "You two take care. You got lucky today."

As if I don't know that. I give him a nod as Lucky's dad bursts from the driver's side door of the van. Lucky is putting his phone in his pocket when he notices his dad running his way. His face crumples, just a little, and then he's being pulled into a tight embrace. Mr. Buchanan hugs his son with all his might, lips moving incessantly, and Lucky's back heaves.

Throat tight, I make my way toward the van. Mrs. Buchanan is helping my mom from the back, and I move that way quickly, offering my hand.

"Ellis," my mom says, voice shaking. As soon as her feet are on the ground, she wraps her arms around me. I have to support her weight with the way her legs are wobbling, but I don't mind.

Lucky's mom gives me a soft, watery-eyed smile before rounding the vehicle toward her son.

"I was so worried about you, baby," my mom says, pulling back some. Her hand lands on my cheek, trembling, and her eyes check me over. I probably look like a mess. Her eyes shift to the house next, and she swallows harshly. "Good God."

"Okay," I assure her, nodding back at the van. "Home?"

My mom nods, and I look over the front of the vehicle, seeing Lucky approach with his parents. With one last glance at the toppled remains of the farmhouse that saved our lives, I guide my mom into the back of the van and follow. Lucky squeezes in beside me, his parents sit up front, and without a word, Mr. Buchanan pulls out onto the road.

We stop at Lucky's rental first, and he retrieves his bag from the back. Thankfully, the car wasn't damaged beyond a few minor scratches, but Lucky agrees to come back for it tomorrow. The absence of noise is heavy inside the vehicle as we drive home, but no one breaks the silence. Lucky grabs my hand, though, squeezing gently and giving me a soft smile. If my mom notices, she doesn't say a word.

By unspoken agreement, we all file into the Buchanans' house when we arrive back. I help my mom, settling her on the couch as Mrs. Buchanan makes tea. Lucky's dad gives Lucky another hug before begrudgingly letting him go, and much to my surprise, he asks if he can hug me, too. I agree, and his arms around me are more comforting than I expect. Once we're settled with steaming beverages in front of us, Lucky recounts the tale from beside me. More than once, a set of eyes travel to the hands we have clasped together, but none of our parents ask, and Lucky doesn't mention it. Mrs. Buchanan is crying by the end.

"We didn't even know you were here," she says through her tears. "We were already so worried about Ellis, but then we got your texts hours after the storm passed, and—"

She covers her eyes, and Lucky scoots off the couch to console her.

"I'm sorry," he says gently, his arm around her shoulders.

She shakes her head. "No, it's not your fault. I'm just... I'm not prepared to lose you. Either of you," she adds, looking my way.

Mr. Buchanan rubs her arm. "We're just so glad you're both okay."

"We are. Promise," Lucky says. His eyes meet mine before returning to his parents. "Ellis and I should get cleaned up, though."

"Of course," his mom says. "The shower's all yours."

"Thanks, but I'd rather use the one next door," Lucky says, standing up and grabbing his bag. "I need a minute alone with Ellis."

No one says anything to that, even as a few looks are exchanged, and I get off the couch, following Lucky to the door. It clicks shut behind me.

The grass is damp underfoot as we walk over to my house. If you didn't know a couple tornadoes touched down nearby, it'd be easy to assume it was just another rainy fall day. It never ceases to amaze me how the storms can leave such destruction and yet never look back.

When I let us into the house, Lucky heads right toward the bathroom. I follow, stopping at the door as Lucky starts shucking his dirty clothes.

"Get naked, Ellis," he says, glancing over his shoulder at me.

My inhale is sharp, but I do as he says, peeling off my clothing one piece at a time. It's not without difficulty, considering the grimy state of them, but Lucky doesn't seem to mind. He watches me as if he has all the time in the world, his eyes tracing over every inch of me slowly. Mine do the same to him as the water heats beside us.

I've seen Lucky dressed down on more than one occasion, but I've never seen him entirely nude. His body is lean, stomach flat with the faint outline of muscle. A few freckles dot his fair skin, but they're not in abundance, and pale blonde hair leads from his navel to his cock. He's gorgeous, every inch of him. I could stare for hours, days, a lifetime, and never get bored.

I never thought I'd have the chance to.

Lucky moves into the shower. "El."

His voice spurs me into action, and I follow, unable to do anything but. The water is hot as it beats at my feet, and steam has already started coalescing in the air. Through it is Lucky, his front toward me. He tips his head back under the showerhead, which quickly drenches and darkens his hair. His eyes are closed, mouth parted, and rivulets of water make their way down his chest, like streams mapping a new destination. I lift my hands to them, following the paths down his skin, and Lucky lowers his head to look at me.

I've dreamed about Lucky throughout the years, whenever I was too weak to stop myself. I wondered what he would look like bared before me. Wondered how smooth his skin would be if I had the chance to explore it. I even wondered at the shape and slope of his cock, imagining what I would do if it was in front of me, as it is now.

But more than that, I wondered what circumstances would bring us together. I puzzled it out—how I might capture him—before eliminating the selfish thought from my head. Lucky wasn't mine to covet, mine to have. And yet here he is. Somehow, mine, by his own choosing. Mine to hold and treasure and cherish. Mine to love freely.

I don't know how this is going to work with the distance between us, and part of me is terrified I'm going to lose him, one way or another. But I never thought I'd get this, and I can't give it back. I can't give it up willingly; I just can't. I won't.

Lucky's irises are the lightest blue as he watches me, like arctic snow. For a moment, I'm reminded of a fox, with cream-colored fur and sharp, cat-like eyes. He's always been wild, my firefly, no matter where he is. And I can see it now in those pale eyes, that spark of something adventurous and free.

He doesn't protest in the least as I step forward and bring my lips to his. They part on a sigh, warm and yielding against my own as the air between us heats, heavy with something more than steam. His eyes slip shut, and my hands drift over smooth, wet skin as I tug his body to mine. My cock fills, but it's an afterthought, not my focus. I'm too caught up in the shape of Lucky's lips—in the feel of them, the top and bottom different. I'm too mesmerized by the soft sighs emanating from Lucky's throat and the way his head tips further back as we fit together, my hands in his hair now and his on my ass.

Maybe I should feel...overwhelmed. Or even nervous. Maybe I should worry what Lucky thinks of me or wonder whether or not I'm doing this right. But none of it matters. It's always been him and me, from the very beginning, it seems. Lucky was right about that. Him coming into my life was a starting point. It was defining, and all that's come after has revolved around him. How couldn't it?

I may still have questions. Concerns, even, skimming the edges of my mind. But when it comes to *this*? There's no room for bashfulness. No hiding from the person who owns me, body and soul. I'm his for the taking, always have been.

And now, he *wants*.

Lucky's tongue greets mine as his fingers tighten against my ass. He draws me closer, grinding against my hip in a way that has my electrical impulses firing. His cock is hard, and I'm acutely aware of the fact that I never got to make him come.

Spinning us both, I ease Lucky against the wall. He blinks his eyes open, watching as I draw back enough to take him in. His chest is flushed, whether from the heat or his arousal, I'm not sure. Maybe both. His cock is tinged a pinkish-red, nearly matching the hue on his chest. I trace from one to the other, mapping the blood flow. Heart to cock. Love to lust.

Lucky inhales when I wrap my hand around him, pumping his shaft. He's warm in my grip, the motion familiar but the feel entirely new, and my own dick throbs in sympathetic pleasure. It's not lost on me that I'm finally touching the only person who's ever played a starring role in my fantasies.

My dreams have nothing on reality.

"God, El," Lucky breathes, finally breaking the silence. His hips hitch into my grip, and he licks his lips, eyes on my face, even as my own have a hard time stopping in any one place. "Would you"—a groan as I swirl my thumb over his crown—"come here? I need... God, I need to know you're real. That this is real."

I don't need him to explain because I understand exactly how he's feeling. I let Lucky tug me forward, bringing our bodies together in a hot press, even as he bats away my hand.

He hikes his leg over my hip and urges my mouth toward his, and the moment we lock together, Lucky wraps his hand around our cocks. I stutter a moan into his mouth, my hips punching of their own accord.

"Yes, Ellis," Lucky says, his voice all breath, lips moving against my own. "Just like that. Don't—*ah God*. Don't stop."

The angle isn't the best considering our height difference, but Lucky's leg wrapped around my hip helps bridge the gap, allowing me to grind against his cock in the tight confines of his fist. When Lucky is sure I'm not going anywhere, he wraps a second hand around our lengths, creating pressure on both sides. I can barely focus on our half-formed kisses as sparks dance along every inch of my skin. My hands scramble for purchase, palms slipping on wet flesh as Lucky encourages me on.

"*Fuck*. Yes, that's perfect, baby. Feel good?"

I nod, breath caught in my throat. I like the way he calls me *baby*. I've heard the endearment before, but on Lucky's lips, it's heated. *Possessive*. It's a claim, a gift I never thought I'd get.

"Want you so much," he says hoarsely, the words like a confession. "God, El, I *need* you. I always need you."

I grunt, chasing Lucky's lips, desperate for proof that he means it, that he's here, that he's with me. His mouth tangles with mine in an instant, hands holding steady as I fuck his fists. Fuck against his cock. The ridge of his cockhead brushes mine as I move, and my entire body feels sensitized, nerve endings crackling and sparking like electricity.

When my balls draw up and I know I can't hold back another moment, I twine my fingers through Lucky's hair and hold him to me, letting him absorb my moan as I jerk and spill between our bodies. He rubs me through it, attention focused along my dick as my orgasm crests for an extended moment—floating,

floating through space—until finally, I crash down on the other side, my mouth still fused with Lucky's, my body pressing his against the wall.

I ease back just a touch as I come to, and Lucky's eyes are blazing.

"Ellis," he groans, hand jacking himself quickly now.

I take over, wrapping him in my fist, pumping as he clutches my arms tight.

"You're beautiful," he whispers among his panting breaths.

I brush his hair out of his eyes as I jerk him, unable to make my voice cooperate enough to tell him *he's* the beautiful one. Always has been. But then Lucky's eyes are rolling up and he's swelling in my hand. My gaze snaps downward in time to catch his cum striping across his stomach and my fist. I can hardly look away, even as I catalogue each and every gasp and stuttered moan that leaves his lips. I bring my eyes to his when I hear my name.

"El."

Lucky's gaze is hooded, and he gently brushes my hand away before pushing off from the wall. In an instant, his arms are wrapped around me, head tucked under my chin, and I can do nothing but hug him back.

He hasn't washed his hair yet, and it still smells like citrus. And the feel of him nestled against me is the best sort of normal. It's *us, El. Me and you. For always.* But it's also something more. Something that has yet to settle into the dirt. A seed, so full of possibilities it's blinding, yet fragile and new, not yet sowed into the earth. It could still fly away, that seed, taken by the wind before it has a chance to grow.

I want to believe that won't be us. That after all we've been through to get to this point, nothing will take Lucky from me.

But how do I keep him? How do I hold onto a creature that's meant to fly?

"Ellis," Lucky says quietly, pulling back from my chest. The steam from the shower has stopped, which likely means we're running out of hot water, but Lucky doesn't seem remotely concerned about that. His focus is on me. "I know today has been a lot, but we're going to figure this out, okay? After we visit with our folks, I'm going to bed with you. Whether that's here or at my parents', I don't care. But I'm not leaving you tonight."

He raises a brow as if in question, and I nod quickly.

Satisfied, he goes on. "And tomorrow, we'll talk. I won't stay gone so long again. I can't..." He swallows a little roughly. "There's no going back for us, El. Not after this."

No, there's not.

"Okay," he says, almost like he's talking to himself. "Okay. Come on then."

Lucky hands me the bar of soap, and we make quick work of cleaning up in the cooling water. We do spend most of the evening with our parents, all of us reassuring ourselves that we're safe and healthy and whole. And when the night is over, Lucky follows me home and climbs into my bed as if he's done it a million times before.

He cries for a short while as the day catches up to him. But I hold him through it, thankful for the privilege, and eventually, his tears dry. It's some time later when he speaks, his voice so quiet and sleepy I almost miss it.

"This is real, El. Me and you, it's real."

I grip him tighter, my heart pounding so hard I'm sure he can hear it. He places his hand over my chest as if in acknowledgement, and his breaths puff lazily across my skin. With the moon lending its soft glow through the window, Lucky falls asleep.

And I learn what it is to cradle a firefly in my palms.

Chapter 24

LUCKY

When I wake, Ellis isn't in bed. My body is stiff after the events of yesterday, so I take a minute to roll around and stretch. The light coming in the window tells me it's likely late morning, so I'm not all that surprised Ellis is gone. Nor am I offended. In fact, I have a feeling I know exactly where he's at as he processes everything that's happened between us these last twenty-four hours.

A smile slips onto my face, and with it comes a familiar swell of butterflies in my stomach. I feel sixteen again, a little love-drunk as thoughts of Ellis fill my mind. Except now, my daydreams are rooted in reality, and Ellis is no longer a boy but a man. A man who had his hand wrapped around my cock just last night. A man who was looking at me as if I was the key to something greater.

I don't know how I didn't see it before. The only explanation I have is that Ellis didn't want me to know. He kept his feelings locked down tight, and I can't even blame him for it. I did the same, assuming they'd never be returned. Ellis isn't like anybody else; I've always known that. He's important to me. Too important to lose.

And maybe that's part of why I never said anything myself. I couldn't stand the idea of losing my friend.

The smell of coffee is the first thing to hit my nose when I step out of the bedroom. I swing by the bathroom first, taking care of morning necessities. Same as last night, I notice the grab bar along one side of the shower. It wasn't there a few years ago. There's a portable shower seat, too, tucked beside the toilet. My chest tugs at seeing the evidence of Mrs. Cole's progressing symptoms.

I find the coffee exactly where I expect to: in the kitchen. It tastes somewhat burnt, having been warming for however long in the pot, but I doctor it with a splash of creamer and drink it all the same. I'm antsy to get to Ellis, but first, I check my phone, knowing Danil will have sent over an updated itinerary for the remainder of our visit to Crete. My sigh is more than a little heavy as I see my new flight plan. I leave tomorrow before dawn.

Once I've drained my coffee, I clean the mug and set it on the drying rack before heading for the back door.

"Morning, Lucky."

I nearly jump at Mrs. Cole's greeting. She's sitting in the living room, a cream-colored blanket on her lap. There's an iced tea on the table beside her and a tablet in her hands, opened to a crossword puzzle. I'm not sure how I missed her when I passed through.

"Morning," I return, stepping her way.

She gives me a smile. "Ellis says you two are dating now."

I almost bark a laugh. Leave it to Ellis to jump forward without worrying about what people would think. He never really has.

The thought makes me smile.

"Yeah," I tell her. "I guess we are."

She hums, nodding as she types out an answer on her puzzle.

"You don't seem surprised," I note.

"No," she says simply. "When do you leave?"

My stomach sinks. "Tomorrow. I, uh... I know it's not ideal. My job, I mean. I travel a lot, and I live in New York, but we'll figure it out. I—"

"Lucky, hon," Mrs. Cole says, cutting me off gently. She sets her tablet aside, hand shaking slightly. Her eyes, unlike Ellis's, are hazel, and they appraise me kindly. "I'm not worried about that. You two have been circling each other for years. I can't imagine you'll let something like distance stop you now that you've finally caught one another."

I don't know what to say to that. Were we really that obvious except to each other?

"Come here," she says, opening her arms. "Give me a hug, and then go spend the day with my son like I know you want to."

I accept her invitation, bending down as Mrs. Cole wraps her arms around me from her chair. My chest feels tight—a mixture of acceptance, love, relief, and worry. When we part, she tweaks my cheek the way she did when I was a child. I can't help but chuckle.

"Thanks, Mrs. Cole," I tell her, hoping she understands.

She gives me a nod. "You'll always be family, Lucky. Don't forget that."

With a lump in my throat, I leave Mrs. Cole to her crossword and head outside, closing the slider door behind me. Instinctually, I check the skyline, but the storms have passed, leaving only blue sky. Even so, a shiver runs down my spine that has nothing to do with the cooling autumn temperatures.

Taking the stairs, I make my way toward the silo. It sits like a towering beacon around the edge of the field, the structure old and weathered but still standing strong. I used to think it looked haunted, but now, the silo is a place of warmth and comfort. I have no doubt that's Ellis's doing.

The door is open when I get there, the interior dim. It only takes a moment for my eyes to adjust, and once they do, I seek out Ellis. I stumble a little when I spot him, and then I come to a stop.

Ellis is in front of the brick oven, his back to me. He's wearing jeans and a long-sleeved shirt. His back is soaked in sweat—a sight that has no right to be as sexy as it is—and a heavy-duty apron is tied around his front. He's not wearing gloves, and I wonder if it's because they'd be a hindrance for such precise work, but the heat from the oven looks immense. An orange glow emanates from within the small window in the brick, and now that I'm looking, I realize there's a ventilation shaft running to the wall, directing excess heat and smoke out of the silo.

I can't believe he did all this.

Instead of alerting Ellis that I'm here, I watch. There's a metal table beside the oven, much smaller than the big wooden workbench in the middle of the room. Ellis turns to it, rolling what appears to be hot, melted glass over its surface. The malleable substance is orange, like the fire, and stuck to the end of a long, metal rod. Ellis lifts it off the table before blowing into the rod, and the glass inflates. He rolls it on top of another instrument I'm unfamiliar with that looks like a metal frame atop a bench, and then he returns it to the heat.

I watch for what feels like an hour, but I'm sure it's far less than that. I can't seem to look away from the steady repetition of the process. I have no clue what Ellis is doing, but he appears to know the steps by heart. He uses tools, too—pliers, smaller rods, and other things I don't know the name of. Before long, he taps the object off the end of the metal rod. I flinch, sure it's going to break, but it doesn't. It sits unharmed, beautifully colored now that the glass has cooled. It's a decorative orb, perfectly round with swirling shades of purple and gold.

When Ellis starts taking off his apron, he notices me. He goes still for just a moment, eyes connecting with mine, and then he sets the apron on a hook. He wipes his forehead before pushing his sleeves up to his elbows.

"Hi," I breathe.

Ellis walks up to me, pinching my chin and moving my head back and forth. I have no clue what he's looking for, but he brushes my hair aside before drifting his thumb across my bottom lip.

"What is it?" I ask.

The softness in his gaze floors me, as does his answer. "Looking."

"You've seen me a million times," I point out, heart pounding.

His expression manages to convey how much of an idiot I am, while also weakening my knees. "Never enough."

Fucking hell.

"I'm going to kiss you now," I inform him.

"Sweaty."

"Don't care."

Ellis grunts when my lips meet his, but he immediately lowers his head enough for me to fall back on my heels. He's hot beneath my touch, a furnace himself, and I hold on like a man starved. No matter how futile it seemed, there was always a piece of me that desperately hoped we'd end up here. I couldn't let it go, couldn't shake the possibility. I wanted him too much, and even now, it's not enough. Like he said, it'll *never* be enough. There won't ever be a time where I don't want this man. Where I don't hunger for him.

Ellis's lips are warm, and his hands cradle my face. I want to bite and claw my way closer, but we only have half a day before night falls, and I promised Ellis a date.

So, with far more patience than I realized I possess, I gentle the kiss and pull back. Ellis's hair is a little damp, curling against his forehead, and his eyes shift between my own, questioning.

"We're going on a date," I tell him.

He cocks his head.

"Here," I explain. "I'll take you out another time. But today, I just want to be here with you."

His eyes drop to my lips. "When do you go?"

My heart clenches. "Tomorrow morning."

"Okay."

"I'm sorry," I whisper.

He shakes his head. "Don't. Lunch?"

"Yeah," I say, running my hands over his forearms. They're strong, just like Ellis, and covered in a dusting of brown hair. A lumberjack, Danil called him. He's certainly built like one. "Do you need to clean up first?"

Ellis nods before canting his head behind him. I'm guessing he has to put out the fire, too.

"How about we meet back here in an hour?" I say. "I need to go grab a few things anyways. Will that give you enough time?"

His lips lift at the corner. "It's a date."

I can't quite resist giving him another kiss after that. When I go, I stop at the doorway for a moment, watching Ellis store his tools. I've always thought Ellis is handsome in a rugged, natural way. There's not an ounce of flash about him. He doesn't flaunt his assets or attempt to flatter others. I'm not sure he even knows how to flirt. But he doesn't need to do any of those things. He draws me like a magnet regardless, his pull undeniable.

With a sigh, I turn to go, but pause once more as my eyes catch on the glass fireflies hovering above. They almost seem to flicker, as if they're alive. With my heart aching for reasons unknown, I head out the door.

It doesn't take all that long to pick up supplies. My mom drives me to my rental car first, and then I head to the store, grabbing ingredients for a simple lunch. Taking a page out of Ellis's book, I set everything up on top of a blanket outside the silo. There's a chill in the air, but the sun is bright enough to keep us warm.

Ellis arrives a little before the hour mark is up, changed and looking freshly showered. I almost stop myself from drinking him in properly before remembering I *can*. If Ellis minds my ogling, he doesn't show it. He sits down next to me, a smile on his face as he plucks at the blanket pointedly.

"You have good ideas," I tell him.

He huffs a laugh.

"Your mom okay?" I check. She seemed in decent spirits earlier, but I know Ellis likes to keep an eye on her.

He nods, giving my leg a squeeze.

"You told her about us."

Another squeeze.

"Is it weird for you, being with a man?" I find myself asking.

He frowns, and I get the sense he's asking me, *Why would it be?*

"I don't know," I answer. "If maybe you assumed you were straight, then—"

He shakes his head quickly. "Didn't assume." He rolls his lips like there's more he wants to say, so I wait. "Not weird. It's you."

There go those butterflies again.

I let out a breath before leaning forward and kissing him. It's small, chaste, but it's Ellis, so it's not so small at all. His stubble brushes against me, his thumb strokes my cheek, and I feel rooted and warmed, sun-kissed and mellow.

When I lean back, I set to work unwrapping the food I brought, if for no other reason than to keep my hands busy and off the man in front of me. At least for now. "Would you tell me about glassblowing?" I ask.

Ellis nods as I plate up our lunch, and like so many times before, we sit and talk and simply *exist* in the same space and time. I don't know how it always feels new, as if there's more to learn. More to discover.

Ellis tells me about converting the silo. About his rudimentary first attempts at shaping glass. He tells me about a workshop he attended and the first piece he decided to sell. I tell him about work, bits and pieces I haven't shared before, and how I'll be going back to Crete to finish up my assignment. I tell him that I'll have to stop in New York afterwards because the magazine is sending me and Danil to Greenland, and I don't have the right gear packed. Ellis assures me he understands, but I get the sense he feels the same urgency as me, wanting to make the most of our last day together.

It's no surprise to me when we end up sprawled out on the blanket, the remnants of our meal pushed aside. I can't keep my hands off him. Or my lips. We start sitting upright, me on Ellis's lap. Then he's lying down. Eventually, I end up under him, all that weight pressing me securely to the ground. He grinds against me, our mouths locked, the two of us battling like horny teenagers.

He never had this, I remind myself. All of this is new for him. It makes it feel new for me, too.

"El," I groan, my legs around his waist.

He grunts, meeting my tongue.

I can't speak again until he draws back. "I don't want you to be with anyone else," I say, my tone a little harsher than I intended, making my frantic words sound more like a demand than the plea they were supposed to be.

He snorts.

"What?" I ask, my breath coming short as Ellis smirks down at me.

He shakes his head, propped up on one arm, his hand toying with my hair. "How many times?" he says. "Only you. No one...but you."

I blow out a slow breath, my heart rate calming. "Right. Okay."

He raises an eyebrow like *you sure you got it now?*

"Yeah," I say, tugging him back down to me. "Just us." His erection nestles against my hip, the thick length of him impossible to ignore. "El. I want my mouth on you."

He goes still before shivering, his lips nearly pressed to mine. He drops his face to my neck, nodding.

"Yeah?" I check, grinding up against him.

He huffs against me, a clear yes.

"Then come on."

Ellis looks confused as I push him away and stand up, but he follows me without question. Considering it's still afternoon, I don't want to risk getting caught out in the open, unlikely as that would be. So I tug Ellis into the field, weaving down narrow rows of corn until we're decently hidden. Then I turn and drop to my knees.

Ellis's chest rises and falls as I unzip his pants and pull them down to his thighs. His boxer briefs go next. One day soon, I'm going to savor every inch of this man the way he deserves. I'm going to worship him for hours, again and again until he's begging me to stop. It won't be rushed, and it won't be in a field of dirt and corn.

But today is not that day.

Ellis grunts as I slip my mouth around his cock. I watch his every facial expression, searching for spots that make him soar. I run my tongue along his shaft and cockhead, ring him with my lips, dig my fingers into his thighs and offer a gentler touch to his balls. The blowjob doesn't last long, but it doesn't matter. I accept the compliment for what it is, and I hoard the memory that's offered to me and me alone.

His cock swells against my tongue before he comes. He tries hard not to tug me down on him, but his fingers in my hair tighten, and I can tell he's losing the battle. I open my throat, letting him do what he needs to as he rides out his orgasm. The sheer size of him towering above me is enough to have me squirming and breathless, knowing he would never harm me, never hurt me. Only protect.

My Ellis.

Wrung dry, Ellis pulls from my lips. "Luck," he croaks.

"Good?" I ask a little cheekily, wiping the corner of my mouth.

He tugs his underwear and pants into place, not bothering to button them, and drops to his knees in front of me. His hands weave back into my hair, and he looks at me. Simply looks.

I've never been as comfortable in silence as I am with him.

Finally, he kisses me, a hard, demanding thing. "Can I?" he asks.

"Can you what?"

"My mouth," he says, hand landing on my crotch.

My hips hitch forward, my long-neglected cock throbbing under his touch. "If you're sure," I get out, even as every fiber of my being shouts in fervent agreement. *Yes, yes, yes.*

"Sure," he says, pushing me gently down to the ground. He doesn't hesitate to open up my pants, even as his fingers skim along my hips and lower abdomen. He takes his time, mapping my skin, laying gentle kisses, and bringing my need to a boiling point, before he finally tugs down my briefs enough to free my cock. He takes it in hand then, his eyes meeting mine.

"There's no wrong way," I tell him. "Don't bite me, and we'll be good."

He huffs a small laugh at that, but there's a smile on his lips, too. Much to my surprise, he lowers his face slowly, turning his head at the last moment and nibbling ever so gently against the side of my crown.

I buck against him, a zing traveling up my entire body as I huff a laugh. "Okay, maybe a little biting," I concede.

His grin would topple me if I were standing.

When the flat of Ellis's tongue drags over the tip of my cock, my eyes slip shut. He sucks me into his mouth, and I have to work hard on controlling my breathing. He glides up and down, his hand holding my base steady as he explores. It's sloppy and unpracticed and by far the best thing I've ever felt in my life. The sun is warm as it beats down on my face, the low leaves of the corn stalks brush my arms, and nothing exists but Ellis and me in this place where we met. This place where we began.

"El," I warn, getting close. He redoubles his efforts, and I bring my eyes to his, knowing it'll send me over the edge but unwilling to miss another moment.

When I come, it's like a punch to my solar plexus, soul-consuming and comforting all at once. It's that feeling of home I've only ever had with him. It's the rumbling of mountains and the kiss of wind through the fields, and it's love. *God*, is it love, wholly, pure, and absolute.

I won't ever love another the way I love Ellis, and I don't want to. He's it. He's always been it. And for the first time since we've known one another, I know, as I look into his brown eyes, that whatever piece of me is tethered to Ellis has a counterpoint. An equal pull.

Mrs. Cole was right. No matter what, nothing will keep us apart. We'll always come back to one another, time and time again.

Chapter 25

ELLIS

"Don't wanna go," Lucky mumbles, his lips skimming mine.

Don't want you to, either. Not yet.

I tighten my arms around him, tossing my leg over his as if I could trap him here with me indefinitely. We've been up for half an hour already, putting off the inevitable. Lucky needs to leave soon.

I'm not quite ready to let him go.

Lucky catches my lip between his, tongue flicking against me before he meets my mouth solidly. We're in my bed again, cuddled under the sheets as if they could somehow hide us away from the rest of the world. I can barely make out Lucky's features. He's bathed in darkness, but the outline of him is familiar. The riotous hair, the shape of his shoulders. Even the feel of his lips is a map I'm quickly becoming accustomed to. I never knew, before now, how intimate the act of kissing could be. Maybe, possibly, even more so than sex, even though my experience in that regard is limited.

I could do nothing but kiss Lucky until the end of time, and I would be content. I'd swirl with him in the sky until we were one, binary stars gravitationally bound to one another.

"Ellis," Lucky says quietly. When his phone pings, he groans against my mouth. "Damn it. Time's up."

I nod, tracing the side of his face. Lucky catches my hand before I can lift it free, bringing his lips to my palm.

"It's not goodbye," he says.

My chest squeezes. "I know."

"Three weeks tops."

"I know," I repeat.

"I'll call."

I know.

"Every day, if I can."

"Luck," I say gently.

He eases out a breath. "I'm going to miss you, Ellis. I always do, but now..."

Yeah. Now, it's going to hurt more.

"Fuck," he mutters under his breath. He kisses me hard for just a second before sitting up and tossing away our covers. It's still dark out, no light coming through the window. Lucky's bag is already packed, sitting beside the door.

We're quiet as we make our way outside. My mom is sleeping, but Lucky's parents are up, waiting for us in front of their house. Lucky heads that way, giving his mom and dad a hug and exchanging soft words I don't hear. Mr. Buchanan ruffles Lucky's hair, and then Lucky comes back over to me. He doesn't say anything—just looks up at me with those light blue eyes.

Sky blue? Robin's egg? I still don't know.

When Lucky wraps his arms around me, it's not a surprise. I welcome the hug, returning it, even as my insides roll. His face burrows against my chest for a moment before he steps back abruptly. Without a word, he turns, and I watch him go, wondering how it's possible to ache so badly for something that's right in front of me.

He's halfway to his car when he spins, striding back over to me with purpose. He doesn't stop until he's an inch in front of me, his palms landing on my cheeks.

"I promise I'll be back soon," he says, voice firm. "It's me and you, right, El?"

I nod against his grasp. *Always.*

He kisses me then. It's an oath, just as binding as his words, and I tuck it inside of me where I know it will keep me warm. He doesn't pull away as quickly this time. When he leans back, he looks at me for the longest moment, his face so close I can see the specks of color that make up his irises, even in the dim light. There are too many shades. Maybe that's why I've never been able to pinpoint it.

"Soon," he repeats.

I nod, and he lets go.

Lucky doesn't stop this time as he heads to his car. He gets inside, shuts the door, and backs slowly down the driveway. It feels as if there's a hook in my chest, pulling tight as his car disappears down the road. I rub the spot, watching dust kick up from his tires.

"Do you know why we named him Lucky?" Mrs. Buchanan asks, stepping onto the grass beside me. The screen door shuts as Mr. Buchanan heads inside.

I shake my head.

"Five is my lucky number," she says. "I was born on the fifth of February, met Ron the fifth of December, and we got married on the fifth of March."

A few birds sing as the sun starts to crest the skyline, sending a gentle pink glow into the dusky dawn. I can't see Lucky's car anymore.

"I was pregnant four times before Lucky came along," Mrs. Buchanan says. "He was number five, and I knew, the moment I held him in my arms, he was our Lucky. Our miracle child."

I look her way, not sure how to respond. I had no idea.

Mrs. Buchanan doesn't seem to expect me to say anything. She goes on, rubbing her hands up and down the sleeves of her sweater. "I know it's hard seeing him go. But Lucky is a fighter. Always has been. He'll come back, Ellis. He knows you're worth fighting for."

Lucky's mom gives me a soft smile, squeezes my arm, and turns away. I stay a while longer, watching the empty road in front of our houses.

It's still early when I head inside, so I'm not surprised my mom isn't awake yet. Marcus gently insisted I take the remainder of the week off, so I make some eggs and toast before settling at the kitchen table with my laptop, in no hurry to be anywhere else.

My fingers start typing before long, the process a familiar comfort by now.

Hey, Luck. I can't help but wonder if I'm dreaming. It feels that way. Less than an hour ago, you were in my bed, so warm and soft tucked between me and the sheets. I've dreamed of you there so many times, I'm not convinced it wasn't another fantasy I spun inside my head. Except... You were here, I know that. You came for me. You came, and you kissed me, and now nothing is going to be the same.

I didn't know you felt it. Maybe I should have. I know you so well; it feels like I should have known this, too. But

I'm fallible. And I didn't see how it could possibly work. I don't have wings, Luck, not like you. I'm afraid of holding you back. But you told me we'll be okay, that we'll figure it out, and I believe you.

I believe you.

I was eighteen when I shattered glass for the first time and told you to go. You didn't listen, not that time. You stayed for me because I was hurting. Because, maybe, you knew I needed you. I still need you, but I let you go. You said you'd come back. You promised.

I believe you.

I'm scared, Luck, but I love you more than anything. I love you, I love you, so please, my beautiful firefly, fly back to me soon. Come back, that's all I ask.

Keep coming back to me.

I consider delivering it. For a moment, my cursor hovers over the button, and I almost click send. But then I save it to my drafts folder like all the others, knowing the first time I tell Lucky I love him, it won't be when he's miles and miles away.

"Ellis, I'm so sorry," Gabby says, her eyes creased in worry. She's wearing jeans and a yellow shirt today, and her dog, Toodles, is sitting on her lap. There's an iced tea on the coffee table in front of her that I poured when she showed up, but she hasn't touched it.

I shake my head. "Okay."

"Still," she goes on, "you wouldn't have been out there if it wasn't for me. When I found out what happened..." She trails off, face pinched. "I feel terrible."

"Not your fault," I assure her. The tornado could just as easily have touched down around here. "Toodles?"

"She's fine," Gabby says, rubbing between her dog's ears. "One of my neighbors found her a few streets over after the storm cleared. She was huddled under some bushes at the side of a house. Gave me quite the scare, but...she's okay."

I nod, and Gabby sighs, petting her dog in a way that seems self-soothing.

"Ellis," she says quietly, her expression almost sheepish. "Is there any chance I could make it up to you? Maybe take you to dinner? My treat."

For a moment, I falter. I suspect Gabby's invite is more than friendly. But I'm not sure how to explain everything that's happened between me and Lucky in the past few days, months, years, even—all of our history and the reasons why Gabby and I could never work. I don't think I'd even have the words if I tried.

"Can't, Gabs," I finally say. "Not as a date."

She nods, not seeming surprised but maybe a touch disappointed. "Can we still chat at work? I like talking to you, Ellis. Unless..." She huffs a laugh, looking down. "Unless I'm being a pain but you're just too nice to say so. I'd get it, I—"

I reach over and tap Gabby's knee, cutting her off as gently as I can. I shake my head and hold up a finger, and Gabby nods, chewing at her lip. I make quick work of grabbing my laptop, and then I type out a message, wanting her to understand. When I flip the screen around, she starts to read.

You're not a pain, Gabby. Not in the least. I like our chats and your stories about Toodles and your gran. You've always been kind to me, and you don't pressure me to be different than I am. I'd like to stay friends if you want that. I'm sorry I can't offer more, but I'm already in love with someone else. Have been for a long time. I hope you can understand.

The smile on her face grows steadily until she's looking up at me again. "Really?" she asks.

I'm not sure which part she's asking about, but I nod yes to all of it, placing the laptop on the coffee table.

Gabby stands up, setting Toodles on the floor in the process, and the next second I'm being wrapped in petite arms and a waft of floral perfume. Tiny dog feet land on my leg, scrambling. "Do I get to ask about her?"

I pull back a little, confused.

Gabby's eyes *are* green. They soften as she takes a seat next to me. Toodles jumps onto her lap. "The girl you're in love with," she says.

"Guy," I correct.

Gabby's eyebrows go up a little, but her smile doesn't falter. "Do I get to ask about him?"

I nod, feeling a touch of heat cross my face.

"Does he live here?"

I shake my head slowly. "Travels."

She purses her lips at that. "So I probably don't know him then, huh?"

No.

"Can I at least see his picture?" she asks. "Oh, what's his name?"

I pull out my phone, sifting through my recent pictures of Lucky. I decide on one where he's holding up a massive blue crab. His eyes are comically wide as he peers around the crustacean, and I can practically hear the laughter bubbling up from his throat. Lucky sent me the picture while he was in Belize.

I show Gabby. "That's Luck. Lucky."

Her mouth opens before her eyes meet mine. "Oh, wow. He's just beautiful, isn't he?"

Yeah. Always has been.

Gabby leans back in her seat, sighing. "So, you said you love him, but what's the deal? Are you two dating? Boyfriends? Friends?"

I slip my phone back in my pocket, my eyes darting toward the front of the house. Lucky is long gone now, but the phantom of him remains. The touch of his lips. The texture of his hair between my fingertips. The words he spoke so quietly against my chest. *"This is real, El. Me and you, it's real."*

We're friends, yes. Always. But we're more than that, too. Lucky is...

He's my *everything*.

Chapter 26

LUCKY

"You okay?" Danil asks, his breath puffing out in front of his face.

I nod, even though it feels like my fingers are about to fall off.

Danil hands me two new instant heat packs. I thank him, squeezing the small packets to activate them before slipping them inside my gloves. I ditch the old ones in the process.

"It's a much better night tonight," our guide tells us. "We should see activity soon."

I sure hope so. Otherwise, we'll be heading back empty-handed.

Danil huddles inside his big, puffy coat that looks like a small down comforter. His hands are tucked away in his pockets, whereas mine are out in the cold, holding my camera at the ready. Our tour guide, Pierce, told me I'd have plenty of time to snap pictures once the show starts, but I don't want to miss a thing. The past two nights were too overcast to see the sky, which means this is our last chance before we return inland.

My track record at the magazine is impeccable, and I'd hate to fail this assignment. If only the weather would cooperate.

Our camp sits behind us as we wait, domed tents lit golden from the lamps inside. Pierce's Alaskan Malamute barks once before settling, making a bed on the cold, hard ground. In front of us stretches water that looks crystalline blue in the sunshine, but now, at just after midnight, it sits dark, like a sheet of black ice. Further still is the Qaleraliq Glacier, a wide expanse of snow and frozen, craggy ground. We hiked along it earlier today, but right now, we're still.

It's early in the season for this, but so long as the night is clear...

"There," Pierce says, pointing off into the distance.

A green light snakes through the sky, there and gone again so fast I barely see it. I hold my breath, waiting for it to return. It does, a whip of light cutting through the star-dotted black. It shifts, shimmers, dancing through the sky like a living thing. A ballet. The light twists, green bleeding with pink and yellow, moving so quickly I can hardly keep up. It's so bright, so *vivid*, the colors stretching through the sky as if they're reaching for the Heavens.

"Did you ever think you'd see the Northern Lights in person?" Danil asks from beside me, his voice quiet.

I shake my head, unable to look away.

"Pictures, Lucky-boy," he reminds me with a chuckle, nudging my arm.

Right.

I hop to, catching the lights within my camera. I no longer feel the cold in my fingers as we watch the Aurora Borealis play out atop the glacier's peak. It's stunning, so much more beautiful in person than pictures could ever properly convey. But I try my best to do justice to the phenomenon, storing the green and pink and glimmer of starlight away behind my lens.

It's nearly three a.m. when we retire to our tents, the light show having dissipated. My fingers itch to call Ellis, but I can't. There's no service this far away from civilization. Instead, I curl inside my sleeping bag, a few heat packs keeping me company and a soft smile on my face, and I count down the minutes until I can hear his voice again.

"Even though that was worth freezing my balls off for, I'm glad to be back in the land of central heating," Danil says.

I huff a laugh, tugging off my boots as Danil sprawls onto his bed in the hostel we're staying at. We have another four days before we leave Greenland, but our camping at Qaleraliq Glacier is done. Danil will be heading back to NYC after this, whereas my plane will take me to Nebraska.

My stomach skips as I think about heading home to Ellis.

"Uh-oh," Danil says.

"What?" I ask, sitting down on the edge of my own cot.

"You've got the face."

"What face?"

"The *I'm-so-in-love-it's-sickening* face," Danil answers, earning himself a smack from my pillow. He laughs, snatching it and tossing it back. "You know I'm happy for you."

"Yeah, yeah."

"Even if I've had to listen to you *hi, baby* this and *miss you, too* that for the past two weeks."

"Mhm," I mutter, raising an eyebrow. "You sound like *such* a supportive friend."

He snorts, tucking his palms under his head. "Although I do wonder at the distinct lack of sexy times."

I wrinkle my nose. "Sexy times? Really?"

"Oh, fuck you, too," he says without venom.

I shake my head. "I can't believe you'd rather hear me having phone sex."

"That's not what I said. I wouldn't *mind* it," he clarifies, grabbing my pillow from the air before it can collide with his face again. He laughs, stuffing it under his head. "But if you're holding off for my sake, you don't need to. I can't imagine the long distance thing is easy, especially considering the recent shift in your relationship."

He's not wrong. It's been a hard couple of weeks away from Ellis, my craving for the man having reached an all-time high. I can't seem to shove my feelings down, not anymore. Not like I used to. It's almost scary, the intensity of my bone-deep desire to hear him, feel him, to be held in his arms. It's *not* just about sex, of course. Not in the least. But I won't lie and say I don't want that, too. Badly.

Still, I chew on my words before answering Danil. "I don't think Ellis would be comfortable having phone sex."

He gives me a pointed look. "Have you asked him?"

"Well, no," I admit. But Ellis has never been particularly comfortable talking about sex.

Danil snorts. "You can be really dense when it comes to him."

"Hey," I grouse, wishing I still had my pillow, if only so I could smack him again. "How would you even know, Dani? You saw us together for, like, all of a hot minute."

"Because I know *you*," he answers, giving me a stern look. "And don't try to tell me I don't. You didn't make it easy, but I *know* you, Lucky. And you know me. Somehow, some way, we clicked. And I've seen the way you dance around him, even still, like you're scared. You don't have to be."

"How can you be so sure?" I ask, trying to hide the quiver in my voice. The truth is I *am* scared. The idea of losing Ellis terrified me before, but now... Now I can barely breathe past it.

Danil pins me with his dark gaze. "Really, Lucky-boy? That man has loved you for years. You told me yourself. You love him, too. You don't have to worry about your heart when it comes to him."

"Sometimes," I say slowly, "you give me such bad advice."

"And sometimes I don't."

"Sometimes, you don't," I agree.

He grins. "Call your man. I'm going to get some rest."

With that, Danil plops my pillow on top of his face, leaving me in relative silence. Our room at the hostel is shared accommodations, but none of the other guests are here at the moment. I grab my phone, not because Danil told me to, but because I'm desperate to talk to Ellis. It's early evening in Nebraska, and he answers quickly, a soft hum coming over the line that soothes my ragged nerves after being radio-silent for the past four days.

"Hi, baby," I sigh out.

A snort has me reaching over and smacking Danil's foot. He tugs his leg back with a hiss, and I walk away, stopping in front of a small window that overlooks the street.

"Luck," Ellis answers.

Everything in me warms.

"Are you off work?" I ask.

He hums his assent. I wasn't sure he would be, considering it's harvest season. Ellis puts in long hours this time of year.

"How's the corn picking?" I tease. He doesn't actually pick by hand, but there are a few small farms in our town that do handpick their sweet corn.

He grunts, and I laugh.

"I saw the lights," I say softly, watching the cars pass by below. It feels almost strange being back here in the city after spending a few days in the wilderness, where everything was hushed and white.

Ellis hums. "Tell me."

"I wish you could have seen them, El. *God*, was it beautiful. I don't even know how to describe it."

"Try," he says gently, sounding as if he's taking a seat.

I turn and sit down below the window, imagining him beside me. "It was like brush strokes. Like paint being splashed across the sky. Except the color didn't stick. It was a constantly changing canvas. A million pictures in such a short period of time, each one breathtaking and fleeting. It almost felt..."

"What?" he asks when I don't go on.

"It almost felt wrong to photograph it. Like... I was trying to capture something not meant to be contained."

Ellis is quiet for the longest time.

"You okay?" I ask.

He makes a small sound. "Miss you is all."

My chest squeezes tight. "I'll be home soon."

"I know."

"I miss you, too."

"I know," he says again.

Other words sit at the tip of my tongue—three big words in particular—but I don't say them. It's not fear holding me back.

We've said *I love you* before, after all. But not like this. And I won't...I won't do it like *this*.

Glancing over at Danil's form, I lower my voice. "What are you wearing?"

There's a pause. "Jeans." It sounds like a question. "And my work shirt."

I bite my lip. "Do you want to get out of them?"

Another pause. "I'll shower later."

"No, I mean..." I clear my throat, praying Danil is asleep, otherwise I'll never hear the end of this. "Are you alone?"

There's a hum, and then a new voice chimes in from further away. "What? Is that Lucky you're talking to? I don't know what you... Oh, sure. Hi, Lucky."

I slap a hand over my face, laughing against my palm. "Tell your mom hi," I mumble.

He does, and I shake my head, unable to fight my smile.

I drop my hand. "Ellis, can you go to your room?"

He grunts, and I wait. A door shuts.

"Are you alone now?" I ask.

A hum.

"El, have you..." I don't even know where to start. Ellis was a virgin before me, and those times we did talk about sex, he didn't express an interest. "Have you watched porn?"

There's a curious hum, followed by, "No."

Oh, God.

It's me. I'm the one who's going to corrupt him.

I blow out a slow breath. "Have you thought about what you'd like to do? With me?"

There's only a beat of silence. "Yes."

My pulse spikes.

"Will you show me when I get back?" I ask. "Will you show me what you've thought about?"

No hesitation. "Yes."

Heat pools low in my stomach.

"I've thought about you so much, El. Even before we..." I lower my voice again, but Danil seems dead to the world. "Even before I knew how you tasted, even before I felt your lips wrapped around my cock, I thought about you. All the time."

"Luck," he croaks.

"I can't wait to kiss you again. I miss that most," I admit.

His sound is an adamant yes.

"Would you stroke yourself for me?" I ask quietly, shifting as my cock plumps. I'm not about to jerk off with Danil in the room, and certainly not in a common space, but that doesn't mean Ellis couldn't.

He groans.

"Is that a yes?" I check.

A hum.

Danil was right; I shouldn't have assumed Ellis wouldn't want this.

"Take yourself out, El."

His bed creaks, and I close my eyes, resting my head back against the wall as my insides pop and light. A grin blossoms on my face as Ellis's soft panting breaths come over the line.

"Are you jerking yourself?" I ask, even though it's obvious. He's not trying to hide his sounds.

He hums a yes.

"Are you still in your jeans?"

Another yes.

"God, that's hot," I breathe, adjusting myself. "I wish I could see you lying on your bed with your pants opened up and your hand around your cock."

He grunts.

"If I were there," I go on, "I'd give you my palm or my tongue, whichever one you wanted." After a beat, I add, "Or my ass."

Ellis groans, a stuttered sound.

"Are you close?"

A grunt.

"I want to hear you come for me, Ellis. I want to remember the sound so I can replay it later when I'm spilling over my fist."

There's a breathy huff, followed by a muffled moan, and my own cock throbs as I hear the evidence of Ellis's orgasm. It washes over me like the most satisfying dunk in a sun-warmed lake, and I let myself be submerged. I let that familiar comfort cocoon me, so much more potent than a physical release.

I exhale slowly before opening my eyes. "Better?" I ask.

"Still...miss you," Ellis huffs out between breaths, but the words sound like a smile.

"Miss you, too, big guy."

"Want to...pick you up," he says.

"From the airport?"

A grunt.

"It's a long drive. You don't have to."

"Want to," he repeats.

I can't keep the smile off my face. "Okay, then."

"'Kay."

I tip my head back against the wall, feeling like I'm floating in blue. "You better not eat all the corn before I get there," I say softly. "I think there's a cob with my name on it."

There's a beat of silence, and then Ellis laughs. It's the most perfect sound.

Chapter 27

ELLIS

Combine harvesters are massive machines. Our headers clear twelve rows of corn at once, which lets us harvest over ten acres an hour, easily. And at ten-hour days, that puts my workload at well over a hundred acres.

Unlike during sweet corn season, field corn is harvested once dry. The machines do all the work, not only snapping the ears of corn off the stalks, but also separating out the kernels from the cobs.

I don't mind the long days. The temperatures are cooler this time of year, and even though somewhat monotonous, it's simple, easy work. The only reason I keep checking the clock today is because Lucky will be here in less than four hours. He's already on a plane, heading this way.

My insides *buzz* just thinking about it. The sensation has been steadily building for weeks, an incessant itch I can't scratch.

He's almost home.

It's six o'clock when I call it a day and head back to the warehouse where my truck is parked. Before I can reach my vehicle, I hear my name called. I stop, pivoting as Riley jogs my way.

"Hey," he says, giving me a smile as he stops in front of me. "I'm meeting a few guys at the bar tonight. Wanna come?"

I pause, mulling over my response. "Raincheck?"

Riley nods, accepting that easily, but I want to explain. Not many people make an effort to include me the way Riley has, and I appreciate it.

"I..." He waits as I formulate words. "Luck is coming home."

His smile hitches up a bit. "Where's he been at these days?"

I huff a laugh. "Everywhere."

He nods, looking lost in thought for a moment. "Are you two a couple?"

I hum a confirmation. "New."

"Really?" he says. "I always wondered back in high school. I thought you guys might have been something then."

I shake my head, hoping he understands.

"Huh. Well, for what it's worth, I'm happy for you guys. You always fit, you know?"

Yeah, I know.

"You, and, uh, Gabby," he goes on. "Were you never..." He lets his question hang, but I think I know what he's asking.

I shake my head. "Friends."

"Okay, cool," he says, nodding a few times. "Well, I'll let you get going. Tell Lucky hi."

I give him a nod, and he claps my shoulder before heading off.

When I get home, I rush through my shower before whipping up a quick dinner that my mom tells me not to bother with. I do it anyway, sitting down to eat with her before grabbing my keys. She chuckles as I hustle out the door.

The drive to the airport is a good hour and a half long, but I don't mind. The time passes quickly as the string between me and Lucky shortens. It's relief when I pull into the airport parking lot, a relaxation of that ache in my chest.

Lucky didn't ask for me to meet him inside, but that's what I do. I wouldn't be able to sit still out in my truck anyways, watching reunions and waiting for one of my own. The minutes tick by endlessly now that I'm here, but I keep myself still, standing near the edge of the long hallway where the arrivals come through.

When I see a flash of corkscrewing golden-blonde hair, my heartbeat kicks up in tempo. There's a smile on Lucky's lips, but his face is tipped down as he walks, a suitcase dragging behind him. My chest rises and falls as he gets closer, and I almost call out. But then he looks up, and bright eyes collide with mine.

Lucky stutters almost to a stop when he sees me, his smile widening. The surprise only lasts for a moment. He picks up his pace, runs, and then, he *flies*.

I catch Lucky in my arms as his suitcase goes clattering to the floor. His legs wrap around me tight, hair tickling the side of my face, and all of that buzzing inside my body quiets to a gentle hum.

Lucky's hands bracket my face as his lips find mine, soft and urgent and warm. "God, I missed you," he mumbles against my mouth.

Missed you, too.

He gives me another slow, drugging kiss that makes me feel as if I'm sinking. "This is such a better way"—a third kiss, so sweet, so smooth—"to come home to you."

I pour my fervent *yes* into Lucky's mouth, losing count of kisses, losing track of time. Our lips come together again and again, and I'm saturated in him, so far under the surface, there's nothing and no one but Lucky.

When he finally draws back, I drop my forehead to his, unwilling to go far. It takes me a moment to realize I'm shaking.

"El," he says gently, fingers skating over my skin. "I'm here for a week and a half." It sounds like a reassurance.

I nod, tucking my face against his hair and breathing in.

He smooths his hands around to the back of my neck, cursing gently. "And to think, I could have had this for years."

My chest twinges. We didn't know. Neither of us knew.

"Now," I say, trying to reassure him, too. *You have me now.*

"El," he says softly, huffing a small laugh when my nose brushes his ear. "You might need to set me down soon. A little old lady is giving us the stink eye."

I shake my head, but I do pull my face out of his hair. Bending down with Lucky in my arms, I grab the handle of his suitcase, and then I straighten back up and start walking. He laughs, his eyes twinkling as I carry him backwards toward the exit. His fingers keep caressing my neck, and a beautiful smile lights his face.

"Danil is going to be so jealous," he says, laying his head on my shoulder.

I don't know why, but I couldn't care less. I keep my arm around Lucky as the doors whoosh closed behind us, and I bring my firefly home.

It's late when Lucky and I get back to our houses. The lights are off inside the Buchanans', but a soft glow emanates from my living room, telling me my mom is still up. Lucky seems to notice the same thing because he tugs me right past my house, leaving his suitcase behind in the truck.

"Do you remember what I asked you?" he says, heading toward the silo. The moon is big and round tonight, lighting our path past the field of dried corn stalks. They're cut low now, the harvest already having been reaped.

My mind skitters back, but I can't figure out what he's talking about, and I shake my head.

He hums, hand still in mine. The air is chilly, but Lucky is in a jacket, so he doesn't seem to mind.

"I asked if you had thought about us," he says, making my heart stutter. There's a whoosh of blood in my ears as he adds, "I asked if you'd show me."

I swallow as Lucky leads me the remaining steps to the silo.

"Let us in," he says gently.

I fish the keys from my pocket, hand shaking as I unlock the door. Lucky waits while I throw it open, and then he tugs me inside, flicking on the lights. He lets me go to pull off his jacket, eyes blazing under the fireflies flickering above. He backs into the circular space, dropping his jacket to the dirt floor.

"Ellis."

I swallow again, pulse racing, cock thickening inside my jeans as Lucky lifts his shirt. He tugs it over his head, letting it slip from his fingers as he continues his slow path backwards. His pants are the last to go. He drops them off his hips, kicking them and his shoes to the side as he reaches the wooden table in the center of the room. He looks ethereal in the warm light from above, his body cast in gentle shadows, pale skin bright.

"El," he says again, drawing my gaze to his. "Show me."

Blowing out a breath, I approach. He wants to know what I've thought of all these years? He wants to know what I've dreamed of on those nights I pondered *why him?* He wants to know what it feels like inside every time I look at his face or hear his voice or see his eyes soften the moment they reach me?

It's a small lifetime that passes in the seconds it takes me to stand before him. It feels like our history, and in a way, maybe it is. Maybe that's what makes love—all the moments, big and small. All the memories piled up one on top of the other, just like those Northern Lights that paint across the sky at the edge of the world. Maybe, when it comes down to it, love is in the act of living. It's choosing—*breathing*—that person every single day.

Me and you.

Lucky lets out a small gasp when I lift him onto the table. His legs part immediately, and I slot between his knees, threading my hands up into his hair. He tilts his head back, eyes feathering closed.

What have I thought of?

I brush my lips across his. "This," I whisper.

He sighs.

I find his pulse-point next, lingering there, feeling his heartbeat thrum against my lips. "This."

When I press gently on the center of Lucky's chest, he drops to his elbows.

"This," I say, bending low to kiss his belly button.

I tug his briefs next, enjoying the catch of Lucky's breath as the band clears his cock. He lifts, and I drag the material off before bending down, hands on either side of Lucky's hips as my mouth ghosts over his crown.

My eyes meet his. "This."

Lucky's stomach contracts as I suck him into my mouth, working the underside of his cockhead with my tongue before letting him pop free. He curses when I hitch up his knees, and his back hits the table.

"This," I whisper, laying kisses across his ass cheek until I reach the center of him. The noise that comes out of his mouth when I flit my tongue across his hole has me repeating the movement. It's the same way Lucky teases me sometimes when we're kissing. The tiniest flick of his tongue, as if he wants me to chase him. This time, it's Lucky chasing me, his hips shifting as I tease him with the tip of my tongue.

"Ellis," he groans, grabbing under his knees. I shift my hands down his thighs, anchoring at his hips, holding tight.

The moan he lets out when I drag the flat of my tongue across him has my cock bucking. I'm so hard it hurts, like a physical manifestation of all I feel for this man. I'm not sure it would have been the same if we had fumbled our way through this interaction when we were younger. I wouldn't have known what to do at seventeen, at nineteen even, or twenty. I wouldn't have had time to understand myself, to know what I like, to have an idea of what *Lucky* might like. Maybe there's a reason it's now.

When I press my tongue inside Lucky's body, he keens.

"El." The word is a gasp. "Do you want to fuck me?"

I nod, my hair brushing the delicate underside of his thigh. I draw my nose upwards and suck one of his balls into my mouth.

He huffs out a breath, lifting his head to look at me before letting it thunk back against the wood. "Then fuck me. Please. Get inside me, El. I need you to—" He moans as I roll my tongue along his sac. "Need you. Just need you."

I nod again before pausing. "I don't..."

"Jeans pocket," he says, letting his heels fall down to the table. They perch at the edge, his body on display as he scoots up onto his elbows again. "Lube and... I want you bare, El. I'm negative. But there's a condom, too, if you'd prefer."

I shut my eyes for a moment, forehead pressed to the inside of Lucky's knee. After I'm fairly sure I can move without falling, I push off from the table and retrieve Lucky's jeans. Both items are inside, as he said they'd be. Two condoms and four packets of lube. I leave the condoms.

Lucky watches me as I stand back up and drop the lube on the table. His gaze travels over me slowly, raking down my chest and stomach as I tug off my shirt. It settles lower still when I push down my jeans. For a moment, the air feels thick between us. Anticipatory.

I step close once I'm nude, my toes digging into the packed earth.

"You're going to stretch me with one finger," Lucky says, spreading his legs wide. "And then two. And then three because you're a decently big fucker."

I huff, Lucky's grin letting me know that's a good thing.

"And then you're going to fuck me, El. Don't overthink it, okay? It'll be good."

I nod swiftly, opening a packet of lube. Lucky pulls one leg up, folding his body in a way I'm not sure I could manage.

"Now," he says.

When I press against him, Lucky's body gives way. I know one finger isn't much of an invasion—I've tried it—but I still go slow, letting Lucky's muscles soften before I add another.

"Have you—" He huffs a curious sound. "Have you done this to yourself?"

I grunt, aiming upwards and curling my fingers along his inner walls. Lucky's head falls back as I massage his prostate, his hair brushing the table as he moans. The sound turns into a chuckle, and he lifts his head.

"Yeah," he says, bearing down on me when I add a third finger. "I can tell. You surprise me, Ellis."

I kiss his leg as I work him open, trailing my lips downwards. My shoulder nudges his leg further to the side, and he lets out one gust of air after another as I feather my lips up the underside of his cock.

"El," he gasps, moaning long and low as I suck him into my mouth. "You gotta stop, or I'm going to come."

I hum, sucking harder, but he traps my head between his legs.

"Stop," he says around a laugh.

I do, easing back. Lucky's gaze turns serious as I look down at him. I rub some lube onto my cock before tugging him to the edge of the table. He wraps his legs around me, heels resting at the top of my ass, and his breath saws out of him in little bursts as our eyes lock.

"Ready?" he nearly whispers.

I nod, even as every fiber of my being is vibrating again, atoms buzzing underneath my skin as if I'm waiting. As if I know Lucky is almost home.

He gives me a nod, and I hold him steady. Hold *myself* steady as I press forward. His body yields around me, hugging me tight as I inch inside him. He encourages me on, saying he's good, that it's good, that *yes, El, that's good, keep going.*

When my hips meet his ass, I stall, my heartbeat going haywire, my lungs pulling and expelling air through my nose. I can hardly think, can barely form coherent thought apart from how *right* this is. How, for the first time, I'm finally, *finally*, close enough. I'm connected to Lucky and him to me, and God, *God*, if I could just stay this way forever.

"Okay?" Lucky asks, his hands on my face, mine holding tight to his hips.

I nod, our noses brushing. *Okay. So okay.*

"Okay," he repeats, fingers tracing over my cheeks and bottom lip. "Show me, El."

I nod again, finding his lips. The sound he makes against my mouth wraps around my heart and tugs. And when I finally move inside him, that moan breaks, shattering apart like glass, both delicate and beautiful.

Powerless against his pull—*always, still*—I show Lucky exactly how I feel.

Chapter 28

LUCKY

This table is the perfect height.

It's an errant thought, but one I latch onto, because otherwise I might float away.

Ellis's dick is big. The whole *guy* is big; let's be honest. I've never quite felt anything like it, but *God*, was I ready. I was so ready for him. It feels like I've been waiting a lifetime. A decade, at the very least, ever since I was a teenager who figured out exactly how not-quite-friendly my feelings were for my friend.

My friend. My...something so much more.

Ellis stretched me enough, so there's no pain. No discomfort. But there's a big something taking up residence inside my body, like a tidal wave rushing steadily toward shore. It's alarming, the gravity of what I'm feeling. How much *more* this is than any other fuck I've had.

Because it's not just a fuck.

It's not.

Ellis stares down at me as he moves, his focus absolute. There's a small bead of sweat on his forehead, dampening a strand of his hair, and his eyes are endless and brown. Beyond him are the fireflies, like little sentinels shining down their light. It's beautiful, all of it. Ellis. The twinkling lights above him. Even the smooth wooden table under my ass. It's like a rustic dream, cast from a fairy tale.

I realize I'm focusing on every single thing apart from what Ellis is doing to me, but that's because if I do—if I think about what his cock feels like, if I think about the way his hips are slapping my ass and how his fingertips are digging into me as if he can't bear not holding on as tight as humanly possible—I might shatter. I might just blow apart into a million tiny fragments, and I'm not ready. I'm not ready for this to end.

"Luck," Ellis croaks.

"Yeah," I breathe out, dragging my fingers through the hair at the sides of his head. His ass cheeks flex under my heels, and he leans forward, dropping a hand near my shoulder. Every time he slams into me, I jump an inch up the table, but he pulls me right back down.

"Am I..." he says, his chest heaving as he stares at my face. "Is... Okay?"

Oh God.

"You're perfect," I tell him honestly. "So good. I—*ahh*. You feel so good, baby. *Fuck*. I'm just trying not to come."

His face flashes in confusion.

"Not ready," I explain. "Not—*God*. Kiss me."

He slows, scooping his hands beneath my shoulders. He lifts my entire upper body off the workbench, hands dragging up my back to my neck, arms holding me steady as our bodies press together and his fingers thread into my hair.

I nearly go off right then.

I feel drugged as Ellis drops his head, fitting our lips together. I cling to him, my heart racing so fast I can hear it in my ears. He doesn't move for a few endless moments, his cock stilled inside my body, allowing me the chance to come down.

"Eighteen," he says, pressing his forehead to mine.

"What?"

"I was eighteen..." There's a pause, and Ellis's fingers curl lazily against my scalp. "The first time I thought...about this."

"Fucking me?" I ask quietly.

He nods, nose brushing mine before he nudges at my cheek. His hands slip down my body, leaving my hair and roaming over my back, down to the swell of my ass. I hang on to him tighter.

"Why didn't you tell me?" I ask, drifting my fingers along his skin.

He shakes his head slightly. "Didn't understand it. Was...scared."

I get that last part.

"I asked you once, though," I recall. "Later, I asked if you were attracted to guys, and you said no."

His head lifts, eyes meeting mine. "Wasn't guys."

My breath catches all over again. "Only me."

He nods, shifting, causing his cock to drag ever so slightly against my rim.

"Luck," he rasps.

"Yeah," I answer, gripping him tight. "Move, El."

He drops his head to my shoulder, tugging my hips until my ass is nearly off the table. I don't for a second worry about falling. Not when Ellis is holding me. His lips find my skin, and slowly, he starts fucking me, his hands moving to my shoulder blades and anchoring. My head falls back as he sucks at my neck, sensation bursting to life in my cock and balls and at every point in which we're connected. I'm not going to last, but I don't think Ellis is, either. Not with the way he's rutting into me now, his careful handling abandoned as he loses his composure.

If I could, I'd make this moment stretch until the end of time. I'd feel the way Ellis's muscles bunch beneath my fingers. Feel the press of his lips against my pulse. I'd feel the way he's burrowing inside of me, making a home for himself there. I'd feel every spark and cascade of pleasure as the length of him drags into me again and again. His damp hair against my cheek. The sound of his pants and grunts and whimpered moans. His fingers digging into my skin and his stomach contracting against my cock.

"El, I'm—"

He drops me carefully down to the table, one hand on my hip as the other circles my dick. My ass is hanging off the edge of the wood, but Ellis has me. And as he jerks me off, fist twisting on the upstroke, I detonate.

The world whites as I come, a blinding flash. I grip the edge of the table, fingertips digging into the wood and back arching as Ellis's cock rubs against me just right. I lose my breath, my entire core drawn tight, my dick pulsing and heart pounding, and I can *feel* it. I can feel the force of Ellis's affection as he drops down over me, body cocooning mine, lips finding mine as he starts to come. I can feel the wash of his release inside my body, feel the near anguish of his groan, can feel the relief in it and the joy and all the words he's never said being pressed against my mouth. I can feel it, and I wrap myself around him, holding tight as my body pings with aftershocks, as Ellis stills, his muscles relaxing beneath my touch.

His lips don't leave mine. We share air as our chests heave against one another, as Ellis's cock jerks once more inside my body. I moan against him, a small sound, everything in me sensitized yet floating at once.

Neither of us speaks for the longest time. Neither of us has to.

When Ellis finally pulls back, his eyes catch mine. For just a moment, I can see the boy he used to be inside the man he is now. I can see the way he used to look at me—the way he still does. It's not lust or even attraction that fuels that familiar expression. It's...understanding. Comfort. A want that runs deep. It's companionship.

Love.

I skate my fingers over his brow, his cheekbones, his red lips. I take in the stubble and the slope of his nose and the notes of honey in his eyes. I see all the facets of the person who stepped into my life fifteen years ago and who—unintentionally—made me fall in love. And it hits me. This is my best friend. The person I know most in this world. And he isn't going away. *This* isn't going away. Not ever.

I knew that; deep down, I did. But I was still scared. Terrified, even, about what this sort of change meant for me and Ellis.

I'm not scared anymore.

Ellis doesn't pull out of my body, and his cock is still at least half-hard.

"Okay?" I ask, even though I know the answer.

He nods.

"Gonna stay put?"

He nods again.

I huff a laugh, stretching out my back. "I'm falling off the table."

I'm not really, but the corner is starting to dig into my ass. Ellis shifts, lifting my hips as he slides me up the table. He steps forward at the same time, and my eyes slip shut as his cock moves inside my body.

"Fuck, El," I groan.

When I open my eyes, his gaze is locked on mine, and my heart stutters.

"You're mine now," I whisper. "I hope you know that."

He leans down, elbows on the table. His hips are still pressed to my ass, and my legs are still around his body. He catches my lips with his own, kissing me once, twice.

"Always yours," he says.

And as the fireflies twinkle above, our mouths dance.

Chapter 29

ELLIS

"Are you kidnapping me?" Lucky asks lightly.

I glance over at him in the passenger seat before refocusing on the road. *Maybe.*

He laughs, and I crack a smile. I hustled Lucky out of bed early this morning so we could get on the road. Where we're going is a good four hours away at the southeast edge of the state. Hopefully, the drive will be worth it.

Lucky sits nestled low in his seat, a warm jacket on and a thermos of coffee between his hands. He sips it every once in a while, content to look out the window and hum along to the radio. I keep my attention on the road, but I can't help but sneak the occasional glance his way. He looks happy, the lines of his face relaxed. There's a smile on his lips that's been there ever since he arrived home last night. And, no matter how hard I try, I can't scrub the mental image of him naked and lying on my workbench from my mind.

Don't even want to.

Lucky's smile grows when he catches my eye, but he doesn't ask me what I'm staring at. I think he's well aware.

When we get to Indian Cave State Park, Lucky perks up in his seat. "We've never been here," he says.

I know.

Lucky hustles out the door the moment the truck is in park. He grabs one of the two backpacks I packed before we left, strapping it on. His grin is wide as he tugs the hood of his jacket up over his head.

"What are we waiting for?" he asks.

I huff a laugh, grabbing the second pack.

We hike for a good couple miles in companionable semi-silence. Lucky takes the lead, following the trail markers and pointing out the occasional animal or landmark. The foliage is beautiful this time of year, the leaves on the trees various shades of red, copper, and burnished gold. There's a definite nip in the air, but it makes for perfect hiking conditions. We stop for a while near the Missouri River, scaring a deer off that was foraging beneath the trees.

"I assume we have lunch in here?" Lucky asks, swinging his pack to the ground. He makes a satisfied sound when he spots the sandwiches I packed. "Roast beef. It's like you know it's my favorite."

I snort, and we sit side by side on the edge of the trail, looking down at the river as we eat.

"Do you like farming, El?" Lucky asks me out of the blue.

I consider the question as I chew my food. Finally, I nod. It may not have been my idea of a dream job when I was younger, but I enjoy my days. I like working the land. "It's...comfortable," I tell him.

He hums at that, looking lost in thought. "You know, I was looking into glass art a bit. You could probably sell your pieces for more online or in a bigger city. They're really good, El."

My chest warms at his compliment, but I shake my head. "Don't need that."

"Even if it meant you could focus solely on glassblowing?" he asks.

I zip the baggie from my sandwich closed now that it's empty and set it aside. Maybe I could earn more from the pieces I make, but it was never about money for me. And I'm not sure how to explain to Lucky that I don't want to turn what was born out of passion for *him* into business. I don't want glass to become about profits and paying bills. I want it to be from my heart. Not my head.

"Farming is stable," I finally say. "That's good enough...for me."

Lucky doesn't push it. He knocks his shoulder into mine, letting out a contented sigh as he looks out over the river and all the natural beauty here in the park. I find my eyes, more often than not, straying to him.

Before we get moving again, the pair of us stop to relieve our bladders. I can hear Lucky snickering as we stand behind our respective trees deep under the forest's cover. I shush him without ire, but he only laughs harder.

When we reemerge onto the trail, I shake my head. *It's like you want us to get caught.*

Lucky only grins. "Come on. Let's go see the caves."

Indian Cave is accessible by boardwalk. A few other visitors are there when we arrive midafternoon. Lucky pulls out his camera to take pictures of the petroglyphs carved into the surface of the sandy-brown cave walls. There's history here.

You can practically feel it in the earth and the air, like an imprint left from those who came before us.

I can't help but wonder what imprints we might leave behind. Me. Lucky. *Us.*

There's a soft smile on Lucky's face when he looks my way. He cocks his head slightly, voice quiet when he speaks. "What are you thinking about, El?"

I clear my throat before answering. "Us."

"Yeah?" Lucky asks, letting his camera hang loose around his neck as he steps close. A small group walks past us down the boardwalk, but once they're gone, Lucky says in a low voice, "Us last night?"

My body flushes at the reminder, even as I shake my head. "Us tomorrow," I tell him truthfully. "And...the next day. And the next."

His breath leaves him in a rush as he looks up into my face, his eyes so light, it feels as if I can see right through them. "What do you see for us, El?"

How do I tell him I see everything? In my most vivid waking dreams, I see everything he'll give me. A life with him, in whatever form that might take. Years of loving him because I know I'll do that no matter what. I see snippets of days just like this one, where we hike or share meals or simply enjoy one another's company. I see *him*. Always him.

"Happiness," I answer.

And that, Lucky doesn't argue. He takes my hand, holding it tightly as we walk back down the boardwalk. It's early evening when we arrive at the park's entry point, having taken another scenic hiking route through the hardwood forests to get there. Despite the fact that we'll need to grab dinner soon, I tug Lucky in the opposite direction of the truck.

"Where are you taking me now?" he asks, an amused smile on his face.

You'll see.

He plants his feet when we arrive in front of the hayride station. "El," he says, looking around at the families and kids waiting in line. "We're not doing a hayride."

Yes.

"Does that say 'haunted?'" he asks, squinting at the sign. "What are we, ten?"

I pull out two tickets. "Already...paid for."

He groans lowly, looking skyward for a moment as if asking for patience, but then he steps with me to the back of the line. "This is worse than the corn maze," he mutters under his breath.

I can't help but grin.

Lucky is determined to keep a scowl on his face as we board the haunted hayride, but it's a poor scowl at best. The corners of his mouth keep lifting, and his hand tangles with mine, fingers softly brushing my own.

"This is so cheesy," he whispers to me halfway through when a ghoul jumps out from behind a tree, causing a few of the kids to scream.

I squeeze his hand.

"Thank you," he adds, head on my shoulder.

My lips curve into a smile.

When we leave the park, it's dark out. We grab dinner to go, eating in the truck as I drive. It's just after midnight when I pull into the driveway, and Lucky follows me inside my house without a word. I can see the lines of exhaustion on his face as we take a quick shower together, making sure to keep quiet so we don't wake my mom. There are no wandering hands this time or steam-filled orgasms. Just washing and a few heated looks.

Lucky is the first to climb under the covers, dressed in long sleep pants but no shirt. He sighs, a happy sort of sound, his wet hair spread behind him on the pillow. I join him a moment later.

"You work this week," he says, not a question.

Still, I nod.

His fingers play with mine. "I think I'll spend some time with my mom while I'm here. I might even see if your mom wants to go to that vintage market a few towns over."

"She'd like that," I tell him.

"Me, too," he says. "You never know what sort of things you'll find in places like that. It's like a treasure hunt. I'll need to edit my pictures from Greenland at some point in the next few days, too, but that won't take long."

I brush an errant piece of hair behind his ear.

"I still need to show you those pictures," he says, sounding sleepy.

I nod against my pillow.

"I like this, El," Lucky whispers. "I like being here. With you. I like *us*."

Yeah.

"Sometimes, I think back, and it's like...why weren't we doing this the whole time? At least, once we were old enough," he adds quickly.

I nod again, knowing what he meant.

"But then, I think about what we *did* have, and I wouldn't change a thing. I'm so glad you're my best friend, El. Even if it took us a few extra trips to get to where we are now, I'm so glad it was you. Is you. Will be *you*."

"Always," I whisper.

He stutters a breath, scooting closer. His leg slides between my own, waking up my cock, and the little uptick of his lips tells me he knows it. Still, he doesn't press for more. Not right now.

"Luck," I say slowly.

"What is it?" he asks, hand trailing through the hair at the side of my head.

I close my eyes, the sensation soothing, even as his fingertips light a small blaze. "Would you ever...fuck me?"

"Do you want that?" he asks, the movement of his fingers never stalling.

I open my eyes. I think I do. "Want everything...with you."

"Then yeah, El," he answers easily. "We'll do that. Anything you want. Everything you want."

"There's...a lot," I tell him.

His smile is a little wicked. "We have time. Don't we?"

Yeah. We do.

"Kiss me?" he asks.

Always.

His lips are smooth when they meet mine. He tastes of mint and smells of oranges, and the fact that he'll be here for longer than a couple days makes it easy to sink into the kiss without the frantic urgency I felt the last time he was here. Having him back, getting this glimpse of what the two of us can be, settles me down to my core. It's the knowledge that Lucky is in this with me. That I'm not alone in my feelings anymore. That, even though it's impossible to know the future, I do know Lucky will be in mine.

The memory of us will be left in the pictures we take, the glass we repurpose. It will be in the wind and the floorboards and the walls of the silo. We'll leave our mark on this world, and we'll do it together because we've always been tied. Lucky came into my life at ten, but he's not leaving.

And when I think of it like that, I realize there's nothing to fear when it comes to us. Adventure can call. Time can, too. But neither will take Lucky from me.

He's already written himself into my heart.

Chapter 30

LUCKY

I find Ellis in the silo when I return from dinner with my parents. It's my last day in Nebraska during this stop, and even though I'm glad I had time to catch up with my folks over the past week and a half, I want to spend my remaining evening with Ellis.

And only Ellis.

There's a pinch in my gut when I think about going back to New York. To my empty apartment and empty bed. But I push it away for now and focus on the man in front of me.

Unsurprisingly, Ellis is shaping glass, still in his worn jeans and navy shirt from work. His body glows in the light from the brick oven, conjuring up the mental image of blacksmiths and knights. I could see Ellis as either. He's always been strong, inside and out. Honorable. Dependable.

The muscles beneath his shirt bunch as he rolls the glass on the metal table beside the kiln. It's such delicate work, yet the man himself is anything but. He's solid and sexy, his movements sure.

With so much force it leaves me nearly breathless, I have the sudden, overwhelming urge to capture Ellis just like this—in his element, looking so confident and serene.

Before he can spot me, I turn around and jog out the way I came. When I step into the silo for a second time, Ellis notices my arrival.

I hold up my camera bag. "Can I take your picture?"

His head tilts, but he nods before going back to his work.

I remove the camera from its case, attaching the proper lens before slipping the strap around my neck. Ellis doesn't seem remotely concerned by my presence as I start snapping pictures. His eyes meet mine once, but then he continues his craft, rolling the hot, melted glass and blowing into the end of the rod. His hands are deft as he works, his focus steady.

I make sure to stay out of his way, but the heat from the oven has me sweating quickly. Ellis is faring no better. His hair is damp, dark strands curling, and the sheen above the collar of his shirt draws my eye more than once.

When Ellis is done, he taps the creation off the rod onto the table. It's a small, rounded robin. An ornament, if I had to guess.

"It's lovely, El."

He grunts his thanks, storing his tools and making quick work of putting out the flames. My pulse is firing by the time he's done, and he stalls, looking at me in question.

"Could I photograph you nude?" I ask.

He blinks at me once, twice, before nodding. I swear my heart misses a beat.

"No one will see the pictures but me," I assure him.

"Trust you, Luck."

I blow out a steadying breath. "Take off your shirt."

He does as I request, tugging the slightly damp material off over his head. He lets it fall to the surface of the wood table, watching me, waiting.

I step toward him slowly before coming to a stop a foot and a half away. I bend down a little, finding the angle that makes him look like a ruggedly ethereal god, lit in the soft glow from overhead and flanked by colored glass I blur with my lens. His skin looks golden, dark hair covering his chest and trailing down the middle of his stomach.

I circle him, taking a few more pictures before I have him sit on the ground, legs bent, knees apart. I crouch between them, heart pounding. My finger flies on the shutter release.

"Pants," I tell him next.

Ellis obliges, standing up to rid himself of his dusty jeans. He removes his boots and socks, too, leaving him standing in nothing but black underwear. His cock, although soft, presses against the front of the fabric in a way that has my mouth pooling with saliva. I move Ellis back until he's leaned against the table, his hands bracing the wood behind him and accentuating the muscles in his arms, and then I step away, bringing the camera up in front of my face.

"You're gorgeous, Ellis."

He doesn't say anything as I continue to photograph him, and I can only hope he believes me. That he knows how much I want him, *all* of him.

"Underwear," I tell him, stepping further back.

Ellis slips his boxer briefs down his legs, his cock hanging heavily between his thighs and swaying as he lifts his feet to remove the fabric. He sets it with the rest of his clothes, completely unabashed in his nudity. His legs are thick and dusted in hair, like his chest and arms. His ass is round and so damn bitable I have to chew on my lip to temper the urge. His cock is nestled in dark curls, and every single inch of him, from his beautiful brown eyes to his trimmed toenails, is perfection in my eyes.

I store this memory—just like the Aurora Borealis and the parrotfish in the Caribbean Sea—in a place I can always return to. But I know, no matter how many pictures I take of the man before me, nothing will ever compare to standing in his presence.

"Turn around," I request, my voice hushed. Hoarse.

He does, giving me his back and planting his elbows on the workbench. He bends one knee slightly, putting his ass and the strong, broad lines of his back on display. He's pure art, and I take a dozen pictures before abandoning my camera for the man himself.

"El."

He turns, and I reach for him, my hands curling behind his neck. I tug him down to me, catching his lips, whimpering into the kiss as I find myself hauled against the hot length of his body. My hands travel downwards, over shoulders, down arms, around to the tight swell of his ass. I moan as Ellis's cock thickens against my hip.

"Want you," I whisper.

His fingers tighten in my hair.

Ellis doesn't object as I spend a good, long minute at his mouth, our lips inhaling, tongues playing. He doesn't object when I break the kiss, either, lowering myself slowly in front of him. His fingers stay threaded in the strands of my hair, and his eyes remain locked on my own as my knees hit dirt. His dick brushes my cheek, and I turn my face, kissing the side of it.

"Do you remember when we were twenty-three?" I say, hands running up his thighs. "I came to visit on Thanksgiving. We were all at my parents', getting ready for pumpkin pie."

He nods, throat convulsing around his swallow as I run my lips up and down the length of his cock. I mouth the base of it before sitting back and pumping him once.

"You were helping with the whipped cream, but the bowl tipped off the counter, making a mess of your clothes."

He doesn't say a word as I run my tongue up his shaft, one hand holding him in place, my other anchored at his hip.

"You went back home to change, but it was taking a while, so I came looking for you."

His brow furrows slightly, and I huff a laugh, my breath ghosting over his crown.

"Yeah, you didn't know that," I say. "Because I found you, your door cracked open, you inside, completely naked, and I froze. I didn't mean to catch you that way."

He shakes his head, eyes hooded. He doesn't care; that much is obvious.

"Still," I go on. "I felt terrible, and I hoofed it back to my parents'. I couldn't get the image of you out of my head, though. Not for a very long time. Not at all, really. There's a million images of you, Ellis, all in my mind. Images of you naked." I lick the head of his cock slowly. "Images of you smiling." I suck him into my mouth, stroking him with my tongue. "Images of you by my side, in so many different places. I have more pictures of you in my head than anything or anyone else."

His fingers sift through my hair, hands cradling my head. His eyes are soft, his cock wet from my spit as it sits against my lower lip.

"I want more," I whisper. "I want so many more pictures, El."

"All yours," he says.

I take him into my mouth then, sucking him down, savoring every pant and quiet groan that leaves his lips. I worship him the way I promised myself I would, taking time to kiss his hips and thighs and belly button. I pull his balls into my mouth, rub a finger along his taint. I play with his hole, even, my own cock throbbing when Ellis wordlessly spreads his legs wider.

When he comes, it's with his dick in my mouth and my finger up his ass. He shoots down my throat with a hoarse cry, his body fluttering around my index finger. I wring out every last gasp and moan I can before pulling back and letting Ellis return the favor.

When we fall into bed later that night and my thoughts shift to New York, leaving an uneasy pressure in my head and heart, I know what I need to do.

The morning comes swiftly. I pad quietly from Ellis's room, leaving the man himself asleep in bed while I start a pot of coffee. As it spits and sizzles, perfuming the air with the smell of bitter roast, I glance out the back window. The sky is light but hazy, early dawn having just arrived. The grass looks damp, silence hanging in the air as the world starts to wake.

When my coffee is ready, I fill a mug and head out onto the deck, grateful for the sweatshirt I pulled on. My feet, however, are bare, so I tuck them up on my chair, drawing the hem of my sweatshirt down under my toes.

I'm not usually such an early riser, but my mind woke me at first light, tumbling around and around, even as I tried fruitlessly to fall back asleep against Ellis's warm, inviting chest.

I spin my phone on the table in front of me, my mug of coffee keeping my other hand warm. I contemplate calling Danil first, but he'd probably kill me if I woke him up this early. Besides, I know he'll support my decision.

For a beat, I wonder what my parents will think. Will they be happy to have me around more often? It's a stupid question. Of course they'll be happy. They never tried to stop me from moving away, but I know they like having me close, too. And they've been nothing but supportive of my relationship with Ellis.

Which just leaves one hurdle.

I finish my coffee before picking up my phone. A chickadee sings as I wait for my boss's secretary to answer. Chelsea won't be in the office quite yet, but I know Beth will be, seeing as it's just past eight in New York. She answers quickly with her standard, overly cheery greeting.

"Morning, Beth," I reply. "It's Lucky Buchanan."

"Oh, Lucky," she says, a more natural warmth bleeding into her tone. "I'm not used to hearing from you so early in the morning. Everything all right?"

"Yeah, of course," I answer, nose twitching as a beam of sunlight drifts through the clouds. I fight the urge to sneeze. "I was just wondering if I could set up an appointment with Chelsea?"

"Of course. Is it urgent?"

"No, not at all. In fact, it can wait until I'm back in New York."

"Sure thing, sweetie," Beth says, typing on her keyboard. "What should I tell her you want to meet about?"

I close my eyes briefly, hearing the gentle repetition of the chickadee nearby. A vehicle passes on the road, a quiet hum compared to the bustle of the city. And if I inhale deeply enough, I can smell the byproduct of the fall corn harvest, like sweet dust and dirt and a hint of earthy, decaying husk.

When I open my eyes, there's a smile on my face. I never thought I'd come to love the damn smell of corn.

"Relocation," I tell Beth, my heart and soul settling as my thoughts turn to Ellis. "I'd like to move home."

Part IV: Blue Moon

Chapter 31

ELLIS

Winter is my least favorite season in Nebraska. Not because of the cold, but because it's idle. Huskers still have plenty to do, even after the harvest: machine maintenance, planning for a new season, ordering equipment and fertilizer, and a slew of other tasks. But I spend the majority of my time in the warehouse building, instead of outside, and after a while, it gets stifling.

I used to take more lunch breaks with my mom during this time of year. But now that she's retired, I've been eating with Gabby. And instead of me traveling to the office next door where she works, more often than not, Gabby meets me here, insisting she likes the change of scenery.

"I think I want to try crochet," Gabby is saying, her chicken salad on the table in front of her. "It seems easier than knitting. Maybe? I don't know."

I shake my head. I've never tried either.

"My gran used to knit," she goes on, "but she can't work the needles anymore."

I give Gabby's arm a squeeze, and she smiles.

"Thanks, Ellis. Would you want to learn with me?"

I pause, fork hovering near my mouth. *Learn to crochet?*

She rolls her eyes. "Yes, crochet. What else would I be talking about?"

Chewing my pasta, I shrug.

Gabby beams. "Great! I'll bring some supplies next week."

I nod, noticing Riley's head turn away when my gaze shifts his direction. The break room is full today, conversation steady like the buzz of cicadas. Not many people wanted to brave it outdoors after our first big snowfall of the year.

Lucky is in Costa Rica right now, where it's sunny and warm. It's going to be a shock to his system when he flies in later tonight. I'd feel bad about it, except I'm too excited to see him. The distance hasn't been as hard as I expected these past couple months. Maybe because we talk almost daily. Maybe because, when we don't, I have the memory of his lips to keep me company. He hasn't been able to fly in as frequently as either of us hoped, but his stays have been full of bundled-up picnics in the back of my truck, evenings with Lucky tucked in my arms and in my bed, and plenty of memorable visits to the silo. And when he goes, knowing he'll keep coming home to me is enough to keep me warm at night.

The calls where Lucky encourages me to wrap a fist around myself while he whispers in my ear about what we've done together—or what he'd *like* to do—don't hurt either.

"Ellis?" Gabby says, giving me a smile. Her lunch is gone now, containers cleaned up. "You were in your head for a minute there. Break is over. I need to get back to the office."

I give Gabby a nod, and she stands.

"See you later. Don't forget—crochet," she reminds me.

Joy.

She snorts lightly, and I can't help but wonder if she was able to read the sarcasm in my expression.

"Have a good weekend," she adds, giving me a wink. She knows Lucky is coming.

I finish my lunch quickly before cleaning up. The break room is nearly empty now, most everyone having gone back to work. Strands of multicolored lights glow weakly along the corners of the room, and a fake snow-dusted Santa waves from the countertop. Christmas is almost here.

I'm just stepping out of the break room when my phone rings. Seeing Lucky's name on the display has my heart beating fast in no time.

I answer quickly, moving to the side of the hall.

"Hey, El," Lucky says, voice nearly a whisper. "Slight change of plans."

My gut sinks.

"I have to make a detour to the New York office," he says, confirming my suspicions. "But I'll see you really soon, I promise. Just don't go to the airport today, okay? I'll explain more as soon as I can."

I nod, unable to get my voice to work. I thought he'd be here for the holidays.

"El?" he asks gently. When I don't speak, he sighs. "It'll be okay. This is good, I promise. Just...wait for me?"

Always.

He makes a soft sound, and for a moment, I think he's going to say something else. But then he goes on in a rush. "I have to get on the plane. I'll be home soon." A pause. "Bye, El."

I clear my throat, the best I can do. After a beat, Lucky hangs up.

I let my hand hang at my side. Someone down the hall opens the door from outside, crossing the threshold in a flurry of cold air and snow. My body rolls in a shiver, no longer quite so warm.

After work, I stop by the convenience store, dropping off my newest piece to Melody. It's the Northern Lights, or at least as close as I could get to recreating them. It took me a long time to get the piece right, and I had to scrap a few attempts that didn't pan out. In the end, I made a polar bear out of mostly clear glass. Streaks of green and pink and golden-yellow flow from one shoulder, along the bear's middle, and down to its tail. Inside, I blew a dusting of glitter.

Melody is ecstatic about the piece. She says it's my best one yet. I give her a smile, but my insides are still aching.

On Saturday, I don't hear from Lucky.

On Sunday, there's a knock at the door.

"I don't understand," my mom says. "He was sick?"

"Yes, ma'am," our guest replies, holding a folder in his hands. He's seated on the couch, crisp suit in place, although the hems of his pants are stained wet from the snow. "He had stage four pancreatic cancer. There wasn't much the doctors could do, I'm afraid."

My mom glances my way, the sadness in her eyes evident. She looks more sad for *me*, though. I'm not sure how I can tell, other than the pain rests along the outsides of her eyes, not within them.

She clears her throat. "And you're here to give us the news?"

The man nods. "That, as well as inform you Mr. William Cole left the entirety of his estate to his son, Ellis William Cole."

There's a long silence.

"Pardon?" my mom asks.

The man nods again, opening his folder. "In his last will and testament, Mr. Cole instructed his assets, including those gained from the sale of his house, were to go to Ellis. It's all here." He passes a sheet of paper over to my mom, who holds it with her usual shaking hand.

Her eyes meet mine again. "Ellis," she says quietly.

I shake my head. I don't need to see it.

My mom sets the paper down. "There was no one else?" she asks.

The man frowns sympathetically. "No. He seemed..." He pauses before saying, "He seemed to live a solitary life. His body will rest here at his family's plot. The service will be held on Tuesday."

My mom nods, looking lost in thought. "Thank you, Mr..."

"Bradley," the man fills in, taking his cue and standing. He holds out his palm, shaking my mother's hand and then coming over to shake my own. "My condolences." He passes me a card. "My information if you have questions."

I nod, and Mr. Bradley steps toward the door. I follow, seeing him out. The black Mercedes that rolls down our driveway through the snow looks out of place.

"Ellis?" my mom says. "Are you okay?"

I close the door, turning her way. I drop the business card on the coffee table before shrugging.

"He...emailed me," I say.

My mom's face scrunches in confusion. "When?"

I think back. "Months ago."

"What did he say?"

"Wanted to talk." I shake my head a little. "Told him no."

"Oh, baby," my mom says, leaning forward in her chair like she wants to come to me. I make it easier, walking her way. She grabs my hand, squeezing tight. "It's not your fault, you know. I probably would have told him the same thing. You didn't know he was..."

Her sentence peters out. *Dying*, she was going to say. He was dying, and I ignored him.

Even still, I nod. I don't feel guilty about it, not exactly. I'm not sure what I feel. A little angry. Because he left us. He left us, and he didn't look back until he was dying with no one else to turn to. Angry because he put me in his will, as if he had a right to. As if he could still call himself my father. Angry that he died, even, through no fault of his own.

And sad. There's a part of me that's sad for the boy I used to be. The one whose dad called it quits. Who up and left as if it were easy. I'm sad for the kid who never got to show his dad the glass he'd collected. Who never got to share about his prom night.

He left, he gave us up, and now he's *gone*. And what for? In the end, he'll be put to ground right back where he started. In the end, he left all he'd gained to a boy he no longer knew. There was no one else. And maybe I'm sad for that, too. Did he ever find what he was searching for? Does he regret it?

I'll never know.

"Honey..." my mom says.

I shake my head quickly, swiping below my eye. "Okay?" I ask her.

She nods slowly. "I am. I said my goodbyes to your father a long time ago. But it's okay to grieve him, Ellis. You don't have to like or even love him for that."

Am I grieving him? Is that what this is? I don't have an answer, so I say nothing at all.

I miss Lucky.

Fear lances through me at the thought. It's a moment. A series of flashes. It's Lucky's voice. *"I'm gonna get out of this town one day, El."* It's my friend, arms outstretched beneath a waterfall. It's his excitement each time he calls and the countless adventures he's lived.

It's the memory of a firefly encased in glass, lifeless and dull.

"I want my life to be...remarkable, El."

My pulse is pounding when I hear a car door shut outside. I let my mom's hand go and step up to the front window, right beside the Christmas tree that sparkles white. The relief I feel is staggering, and my breath breaks with it, stuttering against the windowpane. Lucky is outside. He's here, *here*, and it'll be okay. It'll be okay because everything is *always* okay when Lucky is around.

Except...he's beside his own car, not a rental. And he's pulling suitcase after suitcase out of the back, setting them in the half inch of snow covering the shoveled driveway.

"Who is it?" my mom asks.

I can't answer her. That relief coursing through my body turns brittle and ragged as I step into my boots and head out the front door. Lucky looks up when he sees me, a wide smile spreading across his face.

"El," he says, loud enough for me to hear.

My pulse feels heavy as I make my way toward him. Snowflakes drift lazily down through the sky, landing on my cheeks and nose, tiny stinging bites.

Lucky's expression falls a little once I'm finally in front of him. He cocks his head, brow furrowed at whatever he sees on my face.

"What?" I manage to say, looking at what appears to be all of Lucky's belongings in and beside his car.

He gives me a grin, recovering the excitement he showed up with. "I'm home, El. For good. I'm moving home."

I pull in a breath, the cold aching in my lungs. "No."

Chapter 32

LUCKY

No.

Ellis looks the exact opposite of happy, and everything in me sinks.

"No?" I repeat, not understanding the word or its meaning or why Ellis would possibly be saying it when he should be kissing me.

He shakes his head rapidly, turning around and pacing a few steps away. His hands rake through his hair, and he looks distraught.

"What the hell is going on?" I say, stepping away from my luggage.

He grunts, shaking his head again, barely meeting my eye. I reach for him, but he backs away.

"Ellis..." I say, hurt by his rebuttal.

I think I hear another "No," but then Ellis is walking away.

"Hey!" I call, jogging after him. "Talk to me. What's going on?"

He doesn't answer or slow as he walks past the front of his house, wearing only a long-sleeved shirt, jeans, and unlaced boots. His destination is clear. The silo.

I curse, looking back at my opened-up car. I pull out my phone as I jog after him, texting my dad and tripping more than once over the drifts of snow at the edge of the field. Ellis reaches the silo long before me.

My breath is coming short by the time I catch up. It fogs the air in front of me. "El."

He's pacing the interior of the silo now, the lines of his body drawn tight.

"What's going on?" I ask calmly, heading his way.

His eyes, when they cut over to me, look pained. "Why?" he croaks out.

"Why what?" I ask, trying to catch his arm. He sidesteps, and a small sound escapes my throat. I blow out a breath, letting Ellis pace away. "Why am I back for good? I thought that would be obvious."

"You didn't..." He shakes his head again, not meeting my eye. "Didn't tell me."

"I didn't want to get your hopes up," I admit. "I had to talk to my boss and get everything squared away before I could move back. We just finalized the paperwork, so here I am. I thought I'd surprise you."

The look he gives me is unimpressed.

"What the fuck, El?" I ask, trying to keep my tone even, despite the swearing and uncomfortable gut-swooping. "I thought you'd be happy."

He grunts, and I'm just...shocked. I'm shocked.

"You don't want me here?" I ask, almost in disbelief.

He shakes his head, and *oh fuck*. I sit on the ground, knees bent as I try to catch my breath. *Holy fuck*.

Ellis drops down in front of me, hands on my knees. His eyes are imploring me, but I don't understand.

"Why don't you want me here?" I ask, my voice shaking.

His expression crumples. "Trapped."

"You...you'd feel trapped?" I whisper.

He shakes his head quickly, eyes going everywhere as the silence stretches painfully. His fingers dig into my knees. "Y-you," he finally says.

"Me?"

He nods, but I'm not getting it.

"I want to be here, El. With you."

He makes a frustrated sound before getting to his feet. His pacing resumes. "Like...my dad," he says, the words coming slow. "Leave."

My gut bottoms out, a bone-deep chill blanketing me that has nothing to do with the cold. "You think I'd leave you like your dad did?" I ask. "You really think I'd do that?"

His expression tells me *yes*, he does.

My mouth opens, nothing coming out. "Ellis," I say, a bruise blooming deep in my chest. "How could you think that? How could you think I'd ever leave you?"

"Did," he says, stopping as soon as the word leaves his mouth. His breath perfumes the air in front of him as he turns his head, regret in his eyes as they meet mine.

"Yeah," I say, clearing my throat and pushing myself to my feet. "Ow."

He takes a step forward but stops, the battle in him evident.

"You told me to go," I point out.

He doesn't refute it.

"You practically shoved me out the door."

Again, no defense.

"I would have stayed for you, Ellis! If you'd ever asked, I would have stayed."

He blinks at me, sadness in his expression as he watches the tears run down my face. He takes a big breath before speaking. "Couldn't...have let you."

I look away for a moment, working my jaw. My eyes sting, and I brush my cheeks, wiping the moisture onto my pants. "*Why?* Help me understand, *please*. Why the hell don't you want me here?"

"Trapped," he repeats.

"You think I'd feel trapped?"

He nods, pointing up. I follow his gaze, but all I see are the fireflies twinkling above.

"So, you wanted me to go," I say, trying to parse through it. "And now, what? You'd just make do with me living in another state? You'd be okay with me visiting once a month if we're lucky?"

He nods, even as his face is pinched.

"Well, not me," I say roughly, breath stuttering. "I won't make do with that. I want to be *here*, with you. I want to live with you. Come home to *you*. You're telling me you don't want the same thing?"

"Only thing...I've wanted."

I throw up my hands. "Then why? Why are we even arguing about it? Why do you want me to go?"

He blows out a breath, hands on his head as he looks up, expression pained. "Not...listening."

"I'm trying," I huff out. "But you're not *saying* anything."

In the silence that falls, I pull in a harsh breath.

"I'm sorry," I say, stepping toward him, hand caught midair. "I'm *sorry*, El. I didn't mean that."

He grunts.

"No." I shake my head. "It's not fine. That was a shitty thing to say. I'm just..."

I blow out a breath and close my eyes. This isn't how I expected this day to go. I thought our reunion would be joyful. I thought Ellis would welcome me with open arms and a warm kiss, and we'd celebrate Christmas together, maybe have hot cocoa, and I'd be home. We'd be together, and I'd be home for good, and he'd be *happy* about it.

But he's not happy. And I have to figure out *why*.

"El," I say softly, opening my eyes. He's standing just a foot in front of me, looking as miserable as I feel. "Do you want...*me*?"

He nods, a short, jerky thing.

"This," I say, pointing between us. "You still want this?"

The noise he makes is a wounded yes.

"Then make me understand," I plead, stepping closer. He doesn't back away this time, and I reach out. Tentatively, he places his hand in mine, his skin warm but not warm enough. He has to be freezing without a coat on. "If you can't say it, then write it down or do whatever you need to do. But I need to know what's going on inside your head right now. Believe it or not, El, I can't read your mind."

For the first time, I get a hint of a smile, but it's a tiny thing. Frail.

"Can't ask..." he says, trailing off.

My thoughts hop backwards. "Can't ask what? You can't ask me to stay?"

He shakes his head quickly. A confirmation.

"Why not?" I press. "Because it's selfish?"

He doesn't say a word to that.

"El," I say, tugging his hand until he takes a small step forward. He's right in front of me now, body heat warm through the thin layer of his shirt. His nose is red, brown eyes sad. "I *want* you to be selfish in this. Ask me to stay. Tell me to stay."

He looks like he wants to speak. He licks his lips a few times, clearly struggling. "Can't," he finally says.

My breath whooshes out of me.

He grunts, eyes moving again, looking for answers above us. Finally, Ellis tugs his hand free. He holds his palms out, telling me to wait.

"What?" I ask, watching him head toward the door.

He stops, spins toward me, and does it again. *Wait.*

I hold my hands in the air, but as Ellis disappears around the corner, my arms flop loose at my sides. "Fuck," I mutter, looking up at the fireflies. "Do you know what's going on?"

They don't answer.

It's several minutes later when my phone pings in my pocket. I almost ignore it, but with nothing else to do and my limbs turning to icicles, I grab it. There's a text from my dad letting me know he brought my things inside, but that's not what catches my attention. It's the email from Ellis.

I click it open as my phone continues to ping, more emails coming through. This one is dated in the subject line. Written today. Just now, if I had to guess.

Luck. I've never been good with words. You know that. I don't know how to explain to you that I only want you to be free. You've always had an adventurer's spirit. You're wild and beautiful and tied to the wind. I don't want to keep you here with me. I've never wanted to be the reason you miss out on your remarkable life. I'll be happy with what we have now. If I have you, I have everything I need. You don't need to do this for me.

We were twenty-one when you asked me whether I wanted girls or guys. The answer was neither because it was always only you. No girls. No other guys. No other person has held my heart the way you do. It's been yours since the moment we met, I think. I held your heart that night in your dorm, too. I don't know if you remember that.

I never thought we'd be here, Luck. It's always been me and you, but now, it's really us. It's us, and I promised myself I would never hold you back. I break and bend old jars for you because I won't ever trap you in glass. You're my firefly, and you deserve the life you've always strived to live. You won't lose me just because you're gone. I'll always be here waiting. I just ask that you come back to me.

Keep flying back to me.

I wipe my eyes as the screen blurs. I read the email again and again. And then I look at another. There are dozens now in my inbox, all sent within minutes but dated back years. He's been writing these for *years*.

I work my way through them, my hands shaking.

Hey, Luck. When I woke up this morning, the sky was a gentle cyan that made me think of you.

Hi, Luck. You're here, did you know that? I held your hand less than ten minutes ago, hardly able to believe the flesh and bones beneath my palm were real.

Luck. Hey. I don't like this. There's a distance between us that never used to be there.

Hey, Luck. I can't help but wonder if I'm dreaming. It feels that way. Less than an hour ago, you were in my bed, so warm and soft tucked between me and the sheets.

...It was us against the world, Luck. The two of us, always. Me and you.

...In my weakest moments, I wish you'd stay.

...I'd do it again.

...I love you, my brilliant firefly.

...I was seventeen when I kissed you at Smith Falls.

...If you knew how I love you, would you understand?

...I'm scared, Luck.

...I miss you, my precious firefly.

...I love you more than anything. I love you, I love you, so please, my beautiful firefly, fly back to me soon.

It takes me a moment to realize Ellis is standing in the doorway. He's a blurry image beyond my wet eyes, wavering like a mirage.

"All this time," I say softly, wiping at my face. I shake my head, huffing what might be a laugh or maybe a cry. "Do you want to know what the most remarkable thing in my life is?"

He doesn't say a word.

"El," I rasp. "It's *you*."

Chapter 33

ELLIS

My heart pounds as Lucky strides over to me. He shoves me before grabbing my shirt in both of his fists and tugging me close. We crash together, and he blinks up at my face, his chest rising and falling, blue eyes wet.

"You beautiful man," he says, sounding frustrated but...not. "I love traveling. I love my job. But at the end of the day, all I want is to share it with *you*. You're the one I want to come home to. You're the one I miss every time I'm back in New York. You're the one who makes me happy, who makes my pulse jump like no other high."

He takes a stuttering breath, fog curling around his lips like smoke.

"El... I've had my adventures, but no matter how many, no matter where I go, they always lead me back to you. Do you know why?"

I swallow, shaking my head slowly.

"You say I'm your firefly?"

I nod. *Yes.*

"Well you're my goddamn moon, Ellis. You call, I come."

"I... I never asked for that."

"You didn't have to."

My breath puffs out in front of me, and Lucky goes up on his tiptoes, his lips inches away from mine.

"You had a secret," he says. "So do I. Ready?"

I can't move, and Lucky's eyes ping between my own. His voice, when he speaks, is quiet.

"I love you, too. I have for years. I loved you then, and I love you now, and I won't ever stop. I'm not capable of it. You're it for me, El. You're my big goddamn romance. And there's nowhere else I'd rather be than here with you."

"*Luck.*"

"So are you going to kiss me now or what?" he asks, lips twitching up at the corner. "I was expecting a welcome home. And instead, I got snow-filled boots."

He barely finishes the last word before my lips crash into his. He whimpers against me, his grip on my shirt tightening. It's relief and happiness and the bitter sting of fear. But most of all, it's coming home. His lips taste like home. And if this is what he wants, what he truly wants and not what he feels is necessary, then I'll make sure he's happy here. I'll give him a home so warm and inviting he won't ever regret staying by my side. He'll know he's loved, without fail, without limits, without end.

"Love you," I whisper against his lips.

He lets out a small, happy laugh, looping his arms around my neck. "Again."

"I love you," I tell him, pulling him up. His legs circle my waist, and I hold him to me. I hold him as tight as I dare.

"I love you, too, Ellis," he whispers against my neck. "I'm so ridiculously in love with you, you're going to get sick of hearing me say it."

I shake my head. *Never.*

"We'll see," he says, but it doesn't sound like a warning. It sounds like a promise.

Turning, I flick off the lights. The silo goes dark, but Lucky's hair shines pale gold in the glow of the moon as I walk us toward the house.

"We have to talk about where I'm staying," Lucky says. "I can move back into my old room—"

I shake my head. "With me," I say before blowing out a breath. "Stay with me."

Lucky leans back in my arms, smile wide. He understood. "Yeah, El. Always."

I nod, and within a minute, we reach the house. My mom is in the kitchen when we get inside, and I reluctantly let Lucky down. We step out of our wet boots, and Mom waves us over, one hand lifting off her walking aid.

"Peppermint tea," she says, motioning toward the counter, where two steaming mugs sit.

"Thank you, Mrs. Cole," Lucky says, accepting a mug.

"You boys must be freezing," my mom says.

Lucky huffs a laugh. "A bit."

"Well, your dad dropped off one of your bags so you'd have some dry clothes to change into. Will you be staying here?"

Lucky and I exchange a look, and I nod, encouraging him.

"If it's okay with you, Mrs. Cole," Lucky answers.

My mom waves him off before he can get another word out. "Of course it is. You're always welcome here, Lucky. I'm glad you're home."

Lucky smiles at me over the rim of his mug.

"I'll be reading in bed if either of you need me," Mom says, giving us privacy as she leaves the kitchen.

"Night," I call after her.

Lucky sips his tea. "Should we get changed?"

I nod, and the two of us head to my room. Lucky's suitcase is right inside the door, and he pulls out clean clothes as I head to my dresser. I can feel his eyes on me as I change, and when I look back at him, he's paused, a shirt dangling in his hands and sleep pants slung low on his hips.

He shakes his head a little. "Ellis, do you really not know what you look like?"

I don't answer, and he steps closer, shirt still hanging at his side.

"You're broad, like a mountain. Muscular. Strong. Your presence is big, but you're so gentle and measured. There was never a time I didn't feel safe with you."

I swallow as he comes to a stop in front of me, his fingers tracing the line of my shoulder and arm. When he gets to my hand, his touch feathers away.

"You're breathtaking," he says, looking up at my face, his eyes skipping over my features. "Handsome. Sexy. You have a strong jaw and a good nose." He reaches up, and his finger runs down the latter. "You may not say a lot, but your eyes have always told me everything I needed to know."

His hand settles on my chest, palm warm over the swift beat of my heart.

"I want you all the time, El. You make my dick hard just standing there. But... More than that, I want *you*. Do you understand?"

I nod. I do. Because it's the same way I feel about Lucky.

"Beautiful," I tell him, cupping his cheek.

His eyes feather closed, breath leaving him on a sigh. "Yours," he adds.

Mine.

When Lucky steps back, he tugs his shirt on. We lie side by side on the bed, the room lit by the overhead light. Our heads rest close, hands linked together between us.

"Luck," I say softly.

"Mm?"

I roll over what I need to say. The news we learned right before he showed up. "My dad died."

He jolts slightly, looking at me with wide eyes. "What?"

"Cancer," I explain. "Service...is Tuesday."

He opens and closes his mouth a couple times. "I'm so sorry, El."

I shrug a little.

"Are you going to go?" he asks.

I shrug again. *I don't know.*

He rolls my hand between his own. "Would you tell me about him?"

"Nothing...to say," I reply.

He doesn't push it, and I'm grateful.

"Your job?" I ask.

Lucky nods, seemingly understanding the question. "Won't change. I was already working remotely ninety-five percent of the time. If there's a meeting or event I need to attend in New York, I will. But otherwise, my planes will leave from and return to Nebraska."

I nod, still trying to come to terms with that fact. Lucky will be *here*. With me. He'll live here, and he'll always come home.

"You okay?" he asks softly, fingers trailing over mine.

Another nod. I clear my throat. "Dani?"

"He understood," Lucky says. "I think he was a little bummed I won't be in the city with him anymore, but we'll still be partners, and we'll see each other all the time. He's happy for us." He pauses before adding, "I'm sorry I didn't tell you ahead of time. I think that was a mistake. I just... I thought it was going to be a nice surprise."

I bring his hand up to my mouth, kissing his knuckles. "Doesn't matter now. Costa Rica?"

"You want to hear more?" he asks.

"Always."

He smiles at that, hooking his leg over mine as he talks. "We spent our last day on a whale-watching vessel. There was a big group of us. Tourists, too."

"Whales?" I ask curiously.

His grin lights up his face. "Humpbacks, El. Too many to count, migrating south for the winter. A couple breached the water while we were there, and it was..." He blows out a breath, vision getting lost somewhere else. "They're *huge*. You think you know, but then you see one in person, and it's astonishing that such a large creature can exist in a world that's almost entirely separate from our own. Did you know they sing? The males sing for their mates."

I settle against the pillow as Lucky tells me about the humpback song. How the vocalizations are broken up into parts, some sections repeating the same way a refrain does. How, each season, the song can change and how, sometimes, the males sing in chorus. He tells me how a whale can sing for up to twenty-four hours straight, repeating his love song over and over again.

He also tells me that whales don't only sing in their breeding grounds. They sing while traveling, and some scientists believe it's for practice. So they can perfect their song by the time their migration is complete.

I don't know why, but that hits me. It feels like us, in a way. We had so far to travel to get where we are, but maybe each step was one needed to perfect our song. Have we? Perfected it? I think, maybe, that's a journey we'll keep traveling together.

It's a while before Lucky falls silent, his hand toying with my chest. "El?"

I hum.

"I won't leave like him."

My chest pinches. "I shouldn't...have said that."

"No," he says, shifting until our faces are aligned. "I want you to speak your mind, Ellis. Always. I did move away."

"Different." *Different than what my dad did.*

"Yes, it was," he agrees before swallowing. "But... Leaving you was the hardest thing I've ever done. I did it once, and I won't ever do it again. I missed you every day I was gone. I wondered, more often than once, if I'd made a mistake. And every time I stayed away a little longer, it felt like I was losing my breath. Like I had less oxygen in my lungs. I was starved of it without you, El. You don't make me feel trapped, okay? Never. You're the air I breathe."

"Luck..."

"I even missed the damn corn," he goes on, huffing a laugh. "Don't tell anyone I said that."

I lock my lips, and he chuckles again before sobering.

"I'm staying with you, El. Because that's where I'm meant to be."

And I don't have a single argument against that, so I don't speak a word.

Chapter 34

LUCKY

Ellis leaves early for work. I've gotten used to it the times I've been here. Most mornings, I barely wake while he's getting ready, apart from the moment he places a kiss against my forehead. I always remember that.

It's late morning when I pull myself out of bed, still a little tired after my twenty-two hour car ride the other day. My body is sore, too, but I have a feeling part of that is the residual stress from my argument with Ellis.

Dressed in sleep clothes, I head from the bedroom. Soft Christmas music filters down the hall, making me smile. That smile falls a little flat when I think about what tomorrow is, beyond Christmas Eve.

Mrs. Cole is in the living room when I pass through. "Morning, Lucky."

"Good morning."

"There's coffee in the pot," she lets me know.

I thank her and head for a cup. Mug in hand, I return to the living room, trying to figure out how to broach the topic of Mrs. Cole's ex-husband's funeral. She speaks first.

"Is everything okay between you and my son?"

"Yeah," I breathe out, cradling my mug between my palms. "We're good."

She nods. "And you're back?"

"For good," I confirm. "I'll still be traveling for work, but I already listed my apartment in New York City. Are you sure it's okay if I stay here?"

The look she gives me reminds me of my own mother. "It's more than fine, Lucky. Like I told you before, you're family, and I'm happy to have you here. If anything, I would think it might be difficult for you and Ellis to share the space with me."

I frown. "You know Ellis adores you. He wants to be here, and you've always been like a second mother to me—"

"Precisely," she says, cutting me off. "And I imagine sharing a house with a parental figure when you're an adult in a relationship might have its challenges."

"Oh," I mutter, cheeks flushing hot.

"Oh," she repeats, laughing.

I have a feeling the frequent trips Ellis and I have been taking to the silo haven't gone as unnoticed as we thought.

"I'll just put this out there, Lucky," Mrs. Cole says. "I would be fine living on my own. I know Ellis doesn't want to hear that. He has it in his head he has to take care of me. But I'm still capable of handling essentials without assistance, and I suspect I will be for some time. So if you want to nudge Ellis in the direction of moving out, I wouldn't take that personally, and, in fact, I'd encourage it. Not because I don't want you both here. And not because I wouldn't miss you. But because the two of you should feel comfortable living in your own home without having to tiptoe around. You could always visit. Daily, even, if you wanted."

I swallow, nodding. "Thank you, Mrs. Cole. I'll keep that in mind."

She looks satisfied at that. "Now, did Ellis tell you about his dad?"

I blow out a slow breath. "Yeah, he did, but not until after..."

"After whatever it was that got him all in a tizzy when you showed up?"

I huff a rueful laugh. "Yeah, that."

She nods, looking lost in thought for a moment. When her eyes meet mine, they're clear and bright. "My son is neurodivergent. You know this."

Her serious tone has me sitting straighter in my seat. "Yes. I do."

"He didn't speak until he was three years old," she tells me. "The doctors diagnosed him as autistic early on, but it wasn't until later that they expressed concerns over his selective mutism and ongoing language delays. We started bringing him to a speech pathologist when it was clear his verbal communication wasn't developing at a pace they were happy with. But you know our town. We don't have many resources here."

I nod, and she goes on.

"The speech pathologist's office was an hour away, so twice a week, every week, I would load Ellis up and bring him to his appointments. And then twice a week, every week, I'd spend an hour driving us home, wondering why my son was even quieter than normal. More withdrawn. It took me longer than I'd like to admit to realize what my son had picked up on right away from those appointments. The implication that he needed to be fixed. That something was wrong with him."

My gut twinges, and Mrs. Cole sighs, her gaze on mine.

"Can you imagine knowing the world viewed you as broken at five, six, seven years old? Because Ellis did. And I was reinforcing that notion by pushing him so hard to be *normal*. God, how I hate that word." She shakes her head. "Don't get me wrong—I'm not blaming the doctors. Every child and what they need is different. But that was the point at which I said enough. I apologized to my son, asked him what *he* wanted, and every day from that point on, I made sure he knew he didn't have to be anyone but who he was."

I swallow, my throat tight. I'm not sure why Mrs. Cole is telling me this, but I commit her words to memory, glad to have the insight into this piece of Ellis's past. Although Ellis told me he was on the spectrum shortly after we met, he's never talked much about his early childhood. I've seen the way he's treated, of course. People who look at him strangely or talk to him differently. Kids at school who made fun of him or wrote mean things in the bathroom. It never bothered Ellis—it rolled right off his back, still does—but I couldn't stand it. Didn't they see how special he was? *Is?*

"Now, Ellis's teachers weren't happy with my decision," Mrs. Cole goes on. "They felt Ellis should continue his speech therapy. But when I asked if there were issues with his grades, if he had problems with his classmates, or if he couldn't communicate his needs, they answered no every single time, and, eventually, their complaints grew quiet. What I'm getting at is my son isn't broken." Her voice is firm. "He doesn't need to be fixed. He's bright and kind and good. He's smart and creative. He's unfailingly loyal. And he's happy with who he is, which is maybe most important of all. Many people hear the word autistic, and they think of easily recognizable traits. They think of tics. Outbursts. They think of obsessions with trains. They don't see the shy kid who's fascinated with color and glass. They don't think of the girl with few friends who shows strong leadership skills. But the autism spectrum is as vast and varied as those glass jars Ellis collects. No two situations are the same, and at the end of the day, ASD or not, Ellis is his own person. He's his own unique person just like everybody else. He's not *broken*. He doesn't need to be fixed. None of us are perfect, but I love my son just as he is. And you do, too. Don't you?"

I nod sharply, pulling in a breath. "Yes," I croak.

She smiles, sitting forward in her seat. "Then that's all that matters. But I will say this, Lucky, even though you're not asking for my advice. My son spends a lot of his life inside his own head. I'm sure you know this."

I nod again. "I do."

"He doesn't always pick up on social cues the way a neurotypical person would. So don't assume, when it comes to your relationship, that he understands things the same way you do or comes to the same conclusions. You're going to need to be clear with him. Direct."

"Yeah," I say, dislodging the lump in my throat. "I'm getting that."

"Good," she says, sitting back. "Just don't take it personally if you two have a hiccup like you did last night. I've never seen him love anyone or anything more than he loves you. Trust in that. He won't ever try to hurt you. It's not in his nature."

I blink quickly and look away, needing a moment to center myself. My coffee sits untouched in my hands, and I set it down on the coffee table as soft holiday music continues to play from the kitchen. When I feel like I can finally speak again, I ask, "Have you always known? That he loved me?"

Her smile is soft. Kind. "Yes. But neither of you were ready for it, I don't think. Until now."

I wonder if she's right.

"Will you go to the funeral service?" I ask, changing topics.

She hums. "I think so. I'm not sure if Ellis will, but I won't push him. He'll process his father's death at his own speed."

"I can go with you if Ellis decides to stay," I offer.

"That's sweet, hon, but you should be with him. I already talked to your parents, and they're able to bring me if I need a ride."

"Okay."

"I do have a request, however," she says, a slight gleam in her eye.

"Yeah?"

"Help me make a batch of eggnog?"

I huff a laugh. "You got it."

The next morning, Ellis dons a suit without a word. He looks so incredibly handsome in pressed black, but I keep the thought to myself. It's not the time.

Despite Mrs. Cole no longer needing the ride, my parents accompany us to the cemetery where Mr. Cole is being laid to rest.

I asked Mrs. Cole before we left why she kept her ex-husband's name all those years ago. I've always wondered. Her answer was short and to the point.

"Cole became our family name. He might have left us, but he didn't get to take that away."

The service is short, a small graveside reading attended by less than a dozen people. Each of us sit in our finery, warm coats overtop, our breaths fogging the spaces in front of our mouths. A cardinal sits in the branch of a tree not far off, its bright red feathers contrasting sharply with the white snow all around. Ellis watches it nearly the entire time.

When we go, we stop at Maisy's Diner for a late breakfast. The mood is somber but the pancakes good.

We reconvene at the Coles', the five of us warming ourselves in the living room. Mrs. Cole puts on music again, trying, I think, to return some semblance of Christmas cheer to our group. It works, a little. Expressions become less pinched. My dad asks my mom to dance.

I follow Ellis to the bedroom to change. He's quiet. Has been all day. I don't blame him.

"How're you doing, big guy?" I ask, helping pull his suit jacket off. He lets me maneuver him out of the material before shrugging. "Can I ask a question?"

He nods, changing his pants out for jeans. I get a little caught up watching him unbutton his shirt next, slowly revealing the line of his chest and abdomen. When he glances up at me, I remember myself.

"Are you sad about it?" I ask. "Or do you not feel anything for him anymore? I'm not judging either way. He's been out of your life for a long time."

Ellis sighs, leaving his shirt unbuttoned as he sits at the edge of his bed. I join him.

"I am sad," he says, shoulders hunched over slightly as he rests his hands against the corner of the mattress. "I... I don't get why..." There's a pause. "Why he left. I wish..."

"Things could have been different?"

He shrugs. *Maybe.* "I knew him...as a child. I didn't...didn't know him as an adult." He blows out a breath, forming words.

I wait. "What I forgave then, when...when I loved him... I don't forgive now. I... There's no excuse."

"No, there isn't."

"If I...become a dad," he says, his words sending a jolt to the very heart of me, "I won't ever." His gaze meets mine solidly. "I'll always love. Always be there."

"Yeah," I breathe out, my heart skipping about wildly in my chest. "You'd make such a good dad, Ellis."

He reaches over, squeezing my hand. It feels like a *you, too.*

"Fuck," I mutter, sucking in a breath.

Ellis smiles, leaning in to press a kiss to the corner of my mouth. I pull his face around, planting our lips more firmly together.

"Just think of all the piggyback rides," I mumble against his lips. "Your kid will adore you."

His body shakes with his chuckle. "And...you?"

"They can have your shoulders," I say, swinging onto his lap. He leans back, accepting my weight easily. "So long as you let me ride your front."

He rumbles a hum, his eyes roaming over my face. I cup his cheeks, letting my fingers drift over the coarse stubble there, then down to his chest and the bumpy planes of his abdomen.

"Your mom knows we have sex in the silo," I mention.

He blinks at me, not looking overly concerned. I huff a laugh.

"She also suggested we might want to consider finding our own place to live," I say carefully.

He frowns at that, and I return my palms to his face, hastening to reassure him.

"It was just a suggestion. She knows we might appreciate the privacy. But..." I consider my words, truly not minding our current situation. Not to say I wouldn't mind having Ellis to myself from time to time, too. "But if you want to stay here, I'm fine with that. We'll make it work. Just something to think about."

He nods slowly, and I lean in again, smudging a kiss against his lips.

"Dance with me?" I ask.

He cocks his head.

"Yes, now."

I back up off his lap, holding out my hand. I'm still in my suit, and Ellis is half-dressed, but it doesn't matter. Music is floating lightly through the walls, and even though this day was mired in grief and a twisted sort of sadness, our family is here. *We're* here—me and Ellis, together. And that's not something I'll ever take for granted.

Ellis accepts my hand, standing in front of me. He's a good half-foot taller than I am, but we're a perfect fit as we come together, Ellis's hands on my lower back, mine curved behind his neck.

"Do you remember when we were sixteen?" I whisper.

A smile curls his lips.

I sigh, resting my cheek against his chest. And as snowflakes drift lazily down outside the window, I recall two blue boutonnieres Ellis and I left behind at the edge of a cornfield.

Chapter 35

ELLIS

"Ellis Cole," Lucky says cheekily, grinning over at me from the passenger seat of my truck. "Are you bringing me on a date?"

I park in front of the bar. Holiday lights are strung along the front, and the parking lot is packed. It's New Year's Eve. "Best beer...in town."

He huffs a laugh. "*Only* beer in town." Still, he hops right out of the vehicle, happy as can be. "This will be the first time people in town see us together. Are you ready for that?"

I close my door, coming around to meet Lucky. Without a word, I grab his hand, linking our fingers together.

"Guess so," he says with a smile.

Inside, the bar is busy. Stools are filled, booths are mostly occupied, and patrons are standing around pool tables, festive clothes in place. I spot Riley sitting at a table with a few other guys from our class, Brandon included. When Riley sees me and Lucky, he waves us over.

"Hey," he says, moving from his chair to the cramped booth, opening up space for us. "It's good to see you guys. Have a seat."

"Thanks," Lucky says, letting my hand go as we sit in the two chairs at the end of the table.

Brandon, I notice, looks away. I'm not sure he's forgiven me for breaking his nose, either.

"Guys, you remember Ellis and Lucky," Riley says to the table at large.

There are some murmured agreements, and Lucky and our former classmates start catching up, but my gaze gets caught across the room. It's been a while since I've been in here, and I almost forgot about the picture on the wall behind the pool tables. It's old, sepia in tone and dated back to the fifties. In it, two teams stand across from one another, a thick rope stretched taut between them. A tug-of-war competition. Pulpers versus huskers. It's an old rivalry in our town, but one that doesn't exist today.

I can't help but wonder what Lucky would have become if he'd stayed here after college. Would he have worked free-lance, trying to sell his photography? If he couldn't make ends meet, would he have followed his dad's footsteps and signed on at the paper mill, becoming a pulper himself?

It's not an alternative I like to imagine. He told me he would have stayed for me, but I couldn't have asked him to. Not then. He was just spreading his wings. I missed him while he was gone, the same as he missed me. But I'm not sure I'd change it. He was worth the wait.

"Okay?" Lucky asks me quietly, leaning close.

I give him a nod. "I'm glad...you're you."

He gives me a quizzical look. "Yeah?"

"Mm. Glad you're here...too."

His smile softens. "Me, too, big guy. Want a beer?"

I nod, and Lucky squeezes my leg.

"Be right back," he says before standing and walking off.

Noticing Riley staring off toward the entrance of the bar, I follow his gaze. Gabby gives me a wave as she shucks off the hood of her coat. Her friend says something to her, and Gabby nods, gesturing to me in a way I take to mean *give me a minute.* Riley, I notice, is still watching her.

"Gabby...has a dog," I tell him.

His gaze shifts my way, eyebrows popping up. "Yeah?"

I nod. "Ask her."

He huffs a small laugh, rubbing the back of his neck. "Thanks, Ellis."

When Gabby comes over, her cheeks are flushed from the cold, and she's wearing a big smile. "Hey! I didn't know you were going to be here."

I shrug. *I didn't either.* "Gabs, you know Riley?"

She turns his way, smile still in place. "Yeah, I think so. You work with Ellis, right?"

Riley nods, shifting over now that a couple of our tablemates are gone. "I do. Wanna sit?"

"Sure," Gabby says, sliding in next to him and removing her coat.

"So, um," Riley says. "I hear you have a dog?"

Gabby beams. "I do! Her name is Toodles. Do you like dogs?"

As Riley and Gabby chat, Gabby's friend comes over to the table, claiming Lucky's seat. I turn my head, finding him at the bar. He's passing cash to the bartender, and when he turns around with two pints in his hands, his eyes find mine. I can't look away as he walks over, and when he reaches me, I tug him onto my lap, careful not to disturb the glasses in his hands.

He huffs a laugh, settling on my thighs and passing off one of the drinks. "Getting frisky with me in public, Ellis?" he asks, his words sounding teasing.

"No seats," I defend, hand holding tight to his lower back.

His smile is crooked. "Mhm. You really don't care, do you?"

I cock my head.

"Nothing," he says, shaking his head. "I'm glad you're you, too."

With Lucky's back to the table, he can't keep up with conversation, but he doesn't seem to mind. He sips his beer, one arm around my neck, his weight settled comfortably on my lap. He sways gently, humming to the music in the bar, and I watch him and the way his eyes shift shades, almost as if in tune to his mood.

It only takes a minute before I hear, "Oh my gosh, Lucky?"

Lucky turns at Gabby's voice, a tentative smile on his face. "Yes?"

Gabby squeals. "Holy cow, hi! It feels like I know you already. Ellis just never shuts up about you. Oh, my goodness, where are my manners? I'm Gabby."

Lucky accepts Gabby's enthusiastic handshake before giving me a smirk. "You never shut up about me, huh?"

"Never," Gabby says. "How was Costa Rica?"

Lucky laughs before launching into a shortened rundown of his recent trip, and I hold on to him tight, smelling a hint of citrus as his hair tickles my nose.

It's a good hour later when most of our boothmates are at the pool tables, except for Riley and Gabby, who are chatting animatedly with one another. Lucky leans close, his lips whispering against my cheek.

"Ellis."

I hum.

"I leave for Alaska tomorrow," he says.

I nod, hands tightening on him. My beer is long gone, as is Lucky's.

"For five days," he reminds me.

Not long.

His hand settles on my chest, mouth near my ear. "I need you to fuck me before I go, El."

My cock shifts, and Lucky huffs a laugh, grinding down on me for just a second.

"Take me somewhere?" he asks.

I nod, leaning back enough to catch his eye. The blue is bright. Lucky-blue, I think I'll call it. There's no other name that's enough.

We say quick goodbyes to Gabby and Riley before leaving the bar. It's cold out. Freezing. No snow is falling at the moment, but it still covers the ground. I crank the heat in the truck before pulling out onto the road. I know this area like the back of my hand, so I drive us to an uninhabited road, pulling off into a small turnaround in front of a guardrail. There's no one else down this way.

Lucky unclips his seatbelt when I park. He crawls into the back and shoves the front passenger seat all the way forward. "Ellis."

Swallowing heavily, I get out of the truck, knowing there's no way I can crawl through like Lucky. The air nips at my skin as I round the vehicle and pull the back door open on Lucky's side. He waits as I maneuver myself onto the bench seat, and then he climbs over my lap, his head almost brushing the top of the vehicle.

"I'm going to ride you, El," he says simply. "I need to feel you while I'm gone. Sound good?"

I nod furiously as Lucky grins, and then he's kissing me. It's a spark, near-violent and ember-hot. It's all teeth and tongue and a desperate urge to be closer, and I give in to it, not wanting anything else. Lucky grinds down on my lap, his knee pressed to the door, and when that's not enough, he reaches between us to unzip my pants. His hand is warm when it wraps around me, and my hips hitch into his grip, my breath stuttering as he pumps my shaft.

"One of these days," he says between breaths, "we're going to do this in a bed."

I huff a laugh that dissolves into a groan as Lucky drops to the floor between my legs. How he has room, I don't know, but he squeezes between the seats and sucks me into his mouth. My head clunks against the headrest behind me, one of my legs bent beside Lucky, the other spread around the middle console, foot under the driver's seat. It's cramped and almost too hot, but I wouldn't trade it for the world. Wouldn't dare stop when I have Lucky here with me, showing me with his tongue and his lips and his throat the way he wants me.

My fingers thread through Lucky's hair as he works me over, and I look down, drawn like a magnet to that spark in his eye. His lips are shiny, cheeks rosy and sharp, and his eyes... His eyes are bright and on my person, looking at me as if I'm worth being his sole focus. As if, maybe, out of everywhere in this vast universe, there's nowhere else he'd rather be than here with me.

"Luck," I croak, giving him a small tug when it starts to become too much.

He pops off my cock with a sound that has my gut clenching, and then he reaches for the waistband of my pants. "Lift up."

I do, and with a whole lot of finagling, Lucky gets my jeans and underwear down my legs, leaving them both dangling above my left boot. The right boot got tossed up front, and both our coats go.

"Lift again," he says, grabbing the blanket off the floor of the truck. "Unless you want cum on your seat."

I huff, lifting my ass, and Lucky haphazardly shoves the blanket underneath me. Then he sets to work removing his own clothes, leaving his shirt in place.

"If we get caught, we're screwed," he says, climbing back over me, packet of lube in hand.

I can't help but snort. *Already going to be screwed.*

Lucky laughs, a wonderful, wild sound, before reaching back to prep himself. I take his cock in hand while he does so, jerking him, and he shudders. He makes quick work of stretching himself, and then he shuffles closer to me in the tight confines of the truck. I ease down as much as I can, giving Lucky's legs room to fit on either side of my hips, and with his body folded in a way I could never manage, Lucky holds my dick and lowers himself onto my lap.

His head falls back with his moan, and I grab the back of his neck, holding tight as my entire being vibrates like a tuning fork. Lucky sighs, leaning into the touch, his head lolling slowly forward. He meets my gaze, rolling his hips as his hands land on my chest. I swallow heavily as his fingers dimple my shirt, as he slides up and down on my cock. He brings his lips to mine without a word, and then he rides me.

It starts slow, his hips moving like a dance, his kisses gentle and sweet. But it doesn't stay that way for long. His hands plant against the seat above my shoulders, his lips breaking from mine. His breaths are heavy, hitting my neck as he drops his head beside my own, giving him space to bounce on me harder without hitting the top of the truck. He's warm, and his body grips me tight, his ass milking my cock as he chases his peak.

I help him along as best as I can, hands on his hips, my ass cheeks flexing against the blanket as I tug him down on me harder. My socked foot finds purchase on the floor beneath the passenger seat, and he moans as I thrust upwards, his hair brushing my cheek as he rises and falls.

He reaches for his dick, but the motion causes him to lose momentum, so he abandons it in favor of the roof, planting his hands above his head as he grinds down on me harder. "El," he gasps.

I brush his curtain of hair to the side, cradling his cheek as I wrap my hand around his cock. His eyes flutter shut for just a moment, and then they're opening again, latching onto me. His mouth is open in an O, his cheeks bright red. He looks beautiful, near feral, and he sucks in a shuddering breath as his body starts to clamp down on my cock.

"Fuck, baby," he breathes, grinding, grinding, his eyes hooded. "Fuck, that's—"

And then he's coming, a hoarse cry leaving his lips as he starts to paint my shirt. He throbs in my grip, pulsing out his release, and I can't do a thing other than follow him. I grunt as it hits me, my toes curling against the floor and inside my one boot. I fill Lucky's body, not a single barrier between us, and for just a moment, I revel in that fact. An archaic satisfaction, for sure.

He slumps when it's over, his forehead near mine, his panting breaths loud in the silence of the cab.

"Who needs a bed," he mutters.

I laugh, a chuckle that starts deep in my chest. It shakes Lucky on top of me, and he laughs along, the two of us a sweaty, sated mess. He kisses my nose before sitting back, finding my eyes. His hair is a riot around his head, and I push back the strands after wiping my hand on the blanket. He's so lovely. So utterly gorgeous, and I know, no matter how hard I try, I will never be able to explain to him the depth of what he makes me feel. How he means comfort and safety. How I long for him with an intensity I don't even fully understand. How he makes me brave and, at times, a little fierce, just like him. How, when we're together, all I can see is *blue*. He's blue, and our story is washed in it.

It's waterfalls and a quick beating heart.

It's starlit skies and the feeling of home.

It's paint, splashed across the floor, a messy declaration of loyalty.

It's the look in his eyes, both familiar and exciting.

It's a million shades of relief and compassion, understanding and trust. It's all the memories that bind us together. It's cool and quenching, and it burns like nothing else.

Blue is love. To me, it's love. And that's always been Lucky.

"Love you," I say, hoping the two words are enough.

He sighs, fingers drifting over my arms to my shoulders. "There won't ever be a time when I don't love you, El."

I nearly miss the soft pop of sound over the beating of my heart, but Lucky draws attention to it, his gaze shifting out the window.

"Look," he whispers. "Must be midnight."

I follow his gaze. Fireworks are lighting up the sky, each one joined by a small boom.

"Happy New Year, Ellis," Lucky says. "Should we watch for a minute?"

I nod, and the two of us set to work disentangling and cleaning up. After we're wiped, dressed, and back in our shoes and coats, I set the blanket out—soiled side down—in the bed of the truck. For a short while, Lucky and I watch the fireworks, him nestled in my arms.

"You know what I realized?" he says, breath whitening the air.

I hum.

"All this time... The picnics and the drives in your truck, hanging out in the cornfields and nights like this under the stars... I think we've been dating for years, Ellis, and we never realized."

I huff a laugh, tightening my arms around him.

"Promise me something," he says, turning his face. My lips brush his cheek.

Anything.

"Promise we'll still do this when we're sixty or eighty or a hundred. I want a lifetime with you, El. Me and you. 'Til the end of time."

I draw an X over Lucky's heart.

Promise.

Chapter 36

LUCKY

"You know, if I didn't know you were excited to get back home to your lover, I'd take your joy in parting from me to heart, Lucky-boy."

I snort, sparing Danil a glance. "My lover?"

"Is he not?" Danil asks, arching an eyebrow. "Sure sounded like it last night."

I decide not to comment on that last part. It's not my fault I didn't realize the door to our adjoining rooms was open when I was on the phone with Ellis.

"Let's not call him that," I mutter. "*You* have lovers. I have..."

"Your Ellis," he fills in.

Exactly.

"This is the longest we've been apart since I moved back," I note.

It's been half a year since I relocated from New York to Nebraska. Every time I hop on a plane after an assignment, it's to go back home to Ellis.

Ten-year-old me would have been appalled to know I never escaped the land of corn. But twenty-six-year-old me is older and wiser. He has life experience under his belt and a whole collection of memories from around the world. I've traveled more than most ever will in a lifetime. I've seen pyramids and oceans. Photographed endangered animals and swam with literal sharks. I've *lived*, and I've learned. And not once in the past six months have I regretted moving back to the small, rural town I once couldn't wait to get out of.

Because I also love. I love deeply and with my whole heart. And that, quite frankly, is more important than any other phenomena I could capture with my lens. Love moves mountains.

It moved me.

Danil shifts, checking the time on his phone. "Well, I wish you a happy reunion, Lucky-boy. I need to get to my terminal."

When Danil stands, I do the same, pulling him into a hug. He kisses my cheek before giving me a salute, and then he's off, weaving his way through the airport just as boarding is called for my own plane. I stand in line, a smile on my face as I think about the man who'll be waiting for me on the other end of my flight.

"You're not Ellis."

My dad gives me a big grin, opening his arms. Even though I'm confused, I let him smother me in a hug. "Hey, kiddo. Welcome home."

"What are you doing here?" I ask, hoping my tone doesn't sound as disappointed as I feel. Ellis doesn't pick me up *every* time I fly in—sometimes he's at work—but I was expecting him today.

"I'm supposed to deliver you," my dad says cryptically. He grabs my suitcase from my hand and starts walking toward the exit.

With a stutter-step, I follow. "Deliver me where?"

"My lips are sealed," he says, smiling wide.

My heart takes off at a gallop.

Dad leads me to his vehicle, turning on the air conditioning once we're inside. It's late evening, so the sun isn't at its peak, but it's still a hot summer day in Nebraska.

My foot bounces as he drives. "You can't tell me anything?"

"I could," he hedges. "But I won't."

My foot bounces some more. "How's Mom?"

"Good," he answers. "She and Mrs. Cole had brunch this morning with a few friends."

"And Mrs. Cole?" I ask. It's been a couple weeks since I was home.

"She's good, Lucky," he answers. "Steady."

I nod. With her particular form of MS, she doesn't have periods of remission. Her symptoms get progressively worse over time, but she does have stretches of stability without worsening symptoms, and those periods of time are what we hope for.

The drive seems to take hours, even though I know that's not true. My dad fills me in on what's been going on in town, including a small incident at the paper mill that required them to shut down a fairly important piece of machinery for a day. By the time my dad is pulling into the driveway of my parents' home, I feel as if I'm jittering out of my skin.

The house next door is gently lit. Nothing seems out of place. Ellis isn't in sight.

My dad grabs my suitcase from the back before I can, giving me a nod. "Go ahead," he says. "He's in the silo."

The *thump* in my chest is a physical thing.

The wind is gentle as I make my way around the field. It rustles the leaves of the corn stalks, sending that familiar scent of soil and corn pollen my way. It's somewhat soothing, even as my nerves are frazzled.

The silo is open when I reach it. Ellis is waiting inside.

My footsteps die.

"El," I whisper.

He's standing in front of the wooden table, his hands inside his pockets. A few candles are lit on the surface behind him, flanking both sides of his body. Even more cover the ground, creating a pathway from me to him. I walk it slowly, my pulse loud inside my ears. Ellis never wavers as I approach. His smile is calm. Grounded. He holds out a hand once I'm within reach, and I give mine willingly, the warmth of his fingers familiar and comforting.

"Luck," he says.

"What's going on?" I ask, my voice barely cooperating.

"Made you...something."

Ellis steps to the side, letting me see the center of the table. On it, glimmering slightly from the glow of the candles and fireflies overhead, is a glass heart. An *anatomical* heart. I pick it up gently, the piece fitting perfectly in my palm. It's blue, and something within the substance makes it glitter in the light.

"Ellis," I say, at a loss for words.

"My heart," he says simply. "It's yours."

My breath leaves my lungs.

I twist the heart carefully in my hands. It feels so delicate. "It's beautiful," I manage to say, meeting Ellis's eyes. "*You're* beautiful."

His smile tells me he feels the same. He holds out his hand. "Come with me?"

I don't ask where. I simply return my hand to his.

Ellis blows out each and every candle on our way out of the silo. Smoke drifts lazily into the air with each flame that's extinguished, and when we reach the doorway, he flicks off the lights.

The glass heart feels weighted in my palm as we walk around the cornfield, even though it's quite light. I can't stop staring at it. At the intricate lines and carefully crafted curves.

When Ellis stops in front of his—*our*—house, he reaches for it. I hand it over, and he says, "Wait here."

I do, standing near the driveway as Ellis heads inside, presumably storing the heart somewhere safe. He returns only a minute later, walking around me to his truck and opening the passenger door. I get in with a small huff of laughter.

"Such a gentleman," I murmur.

He tips an invisible hat.

Ellis leads us down the dirt road without a word. I keep sneaking glances at him, wondering where we're going. Wondering why he looks so...*pleased.*

When we park alongside a familiar stretch of road, my gut swoops. "El?"

"Feel like...trespassing?" he asks. "For old time's sake?"

My laugh is more than a little surprised. "Are you serious?"

His exit from the truck is answer enough. Shaking my head, I follow, and Ellis grabs my hand before walking with me past the rows of corn to the bend that leads to the nearby house. I nearly lose my footing when the windmill comes into view.

It's covered in lights. White strands circle the base, curling up the length of the windmill. Even the wide blades at the top are trimmed in fairy lights.

"How?" I sputter, sparing a quick glance at the house.

Ellis gives me a wink. "Got permission."

I shake my head in disbelief.

Ellis's pace is steady as he leads me to the door at the back of the windmill. It opens easily, and the inside looks like a dream. More lights cover the interior, winding up the staircase, giving the space an otherworldly glow. It feels like pure magic as I pass through the doorway, memories of me and El when we were younger flitting through my mind like hazy snapshots.

Ellis gives me a tug toward the stairs, helping move my feet forward. He leads the way, hunching once he reaches the top. Despite his shoulders being so wide they barely have room to slip through the hole, he manages it, holding out a hand once he's up top. I follow him through, eyes blinking at the fairy lights strung across the low wooden ceiling.

"I can't believe you did all this," I say, kneeling before I shuffle forward. The sun has yet to set, but the view out the window is still breathtaking. It's our home, stretching out in front of us, an endless sea of maize and green.

I huff a small laugh. *Damn corn.*

When I look behind me, my breath stutters. "El?"

He's kneeling, too. But instead of being on two knees, he's down on one, hands clasped in front of him. The expression on his face is one I've seen hundreds, if not thousands, of times before, and his lips quirk up a bit at one side, like he has a secret.

He opens his hands without a word, opening the small box within at the same time. The world feels hushed, not a sound reaching my ears above my own soft exhalation. Ellis never speaks. He doesn't have to. Earlier, he gave me his heart. This...this is his life he's offering.

My hand trembles as I reach forward, picking up the ring. It's softer than metal. Silicone, if I had to guess. A thoughtful choice considering my active job. And it's dark blue, so dark, at first I thought it was black.

I slip it on my finger without a word, looking at it for a long moment before I meet Ellis's gaze. His eyes are wet now, lips shaking with his smile. I scoot forward, hands on his cheeks, lips in front of his own. And I kiss him.

It's *yes* and *of course* and *we're going to be so happy, you just wait and see*. It's sixteen years of *Hi. What's your name? Mine's Lucky*. It's knowing no matter how much more time passes, this is my person, and I am his, and we're bound together by fate or choice or, hell, corn for all I know.

It's being somewhere in the middle of a very long journey, and knowing there's no end.

"Me and you, El," I whisper against his lips. "It'll always be me and you."

His mouth brushing mine is an agreement.

We stay at the top of that windmill for hours, my lips bruised from Ellis's kisses. When the sun sets, we watch, the fairy lights keeping us company like little twinkling fireflies. The stars keep us company, too.

And as night rolls over to morning, my fiancé's hand is in mine.

Chapter 37

LUCKY

"Too much?" Danil asks.

I whistle, eyeing my friend up and down. He's in an impeccable pinstriped suit, the coal color suiting his complexion. His dark hair is styled neatly back from his face, and every inch of him, from his expensive watch to his wingtip shoes, looks pristine.

"You clean up nice," I tell him, to which he snorts.

"You're one to talk."

I catch a glimpse of myself in the mirror. My own suit is a light cream color, and my shirt and tie are white. Ellis's, I know, will be the same. I took care when drying my hair this morning, making sure it didn't frizz too badly, but I have a feeling it won't matter once I get outside. The curls have always been unruly.

I floated the idea of cutting it shorter for the occasion, but Ellis didn't like that. He grunted and then proceeded to thread his fingers through the strands and fuck me slowly until I forgot what day it was.

The hair will stay.

"Are you ready to get married?" Danil asks, smiling at me in the mirror.

I nearly scoff. "Are you kidding? I've been ready for a good long while."

"You've only been engaged a month," he points out.

"Dani," I say evenly, "I would have married that man the day he asked."

He hums, squeezing my shoulders. "Fair enough, Lucky-boy."

When there's a knock at the door, Danil heads that way. My mom steps into my childhood bedroom, where Danil and I are getting ready. She's wearing a lavender dress, her hair pulled into a loose, low bun. She sighs when she sees me and comes over to give me a hug.

"You look lovely, sweetheart." She kisses my cheek before rubbing off the lipstick she left behind.

"Thanks, Mom. So do you."

"Are you about ready?" she asks. "Your dad said Ellis is all set next door."

I nod, blowing out a single breath. "Yeah. I'm ready."

She gives me a soft smile. "Oh," she says quickly, holding up a finger. She heads back into the hall, and half a minute later, she returns with a small, plastic box. "For you."

I curse under my breath, blinking rapidly to hold my tears at bay. My mom isn't as successful. One slips down her cheek as she opens the box, removing the blue boutonniere from inside. She helps secure it to my suit jacket, patting my lapel afterward.

"Perfect," she says quietly. "One last thing. Ellis wanted me to let you know to check your email if you haven't."

"Thank you, Mom."

She pats my cheek, and Danil closes the door after her as I head to my old dresser, grabbing my phone from atop. I sit at the edge of the bed as I open my email.

"What is it?" he asks.

"A message from Ellis," I answer hoarsely, finding the email with a subject line dated for today.

With a steadying breath, I read.

Luck. We're going to get married today. Can you believe it? In less than an hour, you'll be my husband, and I'll be yours. I know they say wedding day jitters are common, but I've never been surer of anything in my life.

I was twenty-two years old when I said goodbye to you. College was over, our childhood was over, and it was time for you to move on. I said goodbye to you a lot after that. Each time you came to visit or we talked on the phone, I knew goodbye was inevitable.

I don't have to say goodbye anymore.

I know we decided to exchange simple vows today. To say our 'I dos' in front of our family and friends. And I know that was for my sake because Lord knows I wouldn't be able to give much of a speech on a day like today. But... I promise you this, Luck.

I will love you for all of our days.

I will cherish you the way you deserve.

I will hold you every chance I get.

And I will be closer than that any time you need it.

I will treat you more carefully than glass.

I will hug you before every flight.

I will kiss you all the days we're together.

And I will think of you any day we are not.

I don't know what it is that makes attraction, but I know I bend toward you no matter where on this Earth you are. I feel your pull, and if I am your moon, as you say I am, then I promise to always call you back home.

You are my world, Luck. And even when all goes dark, I will look for you. I will find you, blinking for me in the endless night, and I will be with you always. My brilliant firefly. My love. My Luck.

Forever, I'll be waiting.

"Shit," I mutter, wiping my cheek as my breath stutters. "He wasn't supposed to make me cry before the ceremony."

Danil hands me a tissue, and I thank him, clearing the moisture from my face. It takes me a moment to feel more composed.

Ellis's letters never fail to leave me spinning, just a little.

"You know," Danil says slowly. "I think if I ever *could* have felt more for someone, it would have been you."

I look at him in surprise, pulse hitching. "Dani..."

"Oh, get that look off your face," he says, rolling his eyes. "This isn't some declaration. I'm not coming in like Julia Roberts on your wedding day, all *pick me, choose me,* and I'm not going to quietly pine after you for years to come. It's just..." He fiddles with the pack of smokes in his pocket before holding it up. "You mind?"

I shake my head, and Danil opens the window, leaning against the sill as he lights a cigarette. He takes a drag before bending and blowing the smoke out the window. When he stands upright again, he chews his lip for a minute as if in thought.

"Here's the thing," he says. "I'm not sure if I'll ever want what you do. The permanent partner. The lifetime commitment. But you've made me feel something I haven't for most. It's not *love*...not that kind. But it is... Well, fuck, it *is* love, you know?" He pinches his nose. "Jesus, I'm mucking this up. What I want you to know is that I treasure you, Lucky-boy. You're something special to me, and I'm glad you're in my life."

"Dani," I say softly, rising from the bed.

"We're going to hug again, aren't we?" he says, carefully stubbing out his cigarette. He opens his arms, breathing a put-upon sigh, but there's a smile on his face as he wraps his arms around me, careful not to crush my boutonniere. He kisses my cheek, as he so often does, before pulling back. "I do love you, Lucky. In my way. And I'm happy for you."

"I love you, too, Dani," I admit, voice choked. "And I never did thank you."

"What for?" he asks.

"For reminding me of my courage the last time you were here. I needed that."

"Glad I could help," he says, punching my shoulder lightly. "Now, what do you say? Ready to walk down the aisle?"

I blow out a breath. *I'm ready.*

My parents are waiting for us in the living room. They smile when we enter, and then the four of us head outside.

Ellis and I decided on a simple ceremony for our wedding, not needing anything more. Our engagement was short, but we didn't want to wait. We wanted to be husbands, and soon, we will be. Our gathering is small, just family and a few close friends, with Danil officiating. And as we round the house from the front to the back, everything comes into view.

There are a handful of white chairs set in two rows with a break down the middle. Gauzy white fabric trails from wooden posts, flanking both sides of the unofficial aisle. Blue flower petals decorate the grass, blowing gently in the breeze. And more white gauze is situated up front, creating a backdrop that looks like fluttering clouds.

Mrs. Cole is already seated, as well as Gabby, Riley, and our other friends. And, after giving me another hug each, my parents join them.

But at the center of it all, waiting for me in front of a field of corn, is Ellis, holding up a sign with big, blocky letters. I clamp a hand over my mouth as I read it.

Lucky
Will you marry me?

Ellis is grinning above the edge of the sign, his eyes, even from here, looking wet. Our guests glance between the two of us, smiling, if not a little confused. Our parents, though—they understand.

"What do you think?" I shout at him.

His grin widens, and he drops the sign to his side, revealing his blue boutonniere that matches my own. My stomach flutters as I take him in. He looks undeniably handsome standing there, the soft colors of his fitted suit contrasting so nicely with his darker hair. He looks steady, strong, and determined, and the me of so many years ago never would have imagined he'd be mine.

My Ellis.

"Shit," I mutter to myself, shaking my head. "I'm gonna marry that man."

Danil leans close as soft instrumental music starts to play. He taps the flower pinned to my breast. "You never did tell me the story behind this. The two blue boutonnieres. Your big romance. What happened that day at prom?"

My lips twist as Ellis smiles my way. Our guests are looking back now, waiting for me to step forward for our *I dos*. And Ellis waits at the end of the aisle, ready to accept my hand in his. In mere minutes, we'll be Mr. and Mr. for the rest of our lives.

But for just a moment, we're sixteen again.

My answer for Danil is simple.

"I fell in love."

Chapter 38

LUCKY

I was sixteen years old when I fell head over heels for Ellis Cole.

"Lucky?" my mom calls, knocking gently on my bedroom door.

I pull the covers over my head. "Go away."

"Sweetheart," she says gently. "I'm coming in."

My bed depresses as my mom sits beside me. Her hand lands on my back a moment later.

"There's someone at the door to see you."

"Who?" I ask, refusing to come out. "Ellis?"

"I think you should go see for yourself."

Reluctantly, I pull the covers off my face. My mom gives me a soft smile.

"Go look," she says.

With a great big huff, I climb out of bed and trudge toward the front door. It has to be Ellis. The rest of our classmates are at prom. I try not to let the souring reminder that I'm the only gay kid at school get me down, but, well... It sucks.

When I pull open the front door, readying myself to tell Ellis I'm *fine* and I don't feel like being cheered up, the words promptly die on my tongue. It *is* Ellis, but not like I was expecting. He's standing out in front of the house, wearing a black tux and holding a sign level with his chest.

Lucky
Will you go to prom with me?

I huff an incredulous laugh, my heart skipping. "What are you doing, El?"

He doesn't answer, just gives the sign a shake.

I step outside the door, mouth opening and closing a few times. "Ellis... You don't have to do this. I'm *fine*. It's just a stupid dance."

He holds the sign higher, blocking half of his face.

I look at the sky, shaking my head. My chest feels...tight. But in a good way. Unable to deny my friend, I call out, "What do you think? Of course I'll go to prom with you."

He grins, lowering the sign, but then I realize...

"Shit, I don't have anything to wear."

Ellis points, and I follow his gaze. My dad is standing behind me in the doorway, holding a garment bag.

"Ellis dropped it off," he says.

I grab it without a word, shaking my head again. But there's a big smile on my face as I go change.

When I get back to the living room, Ellis is inside. My rented tux matches his, although his sits loosely around his tall frame, and for a moment, my breath catches. It's not the first time I've looked at Ellis and felt my pulse pick up. It's not the first time I've thought he looked handsome. It's not even the first time I've felt the unmistakable flush in my body telling me what sort of things I'd like to do with my friend given the chance.

But it's the first time I've seen a glimpse of the man Ellis will become. Not because of the tux. But because of the fact that he's standing in my living room in the first place, ready and willing to accompany me to an event he has no interest in just because I told him I wished I could go. He's kind and endlessly patient, and his heart is too big for his chest.

And I think... *Fuck*, I think I might love him.

He opens a small clear box as I approach and pulls out a flower. It's the kind guys give their prom dates. Except, instead of a corsage, it's a boutonniere. It's blue, with white ribbon wrapped around the stem. He has a matching one on his jacket.

"For me?" I ask, aiming for teasing, if for nothing else than to hide the wobble in my voice.

He nods, looking to my mom. She comes over immediately, helping to pin the flower over my pocket. My heart thumps furiously the whole time.

"There," she says, straightening my lapels. "You boys look beautiful. Here, let's take a picture."

Ellis and I stand in front of the couch, and without a word, he takes my hand. I can barely breathe, but I do my best to smile for the camera.

My parents tell us to have a good time before practically shoving us out the door, and Ellis and I head to his new truck. He opens the passenger side first before getting behind the wheel. The entire time we drive to the school, I can't stop staring at the side of Ellis's face, wondering what to do with this scary, warm feeling swirling inside my chest.

The auditorium is filled with our classmates when we arrive. There are banners strung along the walls, streamers hanging from the ceiling, and even balloons floating in clusters around the room. It looks like every picture or movie I've ever seen of a high school prom, and even though it may be cliché, I feel a little bit like a prince with Ellis by my side. I didn't think I'd get the chance to attend my own prom night, but he made my dream come true.

Ellis and I get more than a few looks as we pass through the room, but he doesn't seem to notice. He brings me over to the punch bowl first, offering me a drink, and then we sit at a table as our classmates dance and cheer and pair off in guy-girl combos. I convince Ellis to come with me to the dance floor a time or two, but he mostly stands still as the rest of us jump around in terrible rhythm.

Ellis doesn't say much as the evening wears on, but I'm not surprised. He's quieter in large groups of people. I'm just grateful he seems to miss the snide looks Brandon keeps shooting him. I flip the guy off when Ellis isn't looking.

When it's been a good hour since I last heard Ellis speak, I give him a nudge. "Hey, wanna get out of here?"

He cocks his head, asking if I'm sure.

"Yeah," I tell him, giving his sleeve a tug. "Let's go."

Ellis follows me out of the auditorium into the cooler evening air. It's dark outside, and music thumps quietly at our backs as we make our way to Ellis's truck.

Halfway home, he says, "Didn't want to stay?"

I smile to myself, just glad to hear his voice again. "I had a really good time, El. Thank you for bringing me. I just... I want to hang out with you now. Just me and you."

He doesn't say a word to that, but there's a smile on his face, too.

Ellis parks out in front of his house, and we head toward my backyard, past the old tire swing to the edge of the cornfield. The wind is gentle tonight, and the leaves rustle softly as we walk past the rows of corn, no particular destination in mind.

"El," I say, coming to a stop. He stops, too, facing me. "Thanks again. It's not always easy being the only queer kid around, but you make it easy. So just thanks...for being my friend."

He looks at my face for a long moment, his eyes skipping about slowly. Finally, he holds out his hand. "Dance with me?"

My throat clicks when I swallow. "Right now?"

He nods.

When I take his hand, it's warm and dry. He steps close, one hand at my waist, the other twined with mine. I set my free hand on his shoulder, and then he starts to move. We rotate in a slow circle, the crickets chirping quietly around us. I can't break his gaze. Can't look away from those eyes, so dark in the night. Ellis doesn't say a word, and for the longest time, neither do I.

We dance without music beneath a deep blue sky.

"If I ever get married," I whisper, "I want it to be just like this."

He hums. A questioning sound.

"Nothing fancy," I explain. "Just me and the open air and the people...and person...I love."

"Sounds nice," he says.

"Yeah," I say, voice barely there. My heart is pounding too fast, too out of control, so I add, in a joking tone, "Maybe even in front of the corn. Because, you know, I love it so much."

He snorts lightly.

After a moment, we come to a stop.

"Come on," Ellis says, dropping his hands. "Race you."

"Where?" I ask, but Ellis is already disappearing into the field. I curse, chasing after him, laughing as the leaves whack my arms. My lungs start to burn, but it's a happy sting, and I welcome it, following Ellis's blurring form through the field.

He stops when he comes out on the other side, bending down to catch his breath. I fall right to my butt before sprawling out on my back, arms out wide. I stare up at the stars above as my chest heaves.

"Cheater," I rasp.

He settles down next to me, huffing a breathy laugh. It's long minutes later when he says, "It shouldn't matter."

"What's that?" I ask, turning my head to look at him.

"Who you love," he answers, arms crossed over his knees. "People who judge..." He shakes his head. "Love is big. Important. I think...people could love most anybody...if they only opened their hearts to it."

I watch Ellis, feeling struck. It's not often he gives voice to so much, so it feels big and important that he's doing it now.

"Others...they might come and go," he says slowly, gaze holding mine. "But I'll always love you, Luck. Won't ever stop."

I sit upright, my heart pounding all the way down to my toes. Ellis is bathed in moonlight, his body illuminated enough for me to make out his features. And he means it. I know he does. I can see it in the lines of his face and in the way his eyes are hooked on mine. He means it. He loves me. I'm his best friend. And he's mine.

And maybe that's all we'll be. Maybe, in my lifetime, that's the only love I'll know from Ellis. But it'll be worth it. I don't think another love will come around that's bigger than his.

I draw my finger over the dirt near my leg, writing out the letter E. Next to it, I add L. Ellis plucks the flower from his tux, setting it on the ground below my scrawl. I do the same with mine.

As we sit beside a sea of corn in our wrinkled, black tuxes, our declaration of love on the ground between us, I twist my fingers with his and make a promise.

"I love you, too, El. Always."

Epilogue

LUNA

I was six years old when I caught a firefly.

"Luna?"

"In here," I call, peeking out the window. Papa looks up at me, my baby brother on his hip.

"Ready to go?"

I nod, standing up and dusting off my knees. I climb down the ladder to the top of the stairs, and then I walk—*not run*—down the winding staircase. Papa is waiting at the bottom of the windmill when I get there.

How cool is it that our house has a windmill?

"Come on," Papa says with a smile.

We load into Papa's car, and my stomach flips over. "Where's Daddy?"

"At Grandma Cole's," he says, turning us onto the road. The sun hits my eyes, and I squint at the cornfields as we drive past. Brother kicks his foot in the seat next to me.

"What's he doing at Grandma's?" I ask.

Papa hums. "He had a lot of feelings this morning. He wanted to work on some glass."

"What kind of feelings?"

Papa's blue eyes meet mine in the mirror at the front of the car. "The good kind."

"'Cause of your anniversary?" I ask. I heard Papa talking about it yesterday.

He smiles. "Yeah, Luna. Because of that."

When we get to Grandma Cole's, Papa unbuckles me, grabs Brother, and heads toward the house. I bounce on my toes, feeling antsy, but Papa catches my eye.

"We'll go in a sec," he says. "Let's say hello to Grandma first."

Grandma is waiting for us inside with a smile and a plate of fresh lemon bars. I eat one, legs kicking, as Brother walks around Grandma's wheelchair.

"Watch your fingers," Papa reminds him, but he doesn't say anything back. He's only one.

"How're you doing, hon?" Grandma asks Papa.

He gives her a smile. "Good. Did Ellis stop by on his way through?"

She nods. "Of course he did. Had a big smile on his face, too. Ten years today, can you believe it? Happy anniversary."

Papa looks like he has feelings, too. He squeezes Grandma's arm. "Thanks. Do you want to come to the festival with us?"

Grandma shakes her head, reaching down to play with Brother's hand. "Not this time. Cora invited me next door. Your dad is cooking steaks on the grill tonight. I'm going to stick around for that."

Papa chuckles. "All right. Grocery shopping tomorrow?"

"It's a date," Grandma says.

Papa's eyes meet mine. "Ready?"

I nod, jumping down and licking the crumbs off my fingers. He picks up Brother as I give Grandma a quick hug. She tucks my hair behind my ear when I step back.

"These curls," she says, sounding happy. "Just like your father's."

I look up at Papa. He's smiling down at me.

"I got his eyes, too," I tell Grandma. "That's what Daddy told me."

"That you did," she says, pinching my cheek, but not hard enough to hurt. "Have fun today, sweetie. Bring me back some caramel corn."

I promise, crossing my heart and everything, before running outside. Papa laughs from behind me, but he doesn't tell me to slow down as I hop down the steps and race toward the silo. I hold my hand out as I go, but when the leaves on the corn stalks start to sting, I pull my palm back.

I stop running when I get to the silo. I stand inside the door and call for Daddy, letting him know I'm here because that's the rule. He turns, smiling, and sets down the metal pole in his hand. When he walks my way, I run again, and then he's hugging me.

My daddy is tall, and my feet dangle off the ground as he pulls me into his arms. He feels hot, like the fire, and he hums, the sound tickling my cheek.

"Hi," I say, laughing as I squirm. "Did you get your feelings out? Papa's here to take you to the corn festival."

He chuckles. It's one of my favorite sounds. Daddy doesn't say much, but his laughs always sound nice.

"One minute," he says, setting me down. I stay back from the fireplace as Daddy finishes up. I look around at all the colored glass to keep myself busy. It's like a rainbow in here.

Papa catches up before long, a smile on his face as he sees Daddy. He walks over, Baby Brother still on his hip, and he and Daddy kiss. They do that a lot.

"Almost ready?" Papa asks.

Daddy nods. "Done."

Before Daddy can turn off the lights, I look up at the fireflies. He told me once that they're Papa. That Papa is bright and beautiful and he was born with wings, which is why he flies away every few months. I asked if that makes him sad, but Daddy said no. Because Papa always flies home to us.

The fireflies flicker out as Daddy turns off the lights, but that's okay. They'll be back tonight.

The corn festival is loud when we arrive, and there are a lot of people. My baby brother doesn't like the noise, so he wears earmuffs, and Papa carries him in a baby backpack on the front of his body. We stop for popcorn, and Papa picks up some caramel corn for Grandma. I like the salty kind best. After my brother has a bottle, we go on some rides. Well, me and Papa do. Daddy waits with Brother. Aunt Gabby and Uncle Riley show up, too. They bring Lyle. He's not my real cousin, but everyone calls us that. He's nine, too old to play with me and my brother, but he does go on some of the rides with Papa and me. Uncle Dani isn't here, but that's because he lives in New York. He said he'll come visit for Thanksgiving.

It's almost dark by the time we make it to the corn maze. Papa says we'll leave soon, but we can't go before we do the maze. It's just the four of us again, and Brother is asleep on Papa's chest, his dark hair stuck to his forehead. Papa has a hand on his back as he sleeps, and his other is holding Daddy's. They do that a lot, too.

I give Daddy's other hand a tug. "You promised," I remind him.

He chuckles, letting go of Papa. The next instant, I'm being flung into the air. I laugh as Daddy settles me on his shoulders, and I hold on tight to his head.

"Which way, Luna?" Papa asks.

I try to look over the top of the corn to see the way through the maze, but I can't tell where the exit is. "Let's try that way," I say, pointing at random.

We set off, winding through the paths of corn. I feel like the tallest person for miles. When a light flickers in front of my face, I gasp.

"Look," I whisper. "The fireflies are here."

Daddy stops walking, and for a minute, we all watch.

"Can I catch one?" I ask.

Papa and Daddy exchange a look.

"You can try," Papa says. "But be gentle if you do."

I nod furiously, reaching with both hands toward the nearest one. Daddy grabs a hold of my legs, keeping me steady, and I cup my hands around the flying bug as fast as I can. I bring my hands in front of my face carefully, making the tiniest crack, and peek inside.

"Whoa," I whisper. The firefly glows between my palms.

"Nice catch," Papa says.

I caught a firefly.

I watch it blink on and off. "Hello," I whisper. Another blink. "Goodbye." I open my palms and let it go.

The firefly flies off, and I wonder if I'll ever see it again.

"My turn," Daddy says. He reaches for Papa, and Papa laughs as Daddy kisses him. It goes on for a while.

Papa is smiling when he steps back. He smiles a lot at Daddy. I think that might be love.

Papa bounces Brother gently as we continue forward through the maze. When we finally find our way out, my eyes feel heavy, but I don't say so. I like staying up late. Papa said I was named for the night, after all. He said the moon is his most favorite thing.

Papa and Daddy hold hands as we walk to the car. I rest my cheek on Daddy's head.

"Ellis, look," Papa says. "Is that a blue moon?"

Daddy is quiet for a moment. "Think so."

"It's beautiful," Papa says.

Daddy lifts Papa's hand for a kiss. "You, too, Luck."

Papa sighs. "Happy anniversary, El. Did you ever imagine all this? It's..."

Daddy hums, his hand on my leg squeezing once. "Everything."

"It is," Papa whispers. "I'm so lucky I get to share this life with you, Ellis. I love you. More than I can say."

"Love you always," Daddy replies.

"Yeah," Papa says, voice full of feelings again. "Me and you, El. We don't have an ending, do we?"

Daddy rumbles one of his happy sounds, and even though I try to stop it, my eyes slip shut.

I remember a kiss to my forehead. One to my cheek. Sheets tucked up near my chin, and a *goodnight, my little Luna*. With the big moon awake in the sky, I fall sound asleep.

And in my dreams, the fireflies dance.

The Never-End

About the Author

Information about Emmy Sanders and her complete list of works can be found on her website. Subscribe to her newsletter, join her Facebook reader group, Emmy's Enclave, and connect via email or social media:

www.emmysanders.com

Find online:
www.facebook.com/emmysandersmm
www.instagram.com/emmysandersmm

Printed in Great Britain
by Amazon

40662499R00185